A Chorus Rises

Also by Bethany C. Morrow

A Song Below Water

A Chorus Rises

Bethany C. Morrow

A TOM DOHERTY ASSOCIATES BOOK • NEW YORK

TOR TEEN

This is a work of fiction. All of the characters, organizations, and events portrayed in this novel are either products of the author's imagination or are used fictitiously.

A CHORUS RISES

Edited by Diana M. Pho

A Tor Teen Book
Published by Tom Doherty Associates
120 Broadway
New York, NY 10271

www.tor-forge.com

Library of Congress Cataloging-in-Publication Data

Morrow, Bethany C., author.
A chorus rises : a Song below water novel /
Bethany C. Morrow.—First edition. p. cm.
"A Tom Doherty Associates book."
ISBN 978-1-250-31603-5 (hardcover)
ISBN 978-1-250-31602-8 (ebook)
1. Fame—Fiction. 2. Social media—Fiction. 3. Belonging
(Social psychology)—Fiction. I. Title.
PZ7.1.M6757 Ch 2021
[Fic]—dc23
2021008742

First Edition: June 2021

Printed in the United States of America

0 9 8 7 6 5 4 3 2 1

To the Black girls who loved ourselves from jump.

A Chorus Rises

Chapter I

NAEMA

"Effie," I hear her say, and even though her voice is calm, it carries a telltale vibrato that I register too late. I'm standing across from a siren and there's a call in her voice. Whatever she says next will have power.

"Stone her."

There's no time after that. Not to think, *she wouldn't dare do this to me,* and not to dare her. To tell her that I am through playing nice, that you don't threaten Eloko, and that she and her snake sister had better start thinking of what comes after Portland because they are *never* going to live this night down.

There's no time to run, when what was a wobbling pillar of scales and haunted hair stiffens—and then I do, too.

It hits me in my core. Deep inside my body, something goes hard.

I gasp, but the air doesn't get in. Not really. It comes into my throat but then stops. I can't get it into my chest. That's where my panic starts. Am I going to suffocate? Is being Stoned by a siren and her snake sister actually dying? No one knows. No one's ever come back from the stone. Which means the sisters don't know either, and they're doing it anyway.

I don't know how long it takes from the outside. They're watching me turn gray like the other promgoers in this courtyard, and the man in the cemetery, and the kids in Triton Park—but I don't know if it seems fast or slow. I just know I'm terrified that my lungs will start burning any moment from the air I can't force into them, that the legs I can't feel anymore aren't there, that the stone has broken somehow even though I've never seen it happen. What else am I supposed to think when thinking is all I can do? I can't feel anything, once the hardening starts. It feels like nothing, except that it's spreading.

I want to look down, to see my body, that it's still there. I want to look away so that the last thing I see isn't Tavia Philips.

But there's no time.

Chapter II

Woke Portland: a Year After the Awakening

Contributor | June 2021

Last month, a year after the Awakening, four children gathered in Triton Park. They had been surrounded by their families and members of the Portland community, the way they often were during their nearly decade-long suspended animation. But Mere, Tabor, Wiley, and Ashleigh—first names only, to protect the families' privacy—stand out among the crowd. Partly because of the reverent space they're given, all but close family keeping a considerate distance from the children rarely seen in public. Only a year after being stone themselves, the Triton Park Four still look very much like the sculpture unveiled in the place where their childhoods passed them by.

The anniversary has come and gone, the sculpture christened with colorful wreaths nearly identical to the ones left for the children when they were in stone. The foursome has retreated back into the reclusive cocoon of their families. They probably won't be seen until the next Awakening Day—assuming this is a tradition that continues, and how could it not?

But there were others freed from the stone. It's impossible to forget the few days before the Awakening, when other gray statues appeared in quick succession, leading up to the panic at the prom. Their imprisonments were, thankfully, considerably shorter than those of the children of Triton Park. They were pedestrians mostly, unfortunate and hapless victims. And then, of course, there were the promgoers, with only one known Eloko afflicted—and there was also one siren.

Tavia Philips was never a victim of her best friend Effie Freeman's gorgon spell, but the day she Awakened those who were, she set herself free, too. She won't say so, not on the record at least, but the facts speak for themselves. One day, no one knew there was a siren living in Portland, and the next, we were grateful to have been wrong.

Tavia's reluctance to comment comes as a surprise, given the national attention her YouTube channel, Siren Speaks, has garnered. For the past year, she's gathered quite a following speaking out on the alleged marginalization and systemic oppression she says sirens have faced. Soon, she won't just be a powerful voice in advocacy and activism. This month will see the streaming debut of an original film made about the teenage siren and the day she saved PDX. While one would expect her to be enjoying the fanfare, Tavia intentionally appears to distance herself ahead of the release.

To be fair, she recently graduated from Beckett High, for anyone who forgot this firebrand is actually still a teenager, though any attempt at "average" would be a stretch. Perhaps she's focusing on summer freedom, and college plans. Professor Heather Vesper-Holmes, of the University of Portland, however, provides a much more likely explanation for Tavia Philips to eschew the limelight of Awakening Day.

"Except for Tavia's, the freedom granted by Awakening was from a curse her adoptive sister unleashed," Professor Vesper-Holmes says. She stares out from behind her wide desk, stacked with books and legal pads covered in layer upon layer of scribblings. The thirtysomething academic is hard not to take seriously. Much of her earlier research has been discredited: years of studying sprites under the hypothesis that they were capable of capturing children in stone. But Professor Vesper-Holmes has the distinction of being the one to discredit her own previous work, briefly turning her academic attention to the gorgon who was actually responsible. Now with Effie Freeman nowhere to be found—or studied—the professor has become the first in her field to launch contemporary research on Portland's beloved population of Eloko, prompted by one Eloko's involvement in Tavia Philips's Awakening.

"Tavia had to undo something her sister did. And while Effie, the gorgon who didn't know she was a gorgon at a time when—to be fair—few knew gorgons actually exist, has been all but forgiven, she still chose to disappear. I think that's pretty traumatic for Tavia."

It's a reasonable deduction, and Professor Vesper-Holmes may be right. But if it's trauma, it's also just the kind of origin story you'd expect from a hero in the making.

Chapter III

NAEMA

The first time I sat with Dr. Corey, it was only days after being Awakened, and I opened up immediately, just to prove that I am still Naema Bradshaw. Whatever you think you know about what I can or will do, I promise, you don't.

I say "sat with" because it was not my first time *seeing* Dr. Corey. She's been my pediatrician all my life, but for the past year she's also been my stand-in therapist based solely on the fact that she, too, is Eloko. Which—if I'm being honest—I hoped would be as meaningful as my parents thought it'd be. I mean, if you can't trust an Eloko, you're basically screwed.

"What was it like?" she asked me a year ago, mere weeks after prom. "Coming back."

My eyes didn't wander, or fog, and my breath didn't hitch. People who fluster assume the only way you don't is by force of will, by putting on a tough front meant to disguise that everyone is biting back tears. Like we're all undone, we just refuse to show it. Which is what they clearly need to believe. It's easier than accepting that there are just some of us who aren't so easily shook. So despite the fact that I had really good reason to break into a million pieces, I was pleased to find that I still didn't.

"You're asking what it was like to be Stoned—the thing where you're consumed by gray rock due to a gorgon's curse, not that more fun thing where you're high—or what it was like when the spell was broken, or what it was like to come out of being Stoned and be face to face with your least favorite person in Portland?" I set my chin against my fist. "Which part of 'coming back' do you mean?"

Dr. Corey's not a therapist, but sometimes she does a passable job at pretending.

"Tavia Philips is your least favorite person in Portland? Still, even though it was her voice that broke the curse?"

I could've outed Tavia right there. I could've told Dr. Corey and everyone else how Effie hadn't just happened to curse me; how after years of being part of the network that hid Tavia, the bish sicced her sister on me. But instead I just scoffed and rolled my eyes.

"What do you remember about those first moments?" she asked, like it might not be much.

"Everything. I remember the courtyard materializing like it'd been surrounding me all along."

"Hadn't it?"

"No." I stopped and exchanged blinks with the good doctor for a moment. "It hadn't."

To her credit, she matched my gaze, maybe because of what we have in common. Yes, Dr. Corey's Eloko; she's used to being wise, or insightful, or discerning—whichever word you want to attribute to the characteristic we're said to share due to supposed Ancestral Wisdom. She's used to getting it right, even if sometimes it's by accident. But she hasn't ever been consumed. She knew nothing of the stone, and it showed. So I told her about it. Just a little, and because I could.

"You're *Stoned,*" I stressed, lifting one eyebrow like the distinction I was getting ready to make should've been common sense. It wasn't, but I couldn't help what I knew. I couldn't help that in that room—and in the majority of them since—I am the expert on this. "That doesn't mean you're in*side* the stone."

My pediatrician-cum-therapist lifted her chin.

"I wasn't in the courtyard. I was nowhere. I was in the gray."

There was a hitch then, or more like a glitch. I forgot how to keep my breath and my saliva separate for a moment, and made a kind of abbreviated gargle sound like the last word had been difficult to say. I could've slapped myself. There was no way she wasn't going to read into that, despite that it was involuntary and completely meaningless. I just took a breath, let my lips break into a tight smile, and continued.

"I was a disembodied consciousness, suspended in . . . gray."

The next breath I took rattled in my chest, but at least I had one. At least it had gotten that far.

"What was that like?" she asked, and I might have been annoyed, except that she was genuinely asking. There was a gape to her small mouth, and the hand that usually held her pen above her notebook was lying on it.

I started by shaking my head.

"I couldn't explain it if I wanted to. And you don't want to know."

Who wants to hear that time crashes to a halt—or that it stretches without passing? Or that maybe it does neither, or both?

Who would tell their doctor that what felt like immediately upon being Stoned, my brain wanted to blow through my cranium and escape, except that I had neither. No brain, no cranium. No beginning or end of myself . . . and something worse.

Who would want to say that there is something worse than all that? That there is a quiet that no one but Eloko would've noticed. No one who hasn't been hearing a gentle and occasional tinkling since birth, like a simple wind chime just outside their window, or a delicate bell. Because from the beginning of our lives, we hear a lovely, quiet reminder of our beauty and magic. Other people hear it most audibly when an Eloko first approaches them, but it comforts us as babies, and our parents say we cry less. All through childhood, we hear it in an odd silence and remember who we are, so we're never lonely, and we're prone to suddenly smile. Then we put that sound in our bell charms so we can share it with the world, our unique melodies. No wonder they adore us.

The point is, we're always hearing it, or quietly recalling it. It's never far. It's inside of us, and that must mean that when you're Stoned, while you're there, you don't really exist. It's the only explanation for my melody disappearing with the rest of my body, and the world.

Weeks after being stolen from myself, I wasn't ready to tell Dr. Corey the extent of it.

"And the suspension. Do you feel like you've been silenced?" she asked, like she already knew.

I assumed the alarm that flashed once inside my chest didn't show up on my face. She looked sympathetic, but definitely not You Had The Very Essence Of Who You Are Stolen From You sympathetic.

I am the only Eloko to ever have been Stoned. She couldn't know that I'd lost my melody there. No one could.

Which meant she was probably referring to LOVE.

Officially—or originally, anyway—the app's called Eloko Verified, but we influencers—the Portland Eloko it was designed to attract and amplify—took the Elo and the Ve, and of course our nickname stuck. Why wouldn't it? Someone created it specifically to give us a platform, or at least to make it easier for our audience to follow and engage with us.

I had fifty thousand subscribers the night of junior prom. The next morning, I was locked out. When I was finally ready to venture back out in public—but just digitally—I could see my picture, and my custom banner, and the floral wallpaper of my profile. My featured posts, my pictures, and my streams? Gone. In their place was some nonsense about Sensitive And Potentially Upsetting Content, and something about LOVE Fully Investigating Complaints.

Turns out losing my melody was just the prelude to waking up and seeing what the world would feel like if I'd never had one.

"Were you upset?" Dr. Corey'd asked me then.

I tilted my head from one side to the other, satisfied by the sound and the relief of the cracks.

"Confused, actually. See, I'd just spent six hours out of time and space"—and identity—"so I wasn't immediately sure what *sensitive content* they could possibly have been referencing."

Her eyes drifted to the side, and then she straightened in her chair before concluding, "So you didn't remember."

"I didn't remember what?" I asked, and I didn't adjust. I didn't tense or straighten, or fidget.

"I thought maybe being Stoned impacted your short-term memory? Maybe you didn't remember posting footage of the attack?"

"I remembered," I told her, letting my eyelids sink like the boredom might be putting me to sleep. "I just considered it a public service more than anything. I don't think that's unreasonable, especially since my footage had already been used to help identify victims. It turned out to be pretty useful when kids didn't come home that night. And when someone decided to make an official record."

I didn't mention the University of Portland professor who'd reached out several times by then, first to inquire about archiving the original and full-length livestream I'd made that night, and later to tell me she'd shifted her focus entirely to Eloko study. Like I was supposed to be appreciative. Like she's the first person enamored of us.

Ma'am. Get in line.

"Anyway, I know what you're dancing around," I told her, and ran my fingers through my hair before studying the recently trimmed ends. "Because it wasn't about whether the families of the Stoned were upset over the footage of what happened to their loved ones."

Dr. Corey looked skeptical, and I rolled my eyes.

"I was the Stoned, too. Which is how they walked back that suspension, by the way, because they didn't want to admit that an app I basically helped build—I have the largest number of followers from outside Portland, by the way—was taking the media's side."

She didn't say a thing, because what could she say? She couldn't pretend not to know what I was talking about without looking completely ridiculous, so instead she just looked horribly uncomfortable, like she hoped I'd have mercy on her and not let the awkward silence last too long.

"Despite watching what Effie did, and even though Tavia was right there . . ."

I literally bit my tongue for a moment.

"In less than a day, everyone decided the gorgon was a hapless victim of her unknown powers, and the siren was a conquering heroine. Which means *I* had to be the problem, for capturing it all."

"And then . . ." she ventured, timidly, but not timid enough to keep from repaying my mercy with a rundown of the allegations against me. "The other kids—well, someone—said you'd exposed Tavia. That you'd outed a siren."

"And since that wasn't in the video, I guess you'll have to decide who you believe." And then, precisely be*cause* Dr. Corey's an Eloko, and because there had been no one else whose accusations I'd dignified with an explanation—no one else's I *would*—I told her. "I did not out Tavia Philips."

I let the words rest with her for a moment, kept my eyes trained on hers. It should not have taken that for a fellow Eloko to believe me, whether it was the whole story or not.

Because it was true; I never said Tavia was a siren. I said Effie was. Which, yes, was meant to stress Tavia out, because all three of us knew the truth.

Was it truth adjacent? Doy. Or it wouldn't have been effective.

Did I out Tavia? No.

Did I show everybody that Effie's hair moved on its own? Yeah, but plenty of us already knew that, so. Truly not a big deal. Like, I'm sorry, had no one ever been dragged in front of their classmates? Was I suddenly the first person to feud with my skinfolk? Because I think not.

For the record, I wanted to say, I also didn't start recording until after everybody's True Self had been revealed, and Effie was gorgon-ing all over the courtyard, which—as I mentioned—turned out to be pretty useful footage. It helped identify the Stoned, and it solved the mystery in Triton Park. There was no question what happened to those kids all those years ago, and who had done it—intentionally or not.

You're welcome, PDX.

"They did the right thing," Dr. Corey said, like a concession. "Reinstating your LOVE account."

All of that was a year ago.

I thought things would be back to normal by now. I thought—I just knew!—Portland would be.

In no universe did I think I'd still be meeting with my pediatrician-therapist, that there'd still be anything to talk about, let alone more. New things.

The trash fire has gone full dumpster.

Dr. Corey's holding my phone, because now there's a Please Read Me banner on LOVE, and I don't want to paraphrase it. I want her to see exactly what I saw when I logged on this morning.

To our dear, beloved influencers and users,

We here at LOVE had a single purpose in mind when this platform was launched: celebrate the Eloko who make PDX such a unique and charming place to call home. We wanted a place to admire and adore the magic we sometimes take for granted, and we knew we weren't alone.

That was just four short years ago, but so much has changed since then. We've discovered there's more magic in Portland than we ever knew, and some of it has been hidden because being known wasn't safe.

We are LOVE.

We're committed to uplifting magic in all its forms, and we're going to be taking steps to make this platform more inclusive, so that we aren't just celebrating those who've always had the privilege of celebration. Please continue sharing your concerns and your ideas, because that's what makes this platform magic!

I know she's finished reading the super woke manifesto when she takes a deep breath and her hands settle, my phone sinking into her lap as Dr. Corey lifts her eyes to me.

"Talk to me about this," she says.

"But wherever to begin," I reply, and my laugh is genuine, if misleading. "Oh, I know. We are LOVE."

"Yes?"

"Well, they aren't, are they? They're *Eloko* Verified." I blink a few times. "They're literally using the nickname *we* gave them completely out of context to pretend they've always been about *magic,* when they exist because *we* do."

Dr. Corey isn't on LOVE, but she gets it. She could be.

"So, I'm just waiting for someone to explain to me why they're doing these ridiculous stretches to please people who don't subscribe to the original purpose of an app that no one, I might remind you, is forcing them to use!"

I look around as though in search of the lie, or as though my squad were here, in the office. I can see Priam's adorably smug grin, and Jamie's about to begin her monosyllabic hype woman routine, and Gavin's ready to launch into a sharp-tongued takedown to rival my own.

"I grasp that everybody loves sirens now, I'm just not sure why attacking Eloko is suddenly okay."

And then I feel it again.

The same thing I felt when I read the announcement this morning, standing in the middle of my bedroom, staring down at my phone.

Something like a rush of wind passes through me, almost as though a spirit is entering my chest and moving straight through. I can't help catching my breath, but at least I don't gasp. It takes everything in me not to widen my eyes or gape my mouth, but I keep what I can only hope is a stoic expression, and Dr. Corey doesn't seem to register that anything's changed.

There's no convincing myself it didn't happen this time. This second time it's happening is precisely like the first. I can't explain it, but it isn't something that starts inside me. It's something passing through. Except it feels the way it looks in every cartoon or show or movie where a ghost sweeps through an unsuspecting human. It feels like *someone*. Which, as far as brand-new phenomena go, is more than a little alarming.

There's also the fact that I heard it. As in, I somehow heard this . . . wind move through me—inside me—the way I might hear my melody when no one else can.

And then, I almost say it. The thing I sort of spontaneously spoke aloud the first time this ghost-wind-thing happened.

I need to get out of Portland.

It's true in a way that doesn't exactly make sense, like it's something I just *know*. Despite the fact that I've never, ever had the thought before.

I don't say it to Dr. Corey, which is the important part.

"And you're sleeping?" she asks.

My face scrunches, and my eyes dart around the room.

What kind of segue . . .

"Like at night?" I ask, one brow raised. "Or right now?"

"I know it feels like a remedial question, Ny, but it's important. That and drinking a lot of water."

Yep, because getting Stoned is exactly the same as getting a cold. Thanks, doc.

And she looks up at me like she can read my mind.

"I know this sucks. I wish I was more help, but. There's no protocol for recovering from a gorgon attack. We've done blood work for a year now, and tracked your vitals, and I've asked you what I know seem like such pointless, redundant questions—"

"Because they *are* redundant. And pointless."

A deep breath lifts her chin, and then she brings it back down.

"Right? Can we just say it out loud, finally? You have no idea what you're looking for."

"We have no idea what we're looking for," she replies, and she's lucky she's Eloko, so that instead of coming off like an amateur, her honesty actually comes as a relief. "We've been keeping a close eye on everybody who Awakened, but luckily so far there doesn't seem to be any lasting effect. Nothing physical anyway."

Which just leaves all the mental and psychological possibilities, dope.

"If you're looking for answers, you might reconsider speaking to Professor Vesper-Holmes. She's got as much experience studying gorgons as anyone is likely to get, and she's focusing on Eloko now. In your case, that's a promising intersection. I think you might benefit, and I know she would."

"Of course *she* would," I scoff. "Sorry. I'm not a lab rat."

There's a quiet in my chest. A weird calm that somehow reminds me of the wind I felt before. As though I'm wondering whether that professor might know the source of it, and whether or not it's a post-Stoned thing, or an Eloko thing I've somehow never experienced before.

But she wouldn't. She might have a PhD, but she isn't one of us, and I'm not about to trust a non-Eloko with something like that.

"That's fine," Dr. Corey says, like she agrees with what I didn't say, "but that means for the time being, I'm gonna have to insist you answer my pointless and redundant questions. Like whether or not you're sleeping."

"Yep," I say with a nod. "I sleep."

I'm not gonna tell her that for the past month, Sleep has involved me lying in my bedroom with my eyes wide open because I could swear I heard stones amassing. At which point I throw back the comforter and dash around my room checking the locks on the doors, and then stupidly looking out into the backyard where the little lanterns I used to love make bright spots and leave circles of darkness peppered between them.

Without fail, the thought occurs to me that Tavia might be in any one of these shadows. Her gargoyle might've carried her and she might even be accompanied by her sister, still in a Siren Slave stupor.

I am not about to tell my fake therapist that sometimes I do see her out there—or I think I do. I don't say that the one thing that keeps the scream from getting all the way out is the terrifying fact that in those shadows in my backyard, the Tavia I think I see is completely gray. So I know it isn't really her.

"Okay. Well, that's all my questions. Do you have any for me?" she asks. "Anything you remember about the experience that you didn't before?"

Everything. I remember everything about The Experience, all three hundred sixty minutes of it. I remember the way it stole my melody. And I want to know why it was so easy to disappear. I want to know if our trill, and our melody, and LOVE is all we have, because.

Suddenly every single one of those things seems super unreliable.

Dr. Corey gives me a look she's made the mistake of giving me at least a few times before. It's a gentle earnestness, a silent nudging that always makes me bristle. It's like she thinks that any minute I'm gonna turn out to be a new Naema, and maybe this one is gonna be fragile.

Which, no. Eff that.

"I think I'm good," I tell her, and stand without checking the clock. She isn't a real therapist; this isn't a real session. I'm through, sixty minutes filled or not. "I'll figure it out."

"Naema," she says, and it, too, is a bit too careful. "I know you know that movie's streaming today."

"Oh, you mean that made-for-TV movie about my attacker is finally debuting?"

So what if she thinks by attacker I mean Effie. The girl played her part, too.

"Yes, that one. I hope you'll really think it over before deciding whether or not to watch it. In case it's too much for you."

I roll my eyes again; I am all the way done.

"Dr. Corey, please. Ain't nobody checking for Tavia and Effie's little movie."

Chapter IV

When Eloko Behave Badly, or: a Time to Reframe

Staff Op-Ed | July 2020

It's no secret that many consider Beckett High a kind of mini-Portland. The school with the enviable title of enrolling the highest number of Eloko (in a city known as their self-proclaimed capital) is a microcosm of the strange and magical place we know and love. It therefore wasn't terribly shocking when a phenomenon that's mystified the city for nearly a decade came to a stunning conclusion—and all three players at the center of that conclusion were currently enrolled at Beckett. More fantastic still? The trio was comprised of one siren, one gorgon, and one Eloko.

Microcosm, indeed.

Everyone knows the story of the gorgon, once thought to be the sole survivor of the Triton Park incident, and how she was revealed to be unknowingly responsible. We know that her best friend was a secret siren whose own power proved to be the children's salvation. If that had been the final twist in a story ripe for cinematic retelling, it would have been shocking enough—but there was more.

In the weeks since the Awakening, the internet has been working overtime to piece together the events surrounding it. What's been uncovered is a completely unexpected and seemingly uncharacteristic episode of an Eloko behaving badly. It isn't something often seen, if at all, and it's likely not a conclusion anyone would've been willing to arrive at without video evidence. Which, in another twist, came from the Eloko herself.

On the grounds that she is a minor, we have decided against printing the young woman's name, despite the overwhelming number of views her video received before a magic-friendly platform made the compassionate decision to take it down.

In her livestream, the young Eloko captures the horrifying scene at Beckett High's junior prom when Effie Freeman, the young woman previously known to the public as Park Girl, turned almost a dozen of her classmates to stone under her gorgon form. After Tavia Philips used a call to stop the carnage, the siren is briefly seen pleading directly to the camera. Unaware that the footage was being streamed, and clearly terrified not just for her own exposure, but her friend's, she begs the young Eloko not to release it.

What happened next isn't captured in the video, but it soon became clear that the Eloko herself was "Stoned," a colloquial phrase for the experience of those impacted by the gorgon's power. Initially, discussions about her ordeal revolved around what, if any, impact her magical identity might've made upon her Stoning experience. Speculation quickly gave way to rumors, however, that the Eloko had been responsible for triggering the Stoning. Provocative or not, on closer study it turned out these rumors fit neatly with the tone and content of the footage. Since then, an Eloko accustomed to the flattering attention of her fellow Portland citizens is under a scrutiny she's likely never experienced before.

If activists like Tavia Philips are to be believed, being a siren is a dangerous thing. She points to the recent arrest and subsequent remand of fellow siren activist, Camilla Fox, as evidence. Perhaps the most pointed illustration, though, is that a few short months ago, both young women kept their identities a secret. If that's the argument, then someone capturing the prom attack after instigating the revelation of Tavia's and Effie's identities—even just to their classmates—would be despicable. Considering the Eloko's sizeable following online, it isn't unreasonable to assume the intention was even graver.

But an Eloko using her platform for harm? It's far-fetched—or is it? Because while we in Portland have always considered our beloved friends benevolent and wholly magical, maybe that's been a little myopic. Reductive, even. In this age of parsing and acknowledging the layers of identity one can house, maybe ignoring what the three girls have in common would be a mistake. Not to mention unfair to the rest of the Eloko community.

This is where it gets tricky. No one wants to still be focusing on something as basic as racial identity, especially not in a city known for its progressive values. To hear Tavia Philips and Camilla Fox and a slew of others tell it, however, being a Black woman makes a difference. So we hope it's taken in the most respectful spirit when we state the obvious: all three members of the Beckett prom fiasco were magical Black girls. And *if* that matters, then maybe we've been looking at the young Eloko's behavior through the wrong lens. Maybe it only makes sense when you take into account what the girls—clearly embroiled in a high school feud—have in common. Instead of assigning uncharacteristically malicious behavior to an entire population of Eloko who otherwise have no hostility toward sirens or gorgons, maybe it's time to hold the young instigator responsible as a young woman of color cruelly acting against her own. As difficult as it is to consider those uncomfortable optics, something tells us that a certain well-spoken siren would err on the side of truth.

Chapter V

NAEMA

When I get home, Mommy's rousing from a nap she decided to take on my bed because she's extra.

"Hi, Ny," she says through a yawn, and tries to descend from the tall four-poster bed as though she doesn't have ridiculously short legs. As per yoosh, she's got one hand on her extremely modest baby bump. Her cautious movements usually annoy me to no end since it's a bit early in her pregnancy for all that, but this time I intervene.

"Use the steps," I tell her, blandly, moving the dark wood stool beneath her feet.

Like most of my bedroom furniture, it's heirloom wood, repurposed from ancestral belongings because that matters when you're praying for an Eloko baby. That and—according to Darren and Simone Bradshaw, and plenty of other people—living in an Eloko hotbed like Portland. While planning for a family, my parents were relentless in two campaigns: one, commandeering antiques and hand-me-downs whenever loved ones passed or they were moved into a convalescent home and their things were up for grabs; and two, digging their heels into the PNW and not budging. To hear my dad tell it, they may have burned some bridges to accomplish both, but it was worth it. For years, he stockpiled everything in a locker at one of the local self-storage facilities he owns throughout the state, and when Mommy finally got pregnant, he had everything dismembered, sanded, stained, and rebuilt into custom pieces for me.

They filled the house with family history, but some people said Dad should've gone further. That he should've built it all with his own two hands to be on the safe side, made sure the process was familial from start to finish, but. My father is a literal boss. He knows there's a balance between ritual and right. The wood was the important part, he said, and he wanted it all to be beautiful. Fit for a princess. Because he said he didn't just know I'd be Eloko: he knew I'd be *Naema*. So not only did they give me the master bedroom, they knocked down a wall for my thirteenth birthday so I'd have the elaborate suite of my dreams. Beckett High's Eloko HQ, and intended venue for a historic post-prom bash that obviously never happened. Junior prom, for obvious gorgon-related reasons. Not after senior ball, because—well, nothing about this past year was as fun or energetic as it should've been. I'd be pissed if I weren't just glad high school is done.

When I get back from my appointment with Dr. Corey, my room looks a lot creepier than usual.

"Mommy, what the hell are these wreaths? And why'd you put them around my bed like I'm dying and people are coming to view my body?"

"Oh, Ny . . ." She trails off for a moment because she's finally made it off the bed, and has wrapped her arms around my waist and laid her head against my back. "They came while you were at the doctor's."

"Okay, but what are they? Because they're giving me Triton Park Memorial vibes. And why are they in here?"

"People sent them to the news station after they did a segment on Awakening Day, and the station delivered them today! I put them here, so you'd see them when you wake up, and you'd know there are still so many people who adore you and hope you feel better soon."

"I'm not ill," I snap, pushing through her hold. The part about people still adoring me, I don't dignify. "Get them out of here, please, it looks super depressing."

"They're flowers. I just thought—" She caresses the back of her black pixie cut the way she does when she's playing fragile. It works wonders on my dad. She's petite and she's responsible for my perfect deep brown skin, big eyes, and thick eyelashes, so I get it. I'm just basically her taller twin, and as such, am immune.

"You just thought I'd like to wake up in a crypt? No, thank you. I know you've got preggo brain, but seriously, Mommy."

But she's no more used to rejection than I am, so instead of doing what I've asked, she goes and retrieves a card I hadn't noticed among the mourning flora.

"Look, Ny," she says, thrusting it at me before her hand unnecessarily cradles her bump again. "Read it."

When I snatch the card, she smiles like a doe-eyed Disney cartoon.

"Out loud," she whispers.

"No," I whisper back.

To Our Eloko Princess—Please Post More Content On LOVE, We Miss You!

I accept a second card from her.

You Are Still What Makes Portland Great!

"I can feel you smiling, Mommy. Fine. I'll keep the cards. Get rid of the flowers."

It isn't quite the same as having a constant stream of comments and notifications. It can't undo an entire year—my senior year, if I haven't mentioned!—of being plagued by whispers, and disingenuous smiles, and snubs, and what felt like the whole world's attempt to wrestle away my Eloko-ness. It won't change the fact that the media I never knew to distrust has taken every opportunity to uplift my attacker and disparage me, all while pretending they're protecting me because they don't call me by name.

I wonder how much more useless that flimsy performance will be after today, when Tavia's movie drops.

The level of affirmation and nonmedical attention I am accustomed to has been severely lacking. Despite the fact that I have plans to hang out with my crew—two of whom can always be trusted to deliver some amount of fawning—it isn't like my friends can keep the city from tilting out from under my feet. I mean, they were there when the whole Network Excommunication happened last summer, and they couldn't stop that. But I don't want to spend too much time thinking about the possible limitations of even Eloko friendship on the same day a movie canonizing a siren/gorgon one goes live.

"I'm headed out," I tell Mommy, kissing the top of her head the way pretty much everyone who isn't a small child does.

"I thought that wasn't until later," she says with a pout.

"And I thought this was a bedroom suite, not a sarcophagal chamber, byeee."

My girl Jamie's house is within walking distance, but I drive my beloved Fiat anyway, pulling into the drive behind Gavin Shinn's car, because apparently I'm not the only one who decided to get a jump on hanging out. All we're missing is my Priam, unless he came with Gavin, and I'm so excited to sink into our Eloko oasis that I don't even spare the few seconds it takes to text and let Jamie know I'm here. So when I come around the back and enter her bedroom via the patio doors, I catch Jamie and Gavin completely by surprise.

I know this because Jamie shoots off the bed with a start, and because both of them yelp my name.

The final clue, of course, is what's playing on her sixty-inch television screen. Which Gavin pauses—because in his panic, he must think freezing a huge image of the actress playing Tavia Philips will somehow make it better.

"You guys couldn't have been fooling around, like normal teenagers!" I yell behind me as I storm back the way I came, but not quickly enough not to hear Gavin's calm:

"We're never gonna hook up, like . . ."

"Nyyyy." Jamie's whine tries to catch up as I storm through the backyard, and around the outside of the house.

"Cannot believe you! Jamie!"

"I'm sorry!"

Which is when I whirl around. It's a pretty narrow walkway, between the house and the fence, and Gavin has to peek around Jamie to see me. It'd be hilarious if they weren't betraying me, yet again.

"You can't be sorry the instant you're caught, Jamie, that's not remorse, it's wishing I hadn't found out!"

"Please don't be upset at me!"

"Seriously?!"

"You never said we couldn't watch it!" She bats the unwieldy ivy leaves back toward their lattice, and the leaves defiantly keep hold of her maple tresses so her hair splays like it has a life of its own. Which—naturally—reminds me of Effie, at the pool, the first time we all saw her hair move.

"Are you trying to piss me off?"

"Well, you didn't!"

"And yet, somehow you knew it wasn't cool, otherwise why'd you freak out that I caught you?" Behind Jamie, Gavin has his hands in his pockets. "You good?" I snap. "No pleading apologies from you?"

"If it makes you feel any better, you're not technically in it?"

For a moment I can only blink at him. Why that's supposed to . . . but also how is that even possible?

"You're not, it's some random character named Nina—"

"Gavin," Jamie tries to shush him.

"What, I get that you and Tavia aren't cool, but the movie's about Effie, too, and as far as I can remember she never did anything to you—"

"She was the *weapon,* Gavin!" I yell.

There's a trill like a fragment of an Eloko's already-brief melody, and sometimes we put it in our voices. When we're upset sometimes it just happens, so while the three of us stand on the path beside Jamie's house, our trills mingle in the space between us, reverberating off the walls and the fence, like the echo after cymbals crash. Non-Eloko are enamored with the sound; they also can't tell the difference between trills complimenting each other and trills competing. Mine and Gavin's are doing the latter, but only another Eloko would know.

"I'm going home," I say.

"Ny," Jamie begins, and then Gavin tells her to let me go. And I do.

My city's turned on me. My platform, too. I don't know why I thought it'd be any different with my Eloko crew. After all, we've been splintering bit by bit for the past year.

I'm beginning to realize they aren't feeling what I'm feeling. Which, fine. They didn't have to get used to the slight and usually unspoken chill that comes with a once-adoring audience's disapproval. There were no blog or YouTube posts about a nameless Eloko whose other attributes were exhaustively listed just so no one missed the fact that it was me being discussed.

They weren't the ones slowly coming to terms with the fact that the longer I'm Awakened, the less my world makes sense. Priam, Jamie, and Gavin didn't have to genuinely consider the possibility that the gray I was trapped in while Stoned was actually a portal, not a place, and that I got spit out in an alternate Portland. Because what other explanation is there, really? That everybody's siren fear has really and eternally been forgotten because she released us from gorgon prison? That even Effie is adored, despite being the gorgon in question, because she didn't know she had that power?

It's been clear for the past year that this is not my Portland, and that's not something the three of them have had to face. That in *my* Portland, Tavia Philips is a secret siren I have to help protect from discovery. *I'm* the hometown heroine, or at least generally fawned over. I've got one of the largest followings on LOVE, which means that company is loyal to *me,* not the whims of cancel culture—which surprisingly no one has a problem with when it's directed at me.

This city loves *me.* They don't criticize me for a livestream and still snatch footage to plaster all over local media. The post got me suspended on LOVE, and yet the footage they said was Too Troubling went everywhere. Apparently, it wasn't too troubling to slap on TV.

My friends—my Eloko hive—don't watch the movie that supposedly leaves me out. The movie, I might add, they weren't nearly salty enough about when the production company rolled into town mere months after the Awakening.

Except they *did* watch that movie. Judging by the way Gavin and Jamie reacted during its filming—not to mention neither of them were appalled that it was rumored to be funded by the all-new siren synthesizers—I guess I should've seen it coming last summer.

Maybe if I'd really lit into them the first time Jamie and Gavin betrayed me, things would've been different today.

There had been open casting calls, and I'd found out via LOVE—which I wasn't posting to, but sometimes scrolling through—that Jamie and Gavin had gone to one. Totally unsurprisingly, it had been Gavin's idea, but Jamie had buckled and gone with him, so she wasn't an innocent party.

Shocked doesn't even begin.

Literally anybody else could've pretended that it was just another Portland production and it was harmless to want a cameo, but *my* friends? In a Tavia Philips movie? For what?

I couldn't even flash on them properly, because there was still a small detail they didn't know—that Tavia had instructed Effie to Stone me intentionally. Everybody had dispersed or been consumed by the time that part happened, and based on the way Portland was Upside Down when I got back, part of me thought telling my friends what she'd done would look petty and attention-seeking. Which is really more Gavin's deal.

That and I didn't think I should need to be wounded to deserve a bit more loyalty and consideration than they were showing.

Anyway, after discovering their audition betrayal, I'd muted them in my phone, and Priam promised to take my mind off them with a date day that abruptly ended at Powell's.

That day had been like a ridiculously impressive cornucopia of awful, just a fragrant bouquet of trash events. The first bad omen was definitely the two siren synthesizers we saw between getting out of the car and getting to the door of the bookstore. I knew Priam had seen them, because he'd been tensing up almost as much as I had whenever anything Tavia-related came up.

The first flashed past us on a kid running by, but the second was harder to ignore.

A white girl with long curly hair was standing at the bus stop across the street from the bookstore with her legs wide, chin up, and the white mesh mask covering her mouth. It was all very You'll Never Silence Me and defiant, except for the whole

She Couldn't Possibly Be A Siren thing. She had a photographer capturing her every extremely slight adjustment. Her hair was doing 90 percent of the modeling for her, if we're being really real.

In the middle of the white mesh, there's a flat, white disc. I couldn't see it from across the street, but it's the voice distorter that mimics the powerful vibration in a siren call. If the Not-Quite-Cutting-It-As-A-Model wearing it said anything, she would've really sounded like a siren. By which I mean, it would sound like she was a siren according to the commercial reminding people not to miss the upcoming movie.

Nothing sounds like the real thing. Nothing sounds like a siren call except the sound of Tavia's voice, standing a few feet from me in the courtyard, telling her sister to turn me to stone.

But yeah. Siren synthesizers.

Let's talk about why this was the unfunniest of all the jokes. Not only was Tavia getting a super premature biopic after what she'd done to me, she was getting her very own gadget! That way, there was no grace period before the movie came out! I got to be reminded that it was coming every single time some nimrod was super brave and edgy and wore a synthesizer-dealie!

Amazing!

"One day, Tavia has to hide," I said, while Priam stood a little ways behind me, probably intentionally looking somewhere else. "And six hours after prom, the world is paying to pretend they're just like her."

Priam hadn't answered, and neither of us mentioned that the only accessory previously attributed to sirens was not a toy. It was a collar, a device designed to undo the power in their voice. In the same city where it was legal for cops to forcibly collar sirens, people were now gonna parade around in synthesizers meant to mimic them. I wonder what Camilla Fox would have to say about that, but she's still in police custody, and despite the fact that Tavia's started her own mini-Camilla channel, I'm pretty sure she hasn't said anything, either.

I don't like the girl, but I'm not ridiculous. I can see a couple reasons why she wouldn't want to, I guess.

I don't know how long I stood there staring at a girl who didn't know what to do with her hands, though she'd recently discovered jutting out her pelvic bone was a look. Then a gaggle of preschool/day camp–aged kids came squealing up to Priam and me, grabbing our hands and hugging our legs because they'd heard our melodies.

"I found a princess!" one of the kids told their amused chaperones.

"You did," the woman agreed, smiling, before turning to Priam and me for the inevitable ask.

She wasn't gonna ask if we'd take a picture with the kids; they never did. She was going to ask if she could take a short video—just in case they could catch our melodies on tape.

I turned on my heel before she could get it out of her mouth.

Priam could pose if he wanted to, but I wasn't feeling it. Across the street, a girl in a siren synthesizer was still pretending she had a future in front of the camera and, sorry, but Portland doesn't get to have it both ways.

Inside Powell's, I headed for the corner in the Romance/Coffee room where Jamie, Gavin, Priam, and I usually pop a squat with a stack of manga and comic books. And when I arrived, surprise surprise. The betrayers were already there, one of them toeing the floor like she was preparing to go en pointe, and the other running his hand through his thick hair before tossing his head a bit to get it to fall the way he wanted. Because Gavin Shinn is always ready when the Eloko-obsessed descend on him, and the answer is always yes.

When they saw me, both their eyes got big, Jamie's almost quivering, but they didn't pounce. I knew why when I felt Priam's arm snake around my waist and turn me toward him.

"You told them to come?" I accused him.

"Yes, beautiful. Is that okay?"

"No, Priam, it's not." But I didn't pull away. And not because I very easily get distracted by the way his hair swoops to a point on one side, like it's about to stab the mole under his eye.

Which reminds me. He cut his hair after the school year ended, and never said why. I'd been trying to figure out if it had anything to do with what happened at prom, or since Portland turned into a film set and people started selling interviews. And I really wanted to know if it had anything to do with his new fits of weirdly cagey behavior. Like, he was either pulling me into his arms and calling me beautiful like some blond Noah Centineo character, or he was standing still enough to be stone. The one thing he wasn't doing was telling me why.

"I'm angry," I said, pushing against him now because I knew he wasn't letting go.

"That's all right," and he kissed me. "You get to be. That doesn't mean we stop hanging out with our friends, does it?"

That time I pushed free for real.

"You do know they tried to be part of the movie."

He stopped. Not like he was confused; he knew exactly what I was talking about.

"Priam."

Near us, Gavin took Jamie's belt loop and pulled her toward the coffee because he's such a considerate friend and wanted to give us some privacy. Or because he was guilty and didn't wanna have to actually explain why they did it.

"Did you ask them not to?" Priam was asking, his body free from whatever momentary curse kept afflicting him. He reached for my sides, but his touch was too light. Whatever was going on, I was getting very suspicious. And tired of it.

"I didn't know I needed to," I said, following his eyes to see what exactly was so interesting in the middle distance, and trying to force him to make eye contact again. "Priam!"

"Yes. Would you prefer they hadn't told you?"

"What? They didn't. I saw Gavin's video on LOVE, remember? What is going on with you?"

"Don't get upset, Ny," he said, kissing me again like he'd been paying attention all along. The charming smile returned and he swept a hand through my hair. "Gavin craves the spotlight. You know that. Plus, it loves him."

"So why didn't you, too, since it's no big deal?"

"They didn't invite me."

"And if they had? Then you'd have gone? To be an extra in a movie about her? I thought you said you hated her."

He'd been playing with the charm at the end of my necklace, and paused to take a deep breath.

"I never said I hated her."

"Oh, that's right. You just wish you hadn't met her."

"Yeah."

"Which sounds curiously like something you say when you actually care. But too much."

"I don't wanna talk about— We're here to hang out with our friends, and for you to let them grovel and apologize." But Jamie and Gavin had wandered closer again, and I saw the tick in Gavin's eyebrow, which Priam must've seen, too, because he pointed at him without looking.

"I'm not interested in the apologies of a couple of backstabbers," I said, and watched Jamie's face crumple.

"Ny." Gavin's brow dropped, as I knew it would. "Be nice."

"*Ny*, be nice?" I whirled to face him. "Is everybody high? Why the hell am I supposed to be nice? To anyone? Let alone my best friends who went behind my back to try to get cameos in a trash fire movie glamorizing a girl I effing hate—" I had to stop because my stupid melody was trilling in my voice, and nearby Powell's customers were smiling like idiots. When I started up again, I whisper-growled, "whose story somehow made my city hate me."

"Naema," Priam said, like his heart might be literally sore. "Don't say that."

"This city loves you," Jamie said with an earnestness she couldn't have faked. Poor girl still believed it. "There's a digital vigil for you under every one of your LOVE posts! The ones you haven't selectively and strategically taken down. Which has been totally good for your numbers, by the way."

"Which was the point. Oh." I pivoted like something had just occurred to me. "That reminds me. Just because I haven't been posting my own content doesn't mean I haven't seen yours. Gavin."

All eyes landed on him.

"I can't control what my followers wanna talk about, Ny."

"Well, when your vlog is a very poorly veiled reaction video to some Super Woke video from Tavia's suddenly viral channel about her sirenness being part of Unapologetic Blackness—"

"What's . . ." He turned one way and then the other, gesturing confusion with his hands like some stupid meme. "What's supposed to be wrong with that? It was interesting. I liked the video."

"Funny how quickly the conversation turned into who *isn't* Authentically Black."

"I didn't know it was gonna go there," he said, like for the first time he was actually sorry.

"'Cause there's a lot you don't know, Gavin. But lemme be nice."

"Just. To be clear," Gavin said like he knew he should have stopped talking. "She didn't say that in the video. Rando commenters did."

I opened my mouth to cuss him out.

"Can you help me get something down, baby?"

We all stopped. Because suddenly there was an old lady standing with us, and she'd tapped me on the shoulder.

"What?" Jamie said through a confused snort, while Priam and Gavin looked between the woman and me like they were asking if I could see her, too. "Do you know her?"

The group got only more confused when I exhaled and answered, "Yes, ma'am."

An elderly Black woman told me to do something, what was I gonna say? No? C'mon.

But when I followed her, the woman led me out of the room altogether. She weaved through the city of books and didn't stop until we got to poetry, but I kept quiet. Because by then, I'd figured this wasn't an anonymous and enfeebled octogenarian who'd randomly chosen me out of four teens to assist her. So when we'd passed the information desk and were flanked on both sides by tall bookcases, I waited for her to turn around, and I set my face to I Couldn't Care Less. But like, respectfully, because Elderly Black Woman.

"How are you, baby?" she said, finally.

I hadn't prepared for that. My chest immediately seized, like I'd been hit with a defibrillator. It actually hurt, and I felt like an idiot but I teared up. At that point, it had been weeks since the Awakening, and it felt like the first time anyone asked if I was okay. Dr. Corey didn't count; there was a reason she was asking. The old woman sounded like she really cared.

At first I could only nod my head.

"I'm okay," I said, when the overwhelm passed, and she tipped her head to the side like she was wise enough not to believe me. She rubbed one of my arms and nodded, too. "I mean, kind of. I will be."

"I know you will," she replied.

"I've never met you before," I told her while I casually wiped my eyes.

"You have," she said. "You just don't remember. You've been with us a long time. But I don't come out often anymore, not unless I really need to."

She was really making it sound like it was the mafia, which I guess would make her the donna.

Something had warranted her coming out, and that something had been me.

"I wanted to be the one to tell you," she said, and she kept her eyes locked on mine the whole time, the clear one and the cloudy one, too. "You aren't one of us anymore."

The defibrillator again. After the sting, I was too conscious of my breathing, trying to regulate it so my chest didn't rise or fall too fast or too visibly.

"I figured," I mumbled, without bothering to recount that I'd already told Tavia as much.

"Not just for the moment, baby. It isn't a temper tantrum. It's for good." She insisted on saying it all. "This means you can't be trusted. Not with this."

The donna was saying all of it in no uncertain terms. There wasn't a hint of negotiability, or hesitation. But there was a kind of gentleness like she was sorry for me. Which ordinarily would've pissed me right off. Except for the way she'd started the conversation. And the fact that she'd come herself.

"I know you think she doesn't need it anymore. That maybe none of them do now that she's speaking up, and people are listening. But Portland isn't the entire world, even if it seems that way. And I've lived long enough to know we can't trust the world to take care of us. Not for long. The network'll keep doing what we've always done."

I heard the unspoken *Without you.*

"Yes, ma'am," I said, because I didn't want to say anything else.

If the message had been delivered differently, or if my chest weren't aching, I would've said what I'd been waiting for someone to admit since being Awakened. That what Tavia had done to me should've meant *she* was excommunicated, not me. That she shouldn't get to have a network anymore, that no one should be risking anything to protect a power she could wield so maliciously.

"You're entitled to a defense," the donna said. "And since no one came forward to speak on your behalf, you should be permitted to do it yourself. It won't change the decision any. But I'll hear you now, if you want." Then, before I could answer, she said, "Sometimes when you're strong, people don't think you get hurt. They don't think to help you unless you ask."

I wished she'd stop. talking.

Everything she said hurt, and I didn't have a chance to wipe my eyes this time. I felt the streaks on my cheek, and then she sucked her teeth and reached up to wipe one away.

"I don't have anything to say."

"All right." She nodded again, lines forming around her mouth when she set her teeth together so tightly that it made a kind of grimace. "Thank you for your service."

And I had to get away from her. Away from the reminder that I was exile-able from everywhere. From my city, my platform, my place in all of it—and the network, too. I had to get away from my friends, who wouldn't have understood this even if I could've told them. I had to get out of Powell's, and since literally every one of them had recently let me down, I didn't bother telling anyone when I left.

Chapter VI

UP Professor Wants Portland to Reconsider Eloko Love

Staff Writer | Two days ago

Portland isn't exactly lacking in local celebrities these days. With a first annual Awakening Day on the books, and a commemorative movie recently released to overwhelming local enthusiasm, no one would begrudge us publishing the millionth article on Tavia Philips, Portland's own siren. Even a conjecture-heavy write-up on her mysterious best friend turned gorgon recluse, Effie Freeman, would be considered clickbait. So why is it that Heather Vesper-Holmes, the University of Portland professor who's attained her own level of local acclaim for her theories on the interdimensional nature of gorgons, is shifting her focus and resources elsewhere?

"I think a good researcher should be contrarian, by nature," Professor Vesper-Holmes says when she's made it back to the other side of her desk, and gestured for me to have a seat. "If everyone's already looking at one thing in particular—"

"Like at the suddenly famous sisterhood between a siren and a gorgon?" I ask.

"Like that—then my job is to look at what isn't in focus. It's where my work has the most use. I knew going in that most people wouldn't see the value in studying Portland's most popular magical population," she says, anticipating my hesitation. "Believe me, I get it. We're confident in our relationship with them. We fancy ourselves experts. We're constantly observing

Eloko, after all, whether in person every time we hear that unmistakable collection of notes that make up an Eloko melody, or online, where we know just where to find them."

That's when Professor Vesper-Holmes drops what feels like a bombshell question.

"But what is it we love, exactly?"

"About Eloko?" I ask, and she has to hear the incredulity in my voice.

"Okay, maybe that's an unfair question. Rather"—and it only takes her a moment to reframe it in a way that knocks me off my center—"what do we know about them? What is it that Eloko can do? What's *their* true form?"

That feels like sacrilege, but something about the academic setting in which we're meeting encourages me to ask: Is it fair?

We just witnessed history—the first confirmed gorgon on record. Despite the professor's hypothesis on a second mythologized gorgon more than likely related to Effie Freeman, the named is the only one observed in human, in nearly invisible mirage, and in gorgon form.

"We know gorgons have the power to transform others, with devastating consequences," she says, and there's no arguing that. "Sirens don't change form, but we know their voices carry power. Mermaids transform once, but permanently, and largely retreat to life under the sea."

She briefly sidetracks herself returning to the mythos suggesting that gorgons also retreat for the most part, though perhaps they are among us more often than we suspect, in the mirage form that mimics water, before seeming to recall the self-imposed redirection of her scholarship.

"There's the long-debunked mythos, ancient stories about Eloko being ancestor spirits, and cannibals," and her mouth pulls to one side in an almost apologetic grimace. "I mean, it's observably untrue, and has always gone without saying. But then, it almost begs the question, what *is* the nature of Elokoness?"

For a moment I actually think she's asking me, and if I'm supposed to supply her with an answer, I can't.

"Does it constitute a magical identity, or is it more akin to a caste? We know they're beloved, and we know they're charming," and while she speaks of them, even without being in one's presence, not even Professor Vesper-Holmes can keep from smiling. "They're smart, and they're insightful, and we tend to credit that to Ancestral Wisdom. We adore them for it. But is that the same as a power?"

For my part, I'm stunned silent.

"And does it need to be?"

Chapter VII

NAEMA

My parents have never said anything to me about the footage I took at prom. Over the past year, they've mostly tried to act like that side of things isn't happening, and focused on my recovery with Dr. Corey. I've caught them wringing their hands when they think I'm in bed following the doc's super customized medical advice to Rest Up.

It's been a year since my excommunication, and yet for some reason, when I get home from Jamie's house and power walk down the hall to their bedroom, I find out they're still not over it.

"Do you think they're ever going to ask her back?" I hear Mommy ask my dad, and I pull back in time to keep them from knowing I'm here.

"I don't know, Simone," he answers through a heavy breath, absently scratching at his clean-shaven chin. My mother's the only woman in Portland who doesn't fall apart over a nice beard, so Darren Bradshaw doesn't have one, but you can tell there's something missing in his life by the way he plays with the lower half of his face sometimes. "I don't know why they haven't sent anybody to see about her, I'll tell you that. Kicked out or not. It's been a year, and as far as I can tell she's had it just as bad as the other girl."

"I don't know if that's true . . ."

Wow. So much for family loyalty, I guess.

"I know they feel some kinna way about that video, but it's not like she actually outed Tavia. The girl did that on her own."

"That's not how they saw it."

"I don't care how people *saw* it, that's what was on the video. The world's seen it enough times to know by now. Ny recorded a gargoyle standing in the middle of the high school courtyard, and then that gorgon girl started zipping around changing people, and Tav—"

"Darren," Mommy says, hushing him. I pull all the way around their doorframe, in case they nervously look my way.

"And Tavia," he repeats, in what passes for a gruff whisper to someone with a voice as deep as his, only it's still Quite Loud, "used her voice to calm her down. Just because the girl said it's what Naema wanted, doesn't mean it's Ny's fault. And since when does an Eloko not get the benefit of the doubt?"

At least he sounds agitated.

"The network knows more than the public, Darren." I can't see it but I know she's shaking her tiny head. "They know Ny knew what that girl was. She shouldn't have been recording in the first place; she shouldn't have been so mean."

"Kids fight, period. It's fine. It turned out fine," he says, but I can't help hearing the slight hesitation in his voice. Like even he's not convinced. "They're gonna get over it. She's the only Eloko they have."

I peek back around the doorframe in time to see him swallow Mommy into his arms, and I march away.

I am beyond tired of this, of the endless cycle of finding out everybody still thinks I'm in the wrong. It's been a whole year and my parents are talking in hushed voices, debating whether or not the great network will forgive me despite the fact that I'd told them before prom that I was done. I'd already said I wasn't gonna shield Tavia anymore, regardless. How does it still matter whether or not they're upset at me? When is it gonna start mattering that *I'm* upset?

Screw this.

I turn around and burst into my parents' bedroom.

"Where can I go?" I ask.

They're both still on the bed, legs stretched and crossed at the ankle, only hers end somewhere around his knees.

"Oooh, we haven't done a staycation in a while!" she coos. "We could go back to that meditation hotel, or the Victorian one you like."

"Where can we go that's not in Portland, I mean."

The room gets very quiet, and both my parents stare at me without blinking. Because that is how unfamiliar a concept leaving Portland is. For me, or anyone Eloko-obsessed.

The donna said that Portland isn't the whole world, but it is to us. Boasting the highest Eloko population in the United States, PDX is widely accepted as our capital, so it always made sense that we never left.

Like, never.

Are there other cities in the world? Sure. Do they have their own Eloko populations? Of course. Are they the toast of the town? I have no idea. I assume so. We don't have a network like sirens; we don't need to, so I have no idea what they're accustomed to. If they have a LOVE platform of their own, if they have films or TV shows based in their town, and if that's the majority of what they consume, and whether that media predominately centers Eloko characters. Because that's what it's always been like here. Until last year, the media was just another branch of Eloko fandom.

"What's going on, princess?" my dad asks. Despite its gruffness, his voice is always gentle. When I first came out from the gorgon gray, he was there, in the courtyard. When Tavia rushed off, and the herd of people and cameras chased after her with what I'd hoped at the time was the passion of an angry mob, only he kept his eyes on me. The moment I had legs again, they gave out, and he carried me away.

During the ride home afterward, when I couldn't stop jumping at everything that blurred past my window, he'd asked if it was happening again. He'd kept that up for months, actually, asking if the stone was taking me back, until Dr. Corey explained why it wasn't possible and why it was annoying af.

There's something about what he's asking now that sounds like that's still what he wants to know.

"There's more to my life than prom night," I say, and he nods, which is Darren Bradshaw for I'll Do Better. And then he does. If

I could leave Upside-Down Portland to him, it'd get straightened out and I wouldn't have to go anywhere. But sadly there are some things neither my dad nor I control. Which is really unfortunate for everybody.

"I don't know if you want to go that far," Mommy says, rubbing her belly. "But you could go to the reunion, I guess. I don't know. It's so far. But Carla Ann's hosting it again—"

"Carla Ann's the only one who ever does," Dad interjects like without FaceTime we'd even know that. We buy recordings of family reunions; we don't actually attend them.

"She'd love to have you, and I know your cousin Courtney would, too. Baby Carmen would be over the moon!" She's getting more excited by the moment.

"I can't help noticing how you keep saying *me* now. Like, just me."

The room falls quiet again.

"Ny," and she's using her pouty voice, which she and Dad always claim doesn't exist, but here it is. "I would love to go with you. I wish I could."

"Great, we'll all go."

"You know we can't do that, princess," Dad says.

"I'm pregnant," Mommy announces, like her unnecessarily attentive belly rubbing hasn't given it away. "You know I can't leave Portland right now."

I snort out one of those laughs that make it clear that nothing's amusing.

"I wish I could go with you, do you know how much I'd love to see my sister? The whole family?"

"So come."

Her mouth falls open like there's so much to say, but like it should go without saying.

"No, you're right. God forbid you prioritize the Eloko child you already *have*."

"Don't be like that, princess," Dad says as he finally detangles his arm and my mom's frame, and comes over to hold me instead. "We just want to make sure this baby is as blessed as you are, and Portland is the best place to do that."

"Wait, is that why you've been napping in my room, Mommy? Because of the heirlooms? I'm not sharing my suite with an infant, so feel free to get out of that habit."

"Of course you're not, Naema, no one would ask you to do that." He rubs my back while he speaks.

"No, you're just asking me to go to Bumblescum Nowheresville to visit *her* family, and leave what used to be *my* city, on my own."

"We're not doing any more for this baby than we did for you, darling," Mommy tells me when she's off the bed and either coming to join my dad in comforting me, or else coming to join me in being comforted by my dad. "And look how you turned out. You're exactly what we wanted."

"Maybe it's enough for the baby to be near *me*," I suggest when the three of us are huddled together at the foot of their bed. "Maybe you don't have to actually be in Portland the entire time this time."

"Oh, Ny," she sighs, laying her head on my shoulder. "I'd hate myself if we took the chance and the baby wasn't like you. But you're Eloko. You're so strong, and so vibrant. I just know you're gonna be fine down there, if you really want to go. You're always fine."

I stare at nothing, and feel my muscles tense even while my dad continues to rub my back.

"Just promise me you won't be upset at us for not going," she whispers. "I couldn't bear it."

"I'm Eloko, Mommy," I say, shrugging out of both their arms. "I'll survive without you."

Jamie is always talking, which makes it really glaringly obvious when she's not. When she and Gavin burst into my room unannounced after my group text informing everyone that I'll be summering in the Southwest, she starts off uncharacteristically quiet. Which obviously has to do with the last time I showed up in *her* room unannounced.

"You can cut out the Contrite Quietude, Jamie, it got old real quick."

"So you're not mad anymore?"

"Never said that," I snap, folding a sweater before laying it in my open suitcase.

Gavin has a new girlfriend in tow, a very obvious brand of Portland tourist who makes it their business to gravitate toward the Eloko population as soon as they arrive. I would've put money on her having a LOVE account, too, but. Gavin either doesn't notice what she is, or else he doesn't care, and one is no more likely than the other, to be honest. Point being, I have no intention of learning this one's name.

"Hi, Nina!" she beams, thrusting her hand at me less like she wants me to shake it and more like if I don't, she'll take hold of me. There is no scenario in which she doesn't touch me.

"And this, of course, is Naema," Gavin speaks over her salutation. He does a pretty good job of not cringing, but Jamie does it hard enough for both of them. Not that either of them expect me to remember that Nina is the name of the girl in Tavia Philips's movie. The one who would be me, except she isn't Eloko, and she hasn't selflessly given of herself and her time toward Tavia's safety for years.

So not only did Tavia herself take my melody when she Stoned me, she's managed to do it again in a story memorializing the magic and mystery and love between her and her gorgon sister. Which makes it seem like—and I don't think I'm being dramatic here—at Tavia's direction, the entire world is dead set on erasing who I am. That I'm magic, too, even if it's not the kind that has to be kept secret. Suddenly it feels like the whole world is trying to convince me that being Eloko isn't as wonderful as it had always been—but just for me.

It isn't happening to my friends, even though they've been just as popular.

It isn't happening to Priam, and he dumped Tavia right before homecoming junior year.

It's just *my* Elokoness that maybe shouldn't be paramount. That somehow contradicts the rest of me. Just me who should choose between a magic the whole world loves or an identity they made sure would never be treated as well. That I was born both doesn't make a difference.

That weird ghost-wind sweeps through my chest, in the front and out the back, the way it's done before, only this time something lingers. Like that weird, maybe phantom throb in your throat after trying to swallow a pill without water, it feels like some part of the ghost-wind didn't get all the way through. I feel it, like it's lodged beneath my sternum, and if I was worried about being haunted before, that was nothing compared to not knowing how to get it *out*.

I can hear it again, so clearly that it seems strange the way none of my friends can, and the wind is almost like a collection of whispers. They're hushed and unintelligible, but there's no mistaking what they are.

I am not in the mood for a straight-up possession. But that isn't the way it feels. I should be losing my mind, flipping out because not only am I possibly inhabited by whatever probably meant to go straight through me, but now it's for sure something more than a feeling.

It should crash me right out of sanity, realizing that this really is a full-blown haunting. That there are voices, and they must belong to someone. To someones.

I can't explain why it doesn't. Maybe it's the fact that Portland has been upside down for a while now. Like, sure. Why *wouldn't* this happen? This is fine.

But maybe it's also the fact that these voices aren't mine. There's no confusion about it. The whispers—whatever they're saying—and the ghost-wind itself, they're not coming *from* me. They're coming *to* me. Which is better?

Anyway. In a moment, all of it settles, and I can hear what Jamie's saying.

"I can't believe you're really going through with this."

"It's one summer."

"Before we go to college!"

"Together. In the same city. Calm down."

"Still." She absentmindedly unpacks my luggage to see what

I'm taking with me. "I love this sweater, did we buy this together? But seriously, Ny, why are you packing a sweater to go to the Southwest? In the middle of summer."

"It's a desert, Jamie," I say after I take a deep breath to get myself in order, and then I snatch the garment out of her hands and put it back. It hasn't occurred to me that the weather will be different outside Portland, or predictable, or that it's easily checkable on a weather app. "It cools down at night." That sounds right.

"I can't believe you're doing this to us." She may as well stomp her feet.

"Well, I'm not. Because it has nothing to do with you," and because I feel Gavin sidling up next to me, "and do not say it, Gavin. I don't know who gave you the right, but you can keep that ish to yourself from now on, or lose my number."

"Whoa." He stops in front of me. His fingers are tangled up with his girlfriend's, and he's been taking her on a tour of my suite, which I have *nicely* not interrupted to evict Rando Portland Tourist from what has always been a sacred Eloko sanctuary.

"I'm for real. Stop."

"I heard you," he tells me, but we stare each other down, while Girlfriend's eyes leap between us. I don't *know* that she has a secret recording device, but I totally wouldn't put it past her. She's lapping up all the tea, not at *all* uncomfortable to be a stranger among squabbling friends. And having an audience seems to be giving Gavin that little bit of nerve he genuinely does not need. "So when do the rest of us get to be mad?"

"Pardon me?" I ask, breathing long and slow, because I know this is gonna be good.

"I mean, now that we're all getting dragged into this magical Portland recalibration."

I feel my eyes go wide, and Jamie literally puts her hand over her mouth. Which. Yeah.

"And that's my fault, Gavin?"

"All I'm saying is some professor's talking about Eloko like we're . . ."

No one fills in the blank. Three Eloko standing in an heirloom bedroom, and not one of us can come up with a word for what we are if we aren't magic. Not that we should have to.

"Nobody thinks that," my boyfriend says when he appears in my doorframe.

"Priam!" Jamie bursts out and his name might as well be Oh Thank God.

"Yeah," Gavin continues, like he's not so sure. "Well—"

"No one thinks that," Priam repeats, and it's a declaration. Whatever's been making him standoffish and weird, there's no trace of it in this statement. "That professor doesn't even know if she does."

"Yeah." Jamie's addition bears slightly less conviction, but she's clearly enthusiastic to get there. "Everybody knows what makes us magic." She smiles invitingly, and looks at me.

"Right," I answer her, and then the room falls quiet. If the tourist *is* capturing all this, she really struck gold.

"You guys good?" Priam finally asks, looking between Gavin and me, but I don't turn to face him.

I texted Priam earlier in the day to come over, but he said he and Gavin had plans and they'd be by later. And then Gavin showed up with Jamie and Girlfriend, and no Priam in sight. So whyever my darling boyfriend didn't want to see me, it wasn't likely the other two know any more than I do. Clearly no watches have been synchronized; Priam pulled up alone and after everyone else, and Gavin and Girlfriend have gone back to their touring circuit, which. I don't know if she thinks I can't see her fingering my porcelain figurines, but. Do not test me, tourist.

"We're gonna go get something from the kitchen," Gavin tells him, gesturing to Jamie. "She's already agreed to come skating before she ditches us tomorrow morning, so," and he looks at me, "no take-backs."

"Got it," Priam says as they file past him.

Seconds later, Jamie sings, "Mommy Simone!" and all the excitement I was apparently stifling spills out in the living room while my mom and friends love on one another.

"Good gawd, please close the door," I say, rolling my eyes and throwing myself across the side of my king-sized bed not covered in suitcases and possible clothing choices.

"Have they been working your nerves?" Priam asks, climbing up beside me.

"Don't act all innocent," and my eyebrows crash down over my involuntary grimace. "They're not half as bad as you."

Priam isn't Gavin so he doesn't scold or attempt to correct me. His face does go slack for a moment while he props himself up on one elbow.

"What, did you forget?"

He twists his neck in confusion.

"You were supposedly with Gavin today, remember? Except," and his face goes blank for a moment, before his eyes fall away from me. "Except, right, Gavin was with the girls. And here. And you weren't."

"I'm sorry."

"You don't get to be. You don't get to just say you're sorry, when you haven't even told me what you've done."

"Ny, I haven't *done* anything, you know that."

"Why do I know that?"

"Naema."

And I feel it. That thing I always feel when he says my name, the entire year and eight months we've been together. I'd liked him long before that, but I was always entangled with somebody else, at our school, or otherwise. But *always* an Eloko boy. So yeah. His liking Tavia had felt like a personal slight against me, even though he probably didn't even know I liked him. And he definitely didn't know she was a siren and that I was shielding her.

When he abruptly called it off with Tavia junior year, I was more than a little relieved. I knew he'd come to his senses, and between that Thanksgiving holiday and the beginning of December, he'd started watching my LOVE streams. I'd see his name and avatar bubble up, and I couldn't help smiling. After a couple of times, I started shouting him out in the videos, blowing him a kiss while everyone watched. I just sort of claimed him. It was time for us to happen. And he fell right in.

Except for that one distraction it seems like nobody but me can sense. Throughout our entire relationship, Jamie's maintained that Priam is head over heels for me, but that's just what she's used to. She just takes for granted they all will be, just because they always have been. But he freezes up. At the sight of Tavia, at the mention of her. He always has. He's wooden and awkward at our choir recitals, like he can't just pretend she doesn't exist. He's there to see me, so the fact that he can't just *ignore* her makes me think she was important, which. I've never thought he liked her—that Jealous Nina angle they used in the movie is the absolute laziest—but if it means she has that great an impact on him? Hating her is just as bad.

"Naema," he says it again, like he knows its effect, and he tugs on the ends of my hair.

"Premium." I say the nickname through a sigh, to let him know I am willing to overlook his many faults. He scooches closer and lays his forehead against mine.

"Stay."

"I can't," I whine, even though I don't know why not. Except for the rush of wind inside me that confirms it.

"Stay," he whines back. "Your parents won't care if you cancel your ticket."

When I shake my head, his turns, too, because we're still connected.

"Why leave Portland? Since when is that even an option? Because of Gavin, or, fine, a little bad press? You belong here."

"Just here?" I ask, trying to make it light by putting my trill inside my voice, like a glimmer of soft laughter. "I can't belong in the Southwest, too? I'd like to think I have national appeal."

"You're Eloko," he says, like he's responding to my thoughts instead of my words, and I close my eyes to cherish the sound. "No matter what happens, Portland will always love you best."

Now I squeeze my eyes shut against the rush that swirls into my abdomen again, mimicking a queasiness I never experience. I haven't thrown up a single time that I can recall, and I never feel sick to my stomach.

But there it is again. Like I can no longer just disagree with something, I have to have a physical reaction, too. Conviction that refuses to go unnoticed.

I am not a fan.

"And if I wasn't Eloko?" I ask. I feel his forehead move away from mine and I open my eyes to find Priam scoffing. "What? Why is that such a ludicrous question?"

"Because you *are*, Ny. You're the epitome of Eloko, babe. If you aren't magic, no one is. Nothing a nobody professor says to get her name in the press is gonna change that."

Except that it already has. Where has he been? Where have they all been? How has no one else noticed that whatever Eloko is, and even though it's from birth, it isn't as permanent as we thought—not for me, anyway.

And that's not a consequence of being Stoned. It isn't me forgetting how to be Eloko, or not hearing my melody, because that came back as soon as I got Awakened.

It's something being taken from me. Other people—people who've adored me and treated me like an exception my entire life—changing their minds. So Dr. Corey isn't gonna be of any help. If she hasn't figured it out already, and despite the fact that I haven't told her about the rush and swirl and sometimes nausea I've been feeling, checking my vital signs and sleeping eight hours a night isn't gonna tell us that something changed me on the inside.

Things are changing from the outside . . . and maybe that means that's all Elokoness is.

Totally unrelatedly, I don't know Professor Heather Vesper-Holmes, but I sure can't stand her.

"Don't worry," I say aloud, echoing the rush within, and Priam thinks I'm talking to him.

"I'm not. I'm never worried about you. I just want you with me." He draws a finger along my jawline, and then tips my chin up like he wants to kiss me.

"I'm here right now."

"Hm. But there are people over," he says, his voice dropping suggestively.

"Yeah," I say through a laugh, "that's . . . not what I meant. I was being literal. I'm literally here. I haven't left yet."

"Oh, yeah, no, me, too."

"Okay."

"So we should make the most of it." He makes it sound like a question, or like he's fishing but also wants plausible deniability. "And we're talking about in ways that include our friends, and aren't intimate."

"Right."

"Exactly, that's what I meant, too."

"Good." I smile despite making quite an effort not to.

"So you'll come skating?" he asks, running his fingers through my hair.

"Yeeeesss, I'll come skating. But only because Oaks Park wasn't in that stupid movie, so hopefully it won't be crowded with tourists, aka all of Gavin's future girlfriends."

"Wait. Did you watch it?"

Oops.

"Naema." I can't tell if he's annoyed or just flummoxed. He's wound his neck back and is squinting at me, though. "Are you kidding me right now?"

"Shut up, you watched it, too."

"No." His eyebrows leap so high they're trying to join his hairline. "I didn't."

"Oh. D'aww," and I throw my arm around his neck and curl under him on the bed. "See, that's why you're my favorite."

"You're—"

"Adorable. The word you're looking for is 'adorable.'"

But he grunts and stares off somewhere above my head. "Something like that."

Chapter VIII

Awaken: an Underwhelming Piece of Propaganda

Blog Contributor | July 2021

Editor's Note: *This movie review was intended to be an In Conversation with Ms. Philips. We apologize for any disappointment or confusion.*

If you're in the know, then you already know. A year after the Awakening, there can't be many Portlanders unfamiliar with Tavia Philips's name, but little was known of the story before the story. That changed when her movie hit streaming sites this month, the perhaps slightly underwhelming title immediately becoming the number one locally trending hashtag and viewership more than meeting expectations. And while there were no doubt countless raves written as—or even before—it aired, for the more discerning viewer, it'll leave a lot to be desired—and verified.

Awaken is based on a true story, a disclaimer that tends to get overlooked in favor of the fictionalized account being accepted as fact, but it's important to remember. For one thing, much of the context of the relationship between the two main characters—Tavia and Effie—appears to be gleaned from public record (including Effie's transfer of school districts to confirm when she left her aging grandparents to live with the Philipses) and social media (referring to Tavia's YouTube viewing history, and Effie's already fictionalized accounts of her involvement with the Renaissance faire). Certain story lines, such as the incessant bullying by the resident mean girl at Beckett High, are seemingly confirmed by already well-known events, while other events come across as so dramatic and cinematic they're almost beyond plausibility.

The supposed love triangle involving the two friends and the gargoyle that perched on the Philipses' home is easy enough to disregard as wish fulfillment, completely unsurprising to see in a movie with a teen protagonist and target audience. There are other events—the Camilla Fox protest for one, including a spectacularized version of the activist's arrest being witnessed by an airborne Tavia—that seem to serve an agenda beyond entertainment. In a story about one of very few known sirens, that was the fear, and avoiding it should have been the film's top priority. Instead, and as remarkably few reviews have noted, a story revolving around a heroic use of magical ability for the good of others drifts on more than one occasion into divisive politics that benefit few.

This movie couldn't have been released at a more opportune time. Portland—a city known for its progressively liberal ambience—is feeling particularly amorous. The fact that *Awaken* coincided with Awakening Day is no coincidence, it's good marketing, and if all other critics didn't seem so uniformly under Tavia Philips's spell, perhaps its self-serving messaging wouldn't be alarming. A movie's just a movie, after all.

Unless it isn't.

It's no one's intention to be alarmist, but a word of caution: there are two sides to every story. And if saying so is interpreted as discrimination because this particular story is about a siren? *That* is reason for alarm.

Chapter IX

NAEMA

This is not about explaining myself. In the least. I didn't to Priam, either, because whether there's a movie with even a bastardized version of me in it or not, and despite the fact that I said I was gonna skip it, and regardless that I couldn't care less about Tavia's little rehabilitation narrative, I can also watch it if I so choose. Because—and I can't stress this enough—I am the boss of me.

But, to be clear, I meant what I said.

I *was* going to skip it.

I could not care less about Tavia's thing.

And there was no morbid curiosity about the Nina version of me.

It did occur to me, though, that Tavia Philips was getting the star treatment, and not just from Hollywood types, or whoever slapped her story on the small screen.

Her face has literally taken up residence on LOVE.

Like a billboard for an audience of one, a banner ad promoting her movie showed up in my digital house. It isn't bad enough she's been on pretty much every local podcast, and her channel has eclipsed Camilla Fox's numbers.

This is officially aggression, and there's nothing micro about it. Because for all the Black-tivist rhetoric, she doesn't seem to have any issue with Portland pitting the two of us against each other. Two magical Black girls—thank God Effie disappeared, I guess—and only room enough for one.

The 99 percent not capable of critically analyzing her have

to choose which of us to adore now. Speaking of LOVE—since my account got scoured after prom and someone found every single time I supposedly cryptically dragged Tavia (or they thought I did), and since no one knew anything about her until her Awakening stunt, guess who comes out looking like the model minority?

Let's be clear: she felt unsafe enough to hide from them, she was terrorized by what the world has done to her kind, but their first introduction to her was in service of their children. She won them over with one very specific siren call, and with her noble act of forgiveness.

She must have taken the high road, they'd assumed, otherwise she would have done something dangerous.

It'd be hilarious if it wasn't disgusting to watch.

Tavia's heroism hasn't inspired anyone to look closely at the society that made her hide. Nope. They've instead decided to just treat her like a heroine, and that apparently makes everything all better. They'll listen to her speak, even invite her to do it, but the listening is clearly all they're willing to do.

And what does Ms. I Rise do in the face of them celebrating her while making zero commitments to Dismantle Oppressive Systems, like she's always preaching about now?

She smiles. She waves, and she appears, and she shows up for hair and makeup.

Fine. *Most* of the time.

What's super cute is how I know they'd act surprised that I see through it all, her and Effie. Like being Eloko means I wouldn't. Like—well let's just call a thing a thing: they always acted like being Eloko means I'm not Black. Or that I don't want to be.

I don't have to say this, but I am, and I do, and I see through it.

So I've been thinking. Maybe it's all gone to her head. Maybe she needs someone to make *her* a better person. Because that's what trauma does, isn't it? Isn't that what it did for me? Opened my eyes to the truth about my city and my magic?

According to Professor Vesper-Holmes, I don't have the kind of power Tavia wielded, but I do have the truth. I do have the moral high ground, whether anybody knows it or not. Because

I've spent years protecting a siren, only to have the ingrate refuse to come clean.

So I'm gonna tell them myself. I'm gonna finally let the whole world know who she really is, and I plan on being very careful to clarify. Not All Sirens. Just one.

Just Tavia Philips.

And since I'm Darren Bradshaw's daughter, I know you don't offer on a piece of property without getting comps. Which, for you bagless non-ballers, means you figure out the stats on other properties in the area. It's called due diligence, and it meant if I'm gonna pitch my own movie—

Did I mention that? That the natural clapback is to land my own movie and tell the part of Tavia's story she left out?

Keep up.

—then I need to know what's already on the market. Reviews are fine, but I need to see for myself.

So. *Awake*. Or *Friendship Is Magic: The Effie and Tavia Story,* and chill, or whatever.

Let's just start off right away with how trite and uninventive it is to pretend Tavia and Effie were ugly ducklings. Because, yawn. And it wasn't even like that. Sure, Effie was the quiet type, when she wasn't blurting out snark and then pretending she was an innocent and wilting daisy struggling to bloom with the help of her protective sister, who all along thought she needed protecting, imagine that, and isn't your heart getting physically warm?

Super fictitious triad romance part aside, there's the whole gargoyle sentry subplot, which, to no one's surprise, Tavia thought had to do with her. Whoops, that was an Effie/gorgon thing, girl, sorry. It ain't all about you. Which I feel like I literally told her once, but that didn't make it into the movie. Imagine.

While we're on the subject of the gargoyle/gorgon connection, and Things They Clearly Fictionalized, the whole Renaissance faire thing was a nice tie-in, but it was a bit tidy. The way they turned the lore into Effie's origin story, and created a long-lost father character who also chiseled her community pool boyfriend from stone? I mean. Dope. But also hard to believe her corny hobby played that big a role, not that that's stopped anyone from visiting the Hidden Scales. The local news even did a segment inside the tent, despite the fact that it was pretty underwhelming. A rickety table, and a ledger, or something, and mist.

If there was a portal in there, I didn't see it.

And yes, there was Nina. A Walking Identity Crisis With Relaxed Hair foil character to Tavia's authentic naturalista. And wearing our hair straight is precisely where the similarities end. In the movie, Nina doesn't have a life or crew or shred of an original thought of her own. She's the completely one-dimensional, inexplicably salty high school nemesis that movies and TV shows insist exist in real life. She isn't Eloko, she isn't in the network, and she doesn't see through Tavia Philips's Pretty Little Sad Girl, No One Cares Except All The Folks Sworn To Ride For Me routine. In fact, it's why the prom scene makes absolutely negative sense.

In the movie, Nina rolls up on the intrepid sisters in the courtyard—which, fine, that part sort of happened, except it was just Effie and her boyfriend, and I was just making not completely friendly conversation—and she's flanked by a previously unintroduced entourage of about a half dozen kids—which, nope, because I don't ever roll that deep—and she outs Tavia's sirenness based on receipts she inexplicably came upon off camera and has never had verified. It would have made slightly more sense if the Nina character had been presented as Queen Bey of Beckett or somesuch, but she wasn't. She was just the half-baked antagonist who scowled or sneered anytime the camera caught her so the audience knew she was The One To Hate.

So Nina catwalk-struts up to Tavia and Effie, phone already recording, and announces: Tavia's a siren!

And then the whole of Beckett High's junior class immediately believes her, and they all start demanding that Tavia tell them the truth, and the camera circles an overwhelmed and Barely Keeping It Together teenage girl beset by scoffers, and we whirl around and around because that's how you know the pressure's building, until *bam*!

It happens.

Tavia opens her mouth, and the most beautiful, melodic, yet frighteningly powerful siren call erupts from her lungs, and not only does Effie sprout a tail, and Everybody's Boyfriend sprouts gray skin and wings—while remaining largely gorgeous, which is a complete fiction, because his gargoyle form was not for the faint of heart—but Tavia herself does like a whole Now My Skin Glows And Also I'm Wearing Makeup. Because if there's no glow-up, is this even a poorly conceived high school movie?

Lies on lies on lies, basically, but somehow I'm through it and when the credits roll, I don't shut it off and throw my laptop the way I want to. Instead I write down the names of the producers and affiliated companies, and start researching. I discover that the name with the most traction online is Leona Fowl, a producer whose credit is admittedly near the bottom of the list. And whose name sounds either like a Portland-famous band with an ironic lack of women in it or the name of a little girl taking over for Veruca Salt in an unauthorized sequel.

Aaand when I find her on social media, it isn't pretty. There's a boring Corporate Networker profile that I don't bother looking at, because I'm seventeen, and then there's a Bicker profile that she hasn't used in about four-plus years . . . but hasn't actually deleted. In her defense, she's deleted her profile picture, and four years ago maybe people still thought things could actually get lost on the internet, never to be found again? Whoops.

She clearly did not understand how to use Bicker. Of the dozen Bites she sent—all in the same two-week span—ten of them are to viral personalities and read like an old relative who doesn't know they're not sending a private message.

"Hi [insert handle], my name is Leona Fowl and I'm a producer with It Doesn't Matter. I loved your [article/Bite/who cares] and would love to talk about sharing your story more widely. Email me at [She Really Posted Her Email In A Public Bite, She's Precious]."

I would write her off as mediocre if I didn't hate Bicker to begin with, and if upon checking her IMDB page, she hadn't had a major professional glow-up in the four years since that embarrassingly thirsty display. Clearly she's figured out how to get what she wants, because despite being low in Tavia's credits, she has a slew of other credits and projects, and an increasing number of appearances in articles and press releases. All of which I assume means she's doing the thing.

And since I don't have an email address for anyone else . . .

Dear Leona Fowl.

Get at me.

Priam is still acting like a brat when we get to Oaks Park. I'm trying to be okay with the cold wafting off him, even during the couples' skate while I skate backward so we can pretend it's "prom on wheels." But while we glide across the hardwood, our hair floating on our wind, we just look at each other. The main lights abruptly go dark and the colorful ones sweep over our skin, and the music dares our voices to try to compete, but I don't ask what's bothering him, or where he was earlier in the day, or why he's so hurt that I watched the movie.

Or why I should be okay with something having to do with Tavia Philips hurting him in the first place.

When the love song ends, and I push off a little so that the space between us grows, but not in a way that an amateur skater like Priam would notice, it's meant to seem like inertia. But maybe our eye contact is too constant for that. His expression doesn't change, and eventually I give up on pretense and just smoothly rotate on one quad, going solo so I can twist and twirl when I want to.

I get it; not everybody did ballet and figure skating, and some people really can't figure out how to navigate eight wheels and still look like they invented grace. But I can't say it doesn't get old having to hide that you can, just to have a partner.

Plus the new beat is too dope to waste. Upside-Down Portland, and its alternate version of my doting boyfriend, will still be there when the song ends, and I have to decide exactly how much I'm leaving behind when I get on the plane tomorrow. In the meantime, I loosen up, feel my shoulders start to roll, let all my weight drop into my seat, and weave my legs in and out of each other as I take the turn faster than anyone else. I whip around and groove backward so the other skaters can't help but watch me, my eyes closed for a moment before I have to start checking over my shoulder. Naturally, I work the glances into my dance so it looks like I'm more than just flawless, more than just graceful and rhythmic and impossible to imitate.

Because maybe being Eloko doesn't come with a cinematic power like Tavia and Effie have. Maybe it doesn't mean having a sixth sense, or knowing when to weave, or how to take back the spotlight. But maybe that's what being Naema means.

Listen. Sometimes you've gotta remind folks who tf you are.

Half a dozen songs later, I'm sweating, but working it. I laugh at the smiles I gather, and sweep the strands of hair that've fallen loose from my high ponytail back up, knowing they'll drift right back down. I'm not a naturalista like Tavia and her sister, so I'm not supposed to like the way my relaxed hair gets slick and limp when damp, but I do.

Patting my face and neck, I wave off my admirers before I make the transition from wood to carpet look like a breeze and leave the rink.

A year after Awakening to a city that can't decide if I'm a misbehaving Eloko, or a mean girl who doesn't get to be one anymore, I'm still giving them a show. And when they're not behind a keyboard trying to prove just how righteously outraged they are that *anyone* could mistreat a siren—because they certainly never did—they're still eager to receive it.

Jamie spun around in the center of the rink with me while we lip-synched a song or two, before she and the rest of the group set up shop in the concession area. I find their table and plop down next to a very quiet Priam, while Gavin makes the girls laugh so hard Girlfriend threatens to pee herself and instead spit-takes all over the buffet array of roller rink nachos, hot dogs, and licorice ropes.

Adorbs.

As soon as she darts off to the bathroom, face and chest bright pink, I turn to Gavin.

"What is it with you and these tourists?"

"I don't understand the question," he lies.

"Why would you want to date someone who's only gonna be in town for the summer?" Jamie asks.

"If that," Priam interjects, suddenly remembering how to form words with his mouth.

"Because," Gavin says, calmly. "Then I can date someone else after the summer. If that."

Jamie grimace-pouts, and Gavin laughs, poking one of her cheeks.

"I don't know," I say, through an exhale. "I don't think that's very nice."

"Oop." Jamie pokes him back and they carry on.

"Still sulking?" I elbow Priam before kissing his cheek. He glances at me but doesn't answer. "You need to fix your face. I gave you a minute to get it together. You can't insist I spend time with you and then be a spoilsport, Preemie."

I love a good nickname of a nickname, especially when it's also an arguably unintentional barb.

"Why do you care if I watched it anyway?" I ask, after dropping my voice.

"Can you guys give us a minute?" he says, at full volume. So much for keeping it discreet.

"Yeah, can we finally go skate, please?" Jamie exclaims, like it was her idea. I pretend she annoys me, but I do love her. Some people live for the dramatic showdowns, but Jamie is forever happily interjecting with a distraction—even if she has to fake the happy.

When the two of them leave the table and pick up a returning Girlfriend, Priam turns toward me, pulling his knee up onto the bench so I have to skootch back.

"Okay," I say. "So why are you pissy?"

"I didn't watch it because I knew you wouldn't like it," he says.

"Thank you."

Which isn't the answer he wants, so we just stare at each other for a moment before he starts again. "So why did you?"

"Because as the one who was going to be misrepresented, I didn't think I needed permission to see just how badly." I mean that wasn't the reason, but it would've been a good one.

"So you wanted to see what they told the film people about you, and what you did."

"Yes, Priam."

"Well, so did I."

"Okay, fine, watch it. It's on demand, be free." I roll my eyes, and when they return to him, he's looking off to the side and biting the inside of his lip. "What, is that not what you wanted? I'm saying you can watch it, and I won't be upset."

"I don't want to watch it, Ny, I. I want you to tell me if it's in there."

"If . . . what?" And why are his eyes glassy all of a sudden.

"Homecoming."

I don't have to feign confusion. When my forehead creases and my eyes dart around, it's because I really am not sure what the eff he's talking about.

"She didn't go to homecoming, remember? You broke up. You wanted to know if they showed how you dumped her right before? Because they didn't."

He shakes his head and then drops it into his hands.

"Priam. What are you asking?"

He's really going through it. He rakes a hand through his shorter hair, looking up at me and then closing his eyes like he can't stomach it. For a moment I think maybe what I've started feeling was contagious. Like maybe my Eloko boyfriend is also starting to feel the wind in his core, almost like hearing it, and maybe the pseudo-nausea it culminates into really is an Eloko . . . thing.

"Premium . . . what is it?"

"Not what happened at the dance. At the game."

"What ab—"

"Did they say anything about what happened at the game?" he blurts out in a raised voice, like cutting me off wasn't bad enough.

I lean against the back of the bench and catch my head against my fist, drawing my own knee up onto the seat slow as syrup.

"What happened at the game?" I ask.

I don't feel the wind now. I feel a kind of hiccup in my chest, yes, because when your boyfriend's been cagey and weird, you get worried. But it's finally coated in a warm anger I much prefer. That, I know what to do with.

"You said you broke up with Tavia because she wasn't Eloko—"

He starts to interject.

"Yes, yes, an admitted oversimplification, but pretty much?"

"In a way," he yields, but then lets out a very labored breath after which his shoulders sink.

"But either way. That doesn't make a lot of sense, does it? Because it's not like you thought she would be. And anyway I'm the one who detaches easily, right? The one with impossible standards, who everybody's always trying to please, according to New Gavin, not that I asked anybody to try."

He doesn't say anything when I leave space, so I nod.

"But it turns out something happened. At the homecoming game. Junior year. That you're only just now bringing up, because you're irrationally afraid it's in the movie."

"Why irrationally?"

"Because you're making it pretty obvious that it's something bad, and since we know literally everybody but you has seen it, I'm sure it would've gotten back to you if Tavia outed you."

Now it's Priam's eyes darting around, as though to facilitate the computing process. And then, slowly, he begins to nod.

"Yeah," he says, nodding some more. "I guess you're right."

"So I guess your secret's safe with her."

He's visibly relieved a moment longer before it finally dawns on him that maybe he shouldn't be.

"Unless, I mean. You wanna tell me."

"Yeah." But then he pushes his hand through his hair again in a way I'm starting to suspect guys do to buy time.

I hate it, but the Fed Up I've been rather enjoying gives way a bit to the anxious concern his behavior's been causing. Priam's working up the nerve to make his confession, and pinching Jamie's licorice rope between his fingers even though the soft red candy is staining his fingertips a bit.

"I shouldn't be embarrassed to tell you," he's saying, but then he waits some more.

"Okay, so do it."

"Yeah. We were at the game, and we were having a really good time. And we started making out—"

"You can skip that part—"

"Well, I can't . . . because it's when I bit her."

I squint. "You bit her."

"Hard. Or hard enough to . . . she bled a little. I don't really know how."

"And she freaked out."

"No . . ."

"Wait."

"I did." He runs his hand through his hair yet again, which only serves to draw my attention to how much shorter it is since prom, and how unexpected it was when he cut it off. Except that suddenly it makes sense. If he was worried about someone playing him in a movie, and wanted to look as different from the version of himself they'd be playing as possible.

"You freaked out. Because you bit her?"

He just nods, absently studying the red residue on his fingers, and then rubbing them together so that it smears and spreads.

"I don't get it." I'm talking about the mess he's making right there at the table, and the one he apparently made at the game.

"I've always been sensitive about the lore, I guess. The mythos about Eloko being cannibals back in the day. Aren't you?"

"No," and that makes his eyes snap up to mine. "Literally never. It's silly, and no one believes it anyway. It's something people recall to jokingly keep us humble, and they don't even really anymore." I shrug. "Everybody wants to be Eloko, Priam."

Something almost starts in my center, like the wind is going to start up again, but I keep talking. I say it again, like it's an affirmation that can undo the past year.

"Everybody wants to be Eloko. I've, like, flirtatiously nibbled on boys as a joke, that's how unconcerned I am that someone will freak out about it."

"Well, I was concerned," he says, shrugging one shoulder in a way that doesn't at all convey ambivalence. Especially since he can't look at me. "And when it happened, it just made everything worse, and I didn't wanna wait and see if she believed it."

"Cool." I slide out of the booth. "Well, I'm gonna Uber home now."

"Wait, what?" Priam awkwardly tries to stand and I have to skootch across the bench before he can, at which point I'm already skate-stomping to the shoe exchange, as one does. He grabs my arm, and I turn back to look at him. "Why?"

"Why what?"

"Why are you leaving? And why can't I just take you?"

"Oh, because you've been weird and pressed and obsessing over whether Tavia Philips thinks you're a cannibal all this time, and that's the grudge you've held against her, which, I'm gonna be totally honest, reeks of unresolved feelings, and I'm past tired of being cast as the jealous girl just because I'm observant. So I'm gonna get on the plane tomorrow and fly to Boring-Desert-Crap-Town, and you can get over both of us."

"Naema . . ." His eyebrows knit handsomely, but like. Sometimes guys are cute. That doesn't mean they're worth it.

"I'm not mad, Preemie. I'm vindicated." I wait. "Can I have my arm back? I need to get out of these skates."

And he lets me go.

"I'm taking you to the airport."

"No, you're not," I say, and when he opens his mouth to argue, "Uber's got it. Sleep in. Bye, Priam."

When I take a seat on one of those carpeted stools that's designed to look like it grew out of the floor, I can still feel him behind me. And I can feel the wind beginning to swirl. It isn't like me to change my mind even if I'm wrong— What? A girl can't know her own faults?—but I know that if I hear a certain kind of rush, I'm gonna think this is a mistake. And I don't wanna take back a breakup in less than five minutes. That's such an embarrassing, internet drama thing to do. Even if I don't wanna be doing it in the first place.

I like Priam. The old Priam. The one I crushed on before the Tavia romance. Back when he was more like me. Confident, charming. Okay, and cocky. That Priam would either have brushed it off, or known exactly what to say to prove I've misjudged him. But that Priam started shrinking before we got together, and now he's taking an abrupt breakup—justified, but still—with what I assume is silent confusion and a gaping mouth. So I just don't turn around.

I don't look back.

I swap my skates for my shoes, balancing one socked foot on the other because there is already a mother of a blister forming on the ball of my right foot. The consequence of being a dancing queen in a pair of house skates.

Just because I make things look easy doesn't mean they are.

Chapter X

Love Account: Thegavinshinn

[Group selfie: Gavin, Jamie, Priam, and Naema]

[Caption: No defense required.]

MRSGavinShinn: YES!

LOVEgrl456: Love. This.

LOVEgrl456: #ElokoStrong

Luvgrrl325: I love how Gavin used a radial focus to make himself slightly clearer than the others. 😂 Please don't ever change.

ELO_VE2021: Whenever I see pictures of these four together, I mentally insert myself. Your magical faves could never.

GavinsOTP123: Imagine you and your three best friends not just being Eloko, but also literally the hottest, coolest people alive, hands down, forever.

GavinsOTP123: Hottest coolest ftw.

EloTrash9: I don't know about Naema, but sure.

MRSGavinShinn: We don't do that here. Please return to the ether with that.

EloTrash9: Unpopular opinion, I guess. Didn't know those weren't allowed on LOVE. I love Eloko as much as anyone else, I'm just saying some people's identity is complicated. She's not *just* Eloko . . .

EVOLme: You know Gavin's gonna block you right . . .

LuvLee1: Not sure about that.

ShinnStain7: Gavin's tryna get at Tavia Philips, lmao! Cute group photos aside, I don't think he's caping for Naema anymore, y'all. #staywoke

LOVElorn: Naema's queen of the Eloko. #staymad

LuvLee1: That's not what LOVE said . . .

Chapter XI

NAEMA

I'm at PDX.

By which I mean the literal airport.

True to my word, I Ubered—no recent ex-boyfriend pickup required—and true to *their* word, my parents aren't coming. About which, in her last-ditch effort to curry forgiveness or favor or whatever she was going for, Mommy informed me that I out of everyone should understand why they're staying behind.

And I didn't say as much, but. I'm really not sure I do anymore. I have absolutely no doubt somebody would argue I'm just throwing a princess tantrum because I'm no longer universally loved—and just really quickly, how is it my fault I'm accustomed to a status *they* gave me??—except that's not even what I'm talking about.

I don't wanna think about the stone, let alone talk about it, but. It was real facts.

Someone else's power made my melody disappear. And ever since I got it back, it's been real hard to miss how it's *all* we have—whether I wanna throat-check the non-Eloko professor who decided to question it in mixed company or not. It hasn't gotten much traction—certainly not as much as digs aimed specifically and uniquely at me have—but if this past year has taught me anything, it's that things change. So if all Eloko have is this melody that makes the world adore us, and the world's adoration . . . I'm sorry, that's supposed to be enough, but it really isn't?

And then, every time I think about it, I get that other thing. The Maybe Eloko-Related Rush Of Wind that is getting stronger, and louder, and thicker, if that last one is even a possible characteristic of wind?

Except we've firmly established Portland is the Eloko capital of the country, and I've never heard anything about it in Portland. Of course, there's the possibility that it isn't an Eloko thing in the first place. In which case bringing it up would just intensify the whole You're Not Enough messaging I've been getting loud and clear since prom. Which, trust, doesn't change me? But I sincerely can do without.

Anyway.

I have never been in an airport.

Okay, kind of. I've never been on an airplane, and therefore have never been on the other side of security in an airport. So being at PDX is a super weird experience made weirder by the fact that I'm *not* livestreaming. I still refuse to feed LOVE, though I will continue to strategically delete posts and remove captions because that's just good business, so I'm not capturing it, but like. The chaos and randomness of TSA alone.

I do think I'd feel slightly more like myself with a camera in my hand, and knowing the (mostly) faithful were with me moment by moment. It might improve what simultaneously feels like being borderline anxious, lightly confused, and ridiculously bored. But alas. I remain convicted in my semi-boycott.

Which is why the LOVE staff messaged me first thing this morning.

See, I am apparently an important content creator, or, as they said, Member Of The LOVE Family. Who, despite their pledge to Reevaluate How Their Branding Impacts The Larger World, they're clearly worried about losing.

Pick a lane, friends.

Anyway, during the two hours I have to kill before my flight—and, if you're equally new to air travel, you super do not need to be multiple hours early for a domestic flight, you just don't—I log into LOVE and graciously read the slew of notifications they mentioned in their shameless plea.

Please come back!

Where has the Queen gone?

I s2g if Naema is done with LOVE then so am I 💯💯💯

I can't help but smile. As intended, there are notifications on all of my posts, but there are hundreds of new comments on what is now the latest—a video of Priam and me riding to prom, because that's what I posted immediately before the livestream that got taken down.

And some of the comments are about that. Whole conversations, actually.

FOH everybody who thought she was chasing stats posting that footage only to find out she was one of the Stoned! You're the reason she's gone!

It has been a Y E A R. If her friends weren't here, we wouldn't even have seen what she wore to prom or graduation! I am P I S S E D!

This platform will literally hemorrhage members if she's gone for good.

It already has. This platform'll FOLD if LOVE turns on Eloko like they're planning to.

That's so unfair—where do we go then? It's supposed to be ***about*** *them!*

And the next several comments read like spam. They're repetitive and link-laden, and don't answer anyone in particular.

They read: *KnightsOfNaema* ⚔ *KnightsOfNaema* ⚔ *KnightsOfNaema.*

Okay, Knights of Naema.

Whatever that means.

Below them, my followers and commenters continue their conversations as though uninterrupted. There are inquiries from local journalists about my raw footage since LOVE took down the original prom livestream. They're polite and carefully worded and a complete joke, because despite asking permission, they didn't actually wait for it before sharing the video on every network. There's a new crop of them now, and I guess they're hoping there's more where that came from, since by now it's been seen and spliced a dozen times. As if I'd respond to any of them after the year they've put me through. Choke.

I glance up from my phone at the older man sitting across from me at our departure gate, because I can feel when I'm being watched. When he finally has my attention, he holds up his fingers and pretends to blow. Because he wants me to use my bell charm, and play my melody.

Is it just me or is Portland actually a city of users?

Is being Eloko just dancing, all the time, always at the ready, and I somehow missed it all my life? Because this man is smiling expectantly, and my natural response is to take hold of my charm and play it for him.

Me.

Naema Bradshaw.

My first reaction is to obey. I hate the feeling of that word, because that's not how I would ever have described my life in Portland before. At the thought, the wind sweeps up inside me so quickly that the hair at the back of my neck stands up, and I know. Even if that *is* what being Eloko is about? It isn't me.

"Sorry," I tell the man, and still curl one side of my mouth upward like I'm smiling.

"I thought you guys were supposed to be friendly," he says so quickly it's like he had the retort locked and loaded. He smirks, shaking his head and opening his airport-purchased tome of a book.

I really do try to look somewhere else, mostly because I'm afraid I'm gonna combust if I don't distract myself, and what do you say to someone who would say that in the first place? Where do you begin picking apart the stupidity and audacity, when anybody capable of reason wouldn't have thought it was cool to say at all?

What about not performing on demand is unfriendly, and why do I need to field his disappointment?

I am seething.

And I don't say any of the above for the same reason I haven't defended myself before now, not publicly and not when the donna said I could. I don't serve clapbacks indiscriminately. Despite popular opinion, not everybody deserves the honor. Because seriously. What would I look like explaining myself to people who do not matter?

So I just stare daggers into him. I know he feels them because he clears his throat one too many times, and keeps adjusting in his seat. When the intensity of my gaze doesn't let up, the man furrows his brow like he's really concentrating on the eleventy-first thriller about a grown woman the title still refers to as a Girl.

He's running out of I Totally Don't Realize I'm Being Watched gestures fast.

He straightens his glasses, and I just keep staring, until finally he gives up. The coward gathers his carry-on and jumps up, heading toward the restroom like something just crash-landed in his colon. I don't see him again until we're boarding and he pretends to be thoroughly engrossed in his boarding pass as he passes my seat.

Good. Not everyone can feel shame, and those who can't should at least feel stupid.

The weirdness of air travel doesn't end with boarding. I'd thought finding and taking one's seat was a pretty straightforward endeavor, but I was wrong. Because there is a type of traveler who, immediately upon taking their seat, realizes they desperately need something out of the luggage they stowed overhead. Now they have to get it down, but this troubles the passenger whose luggage is right beside theirs, and they offer to help, which is more an alert that they are aware of the turmoil, and do not wish their things to be touched by a stranger. Then there's the dude who decides he's gonna put *more* things overhead, and so he decides to open compartments the flight staff have already closed, which even an airplane newbie can assume means that compartment is sufficiently crowded, but the dude knows better, no worries, and he opens it anyway. This is when the Tetris championship begins.

There're also at least two other Eloko on the flight, distributed throughout the airplane, and melodies are pinging across the space so no one can tell for sure where exactly we are. I can spot the travelers glancing around to try to triangulate the sources, and before my neighbor becomes one of them, I discreetly slip my necklace inside my top.

For some reason.

Then I pop in my earbuds and return to LOVE.

For some reason.

Back to the livestream of Priam and me, the palpable excitement of preparing for prom, which I mute despite having my buds in.

I've gotten texts from Jamie and Gavin ever since leaving the skating rink last night, none of which I've opened yet, but none from him. Which I guess makes sense, since I broke up with him. Now he can get back to whatever he was doing when he said he'd be with Gavin, I guess.

Still no word from Naema??

Is it just me or has LOVE taken down more of her posts??

Her posts keep disappearing! Why has LOVE turned on its own?

Hi! LOVE team member here! We haven't removed any additional posts, although the account holder may choose to. Thanks for your inquiry!

You shouldn't have removed the last one! Way to censor a Stoning victim!

You have had an entire Y E A R to put it together. She didn't know she'd be Stoned when she posted **other people** *being attacked. They took it down because it was upsetting to the families of the other victims. Google is your friend.*

*I don't need to google it, my dude. It was all over the news for a f*n year, remember? LOVE still should've had her back.*

Looking for a site loyal to Naema? ***KnightsOfNaema*** ⚔

There it is again.

Who the hell are the Knights of Naema? And why do they sound like something out of Effie's timeline?

The captain informs us that there's traffic on the runway—don't people fly to avoid traffic? What?—and we'll be taxiing for at least twenty minutes before we can take off. No need to switch to airplane mode, so I click the embedded link and my phone swaps apps, opening a web browser.

At first it's just a lovely deep purple background and nothing else, but as the site loads, various avatars populate, and their posts, and finally a header. Which is a stretched-out, pixelated picture of me, taken from my LOVE account no doubt, with "Knights of Naema" written over it in some cursive font—purple, of course.

I will say immediately that whoever made this site didn't take into account mobile users. It's sort of a mess, and difficult to navigate without zooming in so as not to accidentally tap the wrong icons. But I get the gist.

Which is, Naema.

I release a slow breath.

I'm everywhere. Aside from the header, my image is used over and over again, because several members have downloaded photos of me from LOVE or from screenshots used in last year's media hoopla surrounding my livestream and used them for their avatars.

From what I can tell, there are only a couple hundred members thus far—despite the moderator spamming my LOVE comment section with the link ever since the app announced they'd be making changes—and the posts are mostly more of my pictures transplanted from elsewhere.

That said, the congregation might be small, but they're active. Most pictures that aren't way too small or distorted beyond recognition have upvotes equaling at least half their overall number. As an influencer myself, I'm impressed. That's a decent level of interaction, not to mention the bursting comments section under every post.

When I toggle to see the site in order of popularity, I find that the most popular post at the moment is a picture of me and Jamie, the day of *this* year's prom. I've basically kept up with Jamie's and Gavin's profiles—mostly Gavin's, because obviously—but I'll be honest. Posts from this past year have a weird, bewildering effect on me. Senior year was a warbly kind of slog, but also somehow a blur, and seeing any particular piece of it paused and immortalized doesn't exactly make sense. Very little of this past year does. It's actually been easier to go back to my own inactive profile from the time before.

Anyway, the Knights had to go to Jamie's feed to get this. We weren't in our dresses yet, but our hair was done and we'd just gotten our makeovers. Priam was our photographer, as usual, and for some reason, we were posing against the tiny hood of my Fiat, blowing kisses, because naturally.

She's gorgeous.

That's the top-voted comment, and I mean. I roll my eyes, but I'm smirking back a grin. Sure it's simple, but it's also impressive in its succinctness. Sometimes less is more.

And more, there are: comments on Jamie and me; comparisons between the two of us, and an unofficial poll on who is Portland's prettiest Eloko with Jamie being awarded the Maybe In The Traditional Sense title, and me winning But Without Question; poetic waxings-on about the length of my legs, complete with competitive descriptions that culminate in a Pirouettes comparison, which I know are those long cookie sticks filled with chocolate hazelnut because the champion commenter was kind enough to embed a picture of the container for reference. I don't know if that goes against the whole Don't Compare Black Girls To Foodstuffs thing, or if that's only about our skin color, but I'll allow it. It does make for a vivid picture, after all.

I completely lose track of time as I scroll, finding photos I completely forgot I'd taken, and laughing at the Knights when they argue over something silly like a proposed favorite accessory of mine, or what genre of music I listen to. When I come across poems or something longer, like a sort of fan-fiction scene wherein the Knight in question usurps Priam, I snort and roll my eyes. I can't make it through them without cringing in a kind of secondhand embarrassment for the poster, and they're difficult to read on my phone anyway, so eventually I just scroll past anything that's not a picture or a poll or a lively comment section.

Full disclosure: that's not the only thing that makes me cringe. Mixed in with the adoration and general fanboying is the impressively rare horndog post. They don't seem to happen often, but they do happen, which makes them more common than is acceptable. Even I can't excuse them: close-ups of some part of my body that wasn't the focus of the original photograph; photos that are clearly not of me—usually with the head suspiciously cropped out, or with a not great Photoshop job of affixing my face to someone else's body. And there are posters who come up repeatedly on that particular brand of content. Posters with names like Nutting4Naema, or something equally unimaginative and pathetic. Members who confess to having cutouts of me in their homes.

I can't wrap my mind around it, but then I've never fangirled over anyone, favorite actor or musician or anyone. Maybe I'm just not getting the concept of fixating on someone you don't know, and another fan would think it's fine? I try not to let it bother me because, for the most part, that's not what the Knights are about. In fact, some of the few downvotes are on the refocused photos that clearly *are* of me. And someone in the comments always brings up the fact that I graduated at seventeen, that I'm still underage, and that anything too racy will be removed.

So when I get to something I can't access without being a member of the forum, my curiosity is piqued.

"Fun's over," I say to myself. But I don't close the browser.

Because there's no way I'm not getting behind that curtain. Even if it means making a stupid burner account that I'll deactivate immediately after.

"Good morning, ladies and gentlemen, thank you for your patience—"

Which means it's time for airplane mode. Whatever else the Knights are up to, I'll have to find out when I land.

I close the browser and check my email before takeoff.

Nothing. Well, nothing from Leona Fowl, anyway. Which doesn't work for me, so I read the message I sent her to see what was so unenticing.

Catalogue of factual errors in the movie? Check.

Valid criticism of the production's dependence on stereotypes and tropes? Check.

Thinly veiled suggestion that there is more to Tavia and much more to *my* story? Check.

Honestly, I'm totally perplexed by the lack of response, especially given that I supplied not only my reply-to email address, but also my cell and my home phone number.

Following up on that will have to wait until I land, too.

I don't quite know how to explain it . . . but it's quiet when we land.

Like before your eardrums pop, when there's pressure blocking the outside world, and everything's muted. Except even after I gyrate my face and jaw enough to unclog everything impacted by the altitude, the quiet persists. Like I've been in a really loud party and just come outside—except it's been all of my life. It's the same kind of stunning calm I couldn't have known until after the first time I felt the wind, because it was the wind's absence.

Air travel's weird.

I knew there wouldn't be a network welcome wagon in the Southwest, after what happened with the donna and the whole excommunication dealie. But it occurs to me as I'm deboarding that I don't even know if there's a network down here at all. Or if anyone in my mom's family is part of it. If they like sirens more than they like Eloko. And I don't know if networks share exile information . . . which I hadn't thought of. So I guess there's a chance that someone I'm about to spend the next couple weeks with still has something against Uppity Eloko, which is a phrase I've heard a few times over the years between Mommy and her sister Carla Ann when they're complaining about family criticizing us, *and* that someone knows that I am Not To Be Trusted. And I won't know who.

Cool.

The thought is as welcoming as the absolutely death-defying heat. It's like a sweater that wraps around me as soon as I'm off the plane and inside the jetway. It's seeping in between the accordion folds or something, and besides the jeans and T-shirt, the knee-length floral kimono I wore to de-basic the outfit is too much. My hair is down and that's immediately a gd torment.

I regret everything. Every life choice that's led to this moment, and this heat. I would take it all back, given the chance, because I do not understand how people are alive and living in the Southwest.

This is nonsense. Cheezus.

I don't notice my cousin Courtney until he's right beside me, and that could be due to the heat and the genuine mental power-down it's causing, or the fact that I haven't seen him since he came to visit me in Portland almost ten years ago. At which time, he for sure wasn't taller than I was, and he also didn't have a bleached blond coily mushroom top with a super-clean fade. I didn't know they had style down here, but maybe it just runs in the family.

"Hey," I say, but of course he's not equally surprised, since he clearly saw me from a distance and made his way over.

"Sup," and then he leans forward, hands in his pockets, and nods toward the carousel. "Those two yours?"

"How'd you know?" I ask, but when I look over there's a flamboyance of black and gray luggage serpentining along, and just one matching set of coral-and-turquoise suitcases with a capital *N* embroidered in thick mustard thread.

"Girl, please," he snarks before making his way over and hoisting them off the conveyor belt.

So no hug, but he'll get my luggage.

Courtney is my Aunt Carla Ann's eldest. We used to call him lightskint because he got his dad's buttery light brown complexion, and because it was a way to balance out all the annoyingly frequent compliments his fairer skin got from people. He was really never that fair, to be honest, and he's less so now, so I take it he spends a lot of his time in the oppressive sun I can almost *hear.*

It's so doggone hot.

I can't even think. We're all the way to his weird pickup/SUV hybrid thing—which is doing entirely too much with its category-breaking design—before I realize he's led me out of the airport.

"Where's Carmen?" I ask.

"You mean Little Bit?" he asks. "I'm surprised you know her name." He snorts.

"Excuse me?"

We've both opened our doors and are staring at each other from opposite sides of his ugly car.

"Whatchu need?" he says, eyebrow cocked. This boy definitely plucks.

"Imma need the attitude to dial down, for one thing."

"Oh, for real?" He's amused.

"For real. It's hot. I just got here. You can act like you have some sense till you know me better."

Now he gets in the car, smirking like a handsome asshat.

"Till I know you better?" he repeats, face scrunched up dramatically. "I know you well enough, Nina." He gets behind the wheel.

Son of a.

I guess Upside-Down Portland decided to stowaway with me.

"Naema." I'm not getting in this car until I'm good and ready. "It's Naema, *Corey*."

This time when he looks at me, his hand on the steering wheel like he's ready to go, he lifts his chin.

"Huh. Okay."

I figured he'd remember that.

He liked me fine when he spent the summer before fourth grade in Portland and told me he'd always hated his name, that he'd been getting picked on at school for supposedly having a girl's name, and that he wanted me to tell all my Eloko friends his name was Corey instead. He'd asked me to tell them he was Eloko, too, but there was no way of selling that. They'd know. So instead we told them we were closer than twins, and that we could read each other's minds. For that, we practiced little tells so that when we had to prove it to people, we could hold something behind our backs and we'd be able to signal what it was. Because we kept the things we'd use to prove this psychic connection on us, and eight-year-old kids aren't super smart, so nobody thought to protest the use of things already on our person.

Carmen, Courtney's younger sister, was a newborn then, so it was like we were both still only children.

We were close. Really close. When his family came back to pick him up, we promised we'd keep in touch every week, and we were pen pals for a long time. Then he asked me to spend the summer before middle school at his house, even offering to push Carmen off on our childless Aunt Toni, who he said only spoiled his little sister anymore anyway. I can't remember what happened, but I never did make it down, and I don't remember why, but we stopped writing around that time, too.

"You wanna get in and close the door? Maybe stop wasting my a/c."

I snort and toss my hair over my shoulder before climbing aboard. "Ain't nobody worried about your little air-conditioning."

"How air-conditioning gonna be little?" he asks, laughing, and starts driving with one hand while the other arm drapes lazy in his lap. "Y'all stupid."

I'm barely containing a smirk because by y'all he means me and Auntie Carla Ann, who is notorious for reducing everything and anything to smallness when she's annoyed. I haven't seen her any more recently than I've seen Courtney, but she and my mom FaceTime pretty regularly, so I know she still does it.

We drive in comfortable, amused silence for a minute, and he keeps snorting before shaking his head. And then he tries to ruin it.

"That ain't the voice you use in those little livestreams of yours."

"What's that supposed to mean?" I ask through a sigh, keeping my head facing front since I can see with my peripherals that he's done the same, only cutting his eyes at me like he doesn't care much about what he's just said.

"It means what it means. You got a whole 'nother way of speaking when you post."

"So you watch my posts." I refuse to go where he leads.

"So you didn't know your cousin watches your posts."

"Boy, I have fifty thousand subscribers. And you aren't one of them, I know that."

"Oh, would you have noticed?"

"Yep. So you creep, but you don't comment, or subscribe, and it's *my* fault I didn't know you were there." He doesn't grunt or snort or scoff at that. "I guess communication only goes both ways in Portland."

And then, before I can stop myself: "*Had* fifty thousand."

Now he turns to look at me, while we idle at a stoplight.

"You think that's from the glitch, or you really think you lost some?"

So I guess he noticed the deactivation.

"Anyway." I don't return his gaze. "What's good to eat?"

"Hah. I got you," he says, flicking on his turn signal like I just started something.

"Oh, it's that good?"

"Just wait. Wheeeew, you ain't ready." And the easy laughter is back. Like the summer we spent together in Portland was yesterday, and everything in between never happened.

Chapter XII

Upside-Down Portland refuses to let me go.

When my nine-year-old baby cousin, Carmen, comes bounding out to the garage to meet Courtney and me, she's got a very familiar and fashionable white mask shoved down beneath her chin and I have to actively keep myself from recoiling.

Courtney made clear he'd seen the movie—or at least knew enough about it to call me Nina—but I was hoping the rest of the family hadn't. I can't imagine Mommy hasn't told Aunt Carla Ann . . . everything, but for once I was planning to happily stay out of grown folks' business and pretend I didn't know she knew I was Stoned. Now I'm struggling to understand what sympathetic, Naema-concerned conversation could've taken place and *still* resulted in everybody not only watching the movie, but also *buying a siren synthesizer.*

For the sake of full disclosure: yes. Sprite synthesizers came first. We had them when I was a kid. We used to play with them in parks, if you can believe it. Which obviously fell out of popularity after four kids were turned to statues by what we all thought were mischievous sprites. In a stroke of genius or, as I like to call it, We Are Not Recalling Our Cash Cow, a new ad campaign specifically advised against using the toy outside. Like anybody was gonna listen to an advisory like that.

Those first ones were like call center headsets, and they came in pairs with wristband speakers. We'd cast our voices—distorted and whispery like sprite sounds, of course—across wide spaces or wherever. The most fun use was the one advertised, which involved having a slumber party and secretly wearing the wristbands around your parents while one kid went into a different room and started making creepy sprite rhymes. And, of course, your parents would pretend to freak out and think a sprite had gotten into the house. It had started as a game, and then had become a bit like social therapy. Turning sprites back into something troublesome but harmless, who just wanted to play. They got harder and harder to find after Triton Park, at least in Portland, but I bet anything that's just one of the many things that the movie will change. Sprites have been exonerated, after all.

Eloko synthesizers were next, and those were designed to look like bell charms. Now, those took a few tries to take off: for one thing, our actual Eloko charms are a trademarked design, and at first toy makers were trying to make them almost indistinguishable from the real thing. I distinctly remember some little girl with blond highlights at the tender age of We Were In Elementary School showing up after Christmas with a knockoff hanging around her neck, back when they were a little too exact. I'd had mine since forever, so it's not like I personally recall what it took to get it, but my parents said the process of verification was built into the design, since my unique melody had been mapped and programmed into the bell. Having one meant people knew at a glance that I really am Eloko. So having a knockoff designed to look like mine? And one that had a synthesized three-note melody the same length as ours already programmed into it? Sacrilege. The only justice was that there were a lot of repeats, kids who got the same melody, and then it sort of spiraled into that—trying to find matching melodies between friends. Which would've been fine, if the charm didn't look too much like ours.

Anyway. We let it go once the toy design got swapped from our proper bell, which is filigreed so that we can activate it with our breath, to something called a "chanticleer bell," which is completely the wrong shape and looks more like those nasty pink snow globe snack cakes. But that little girl I went to elementary school with had an earlier design, so. Naturally she attracted my rage. If memory serves, I worked "Lizzie is a pathetic liar" into several classroom exercises, and fashioned it into a catchy little ditty during jump rope at recess. She ended up going home early with a "stomachache," but she didn't wear the necklace again.

And guess what? No one called me a mean girl, isn't that interesting. Back then, people seemed to grasp that something was being taken from me, and it wasn't wrong for me to check her for it.

The point is, synthesizers have long been a thing, and the last time there was a craze over them, it was because people wanted to be us. So guess what it means when my baby cousin is wearing one designed to make her sound like a siren.

For real. Where is *my* network?

"Naema!!" Carmen squeals like we haven't seen each other in days or weeks instead of Since Before She Can Remember. I smile wide at her, because finally, a proper reception, and I let her throw her arms around me.

"Beware the sweat, I'm so sorry," I say into her microbraids. As people apparently do, Courtney drove us into an air-conditioned garage and closed the door behind us before we opened our doors, and Carmen must've waited for that before opening the door to the house.

It's like living on a submarine or something. The air must be contained. The heat must not be let inside.

"I can't believe you're heeeeere!" she says, ignoring my warning/apology and giving me the Aunt Carla Ann squeeze-twist-bend hug I didn't know I've been missing. It feels designed to test and verify a full range of upper-body motion. "Y'all made me wait my entire *life*!"

"I mean, technically, yeah," Courtney says as he retrieves my bags. So that's gonna be a thing, apparently; that whole We Haven't Seen You In A Lifetime thing.

"Mama said you could have my room and I can take the fold-out, but she said if you let me, I can stay in my room with you." This little girl can talk. The speed, friends. Jamie could never. "And I have a full, too, so we can both totally fit!"

What is being discussed right now.

"Do you have any idea what Naema's house looks like, Carmen?

She had a bigger bed than our parents when we were *your* age. Ain't no way she's gonna have a sardine sleepover with you for two daggone weeks, Imma tell you that right now."

"She didn't say no!"

"She didn't have to, Little Bit, I'm telling you."

"I don't know who told your brother he speaks for me," I say, finally getting my bearings. Between the Slightly Cooler But Muggy Garage and the whole siblings thing, I'm a little slower on the uptake than normal.

"Told ya!"

"Oh, you wanna suffer to prove a point?" Courtney sneers at me, but it's so aggressive that it's clearly for comedic value. His toasted shea butter–hued skin goes from smooth to neatly folded, and his lips curl like he's doing an impression.

"I'm a very docile sleeper, Courtney," I tell him, blinking slow like he's a bore. "By the way, your hair matches your complexion, just so you know."

"That's what *I* said!" Carmen chirps, excitedly.

"Wooow," he says, looking between his sister and me.

"It's a little matchy-matchy." I shrug with one shoulder.

Courtney nods and then shakes his head, his favorite combination apparently, and takes my things into the house.

"So we can share my room while you're here??"

"Of course we can!"

I side-snuggle Carmen, who's taller than I was at her age, so her shoulder fits snugly in my armpit, and even though I keep looking at it, I resist the urge to ask about the siren synthesizer she's wearing. I already know what it is, and there's no way she'd believe me if I pretended not to. I know I said kids aren't super smart, but she's family, so she might be. And anyway, even if nobody's in the network down here and they don't know I used to shield a siren, at least Courtney's seen both the movie and my livestreams. So they probably know I outed one. Allegedly.

I could ask her *why* she's wearing it, but. That seems just as disingenuous. I know why. Because it's fashionable to be a siren now, thanks to the same girl who tortured me.

In the still air of the garage, just when I think that maybe leaving Portland was a mistake, that maybe I should've stared down the incessant noise and vilifying and character assassination, I feel a cool and calming whirl of wind inside my chest.

I breathe.

I still don't know what this wind is or why it's been happening, but. It's helping. It's like having a center, despite the way the world has shifted around me. Right now, it's helping me extend grace.

Carmen's a child. She's celebrating someone who looks like her being celebrated. Whatever I wish would've been taken into account—for instance: of course you can have a synthesizer, Little Bit, but maybe put it away while your embattled Eloko cousin is here—it's not like anybody knows what Tavia did to me.

Yet.

The Extend Grace wind is light, but encouraging. Even though I now fully understand that you never seem to get credit for grace unless you humblebrag about it. Document it and then share it under the guise of encouraging other people or being moved by the reaction of the person you gave the grace to. Philanthro-posts, if you will. They've never been my style, so maybe that's on me.

I didn't vlog about what I did for Tavia, so when I posted about anything else—my rightful oughts against her, for instance—well, at the time, it was fine. Now, not so much. Instead of being proclaimed Humble Queen Naema for not needing internet cookies over being a decent human being, apparently now the consensus is that I've never done right by anyone, ever, because you can't find a post about it on LOVE.

Which is actually why I'm conflicted over the video I *do* find the next time I log onto Knights of Naema.

I endure a solid hour of Aunt Carla Ann telling me she's gonna let me get some rest and then proceeding to tell me a million stories about people I don't know or remember, or asking me a grillion questions about Mommy's pregnancy (a) like there's much to tell and (b) like she doesn't watch it in real time on a daily basis. Baby cousin Carmen aka Little Bit is bouncing between us the entire time, until finally the two of them plus Uncle Deric *have* to leave me be because family reunion prep calls them away from the house.

Courtney's disappeared into his own room, so when I shut myself in Carmen's, I'm alone at last, and resolved to make a Knights of Naema account so I can see the members-only content. But when I get back to the site, there's a new top post.

It's another transplant from my LOVE account, and it genuinely takes me a minute to recall what it is. The thumbnail is me, in my droopy purple beach hat whose brim can be curved so it hides one of my eyes. Which is obviously what I've done. Iconic.

There's text in the top left and bottom right of the image, and it reads: GIRL, BYE and FED! UP!

And I remember.

I don't read the KoN poster's caption, if there is one. I just play the video.

You guys know I don't usually do this, and I look away for a moment and take a deep breath, before facing my phone again. *But there are times even the happiest person gets pissed all the way off.*

I can feel it. The tension in my chest and shoulders while I was taping. The rage seething out of me as I'd driven home from the construction site that morning. I couldn't call my friends, couldn't tell Priam what had just happened, even though it was partially about him. Because Tavia had summoned me to an early morning meeting that day, and I was acting within the confines of my network oath. Which said I would shield and protect Portland sirens from exposure, suspicion, or threat of harm.

So I couldn't tell anyone that she'd not only had the nerve to summon me at Bright And Early O'Clock, but that when I didn't respond with the proper deference—when I questioned why she would've done something as stupid as using a siren call in front of Priam's police officer dad—she snatched my phone out of my hands, and finished by threatening me.

"Don't cross me," she'd said.

Like, bish, whet?

In Carmen's room, I realize I've covered my mouth with my

hand, while I watch the me in the video struggle to say anything without saying too much.

Listen. There are different kinds of magic in this world, thank gawd. That's what makes the world amazing, right? And there are some kinds of magic only some people can be—

Video Naema curls her lips into her mouth, and her one visible eye wanders. Because she's trying to be so careful, even in her palpable rage. She shakes her head, and then pushes her lips out like she's asking for a kiss.

I remember the congestion. Believing in what I'd promised to do, and despising the individual who required it, and being totally helpless to express it. No matter what she did. No one who wasn't a threat to her thought she could be a threat to anyone else. Or just a pain in my behind.

They wanted me in the network because of the trill in my voice. Because if ever a siren needed to employ some misdirection, I could try to take credit for the call that was heard, and charm the hearer. Being Eloko meant I was the least at risk. I could absorb the impact, be the soldier who falls on the live grenade, because that's what you do when you have a privilege someone else needs. And even though my parents presented it to me without applying any pressure at all, I agreed.

No magic, indeed, Professor.

The network needed me because I'm Eloko, but they made it seem like Tavia was more Black than I was because I was Eloko.

"Thank gawd you're Eloko," and also: "You can never truly understand the struggle because you're Eloko."

So the me in the video, the one who knew before I could really understand that I basically wouldn't have a place in the community if I *wasn't* in the network—she was Black enough to be in it, but never Black *enough*. And when the community that loved her was predominately made up of other people, it wasn't a hurt she could ever discuss. And never in those words.

So she said it the best way she knew how.

There are some kinds of magic only some people can have, and maybe they think that makes them more real than the rest of us. It clearly makes them think they have some kind of power over the rest of us, but beloved. It's only as much as I allow.

I'm Eloko, whether you like it or not.

The livestream capture includes all the original reactions and running commentary from when I posted it on LOVE, and the bell charm emojis explode all over the screen, along with overzealous shouts of support and allegiance.

I know when Video Naema catches sight of them because her eye sparkles, and I see her chest rise. But also because I remember it. I remember remembering.

I. Am. Naema. Bradshaw.

I remember the surge that rushed through me. Which is interesting, considering that I've been feeling the wind now—but that isn't what I felt before. It wasn't calming, or centering. It was a tingling right beneath my skin; an electric surge, like you get when the audience goes uproarious during a jaw-dropping, window-shattering gospel choir performance.

I'm Eloko first.

Don't cross you? And Video Naema laughs, joined by a burst of laughing emojis from the viewers. She whips the purple beach hat off, shaking free a cascade of wet, wavy hair she didn't get a chance to blow-dry before getting Tavia's text.

The screen goes pink and silver with hearts and bells.

Girl, bye.

And even though I always let the video continue while I went about my business in the still-visible background so that my viewers would continue emoting and messaging, on the Knights of Naema site, it cuts right off.

I need a moment, so instead of reading the caption on the post, or the comments I know will be underneath, I take a deep breath and let my gaze drift around Carmen's room. There's not much to look at, if we're talking space. There's a delightful matching bedroom set that looks like she saw an ad and got everything in it, most of it white. White sheer curtains cover the window to the side of the bed. They're moving but it's due to glorious, recirculated air. The sight makes me close my eyes to see if the wind is there. And whether it can tell me how I feel.

Because I remember so much about the morning I filmed that video. Almost everything. And I wish the conviction was part of it.

I can't point to anything Video Naema said that doesn't track, but. Somehow I don't *feel* it.

She was right. I know that. But something's missing. Upside-Down Portland has made sure of that.

When it's been several minutes and no wind is swirling in me, I return my attention to the forum and see what the Knights had to say.

#ElokoFirst.

They've made it a hashtag and an apparent mantra. It's all throughout the comments, and they unanimously love me more for it. That I've always identified that way.

Which I have. They're my own words.

But.

Courtney bursts through Carmen's door without knocking, and then just stands there, super casual and chill.

"What're you doing," he asks like it's a statement.

"Minding my business," I respond.

"C'mon." He gestures with his head.

"What?"

"We gotta go run an errand for my mom. It's for the reunion."

"You mean *you* gotta run an errand."

"Naw, I'm pretty sure I said 'we.'"

"I'm jet-lagged, Courtney, I think I'll probably just stay in the air-conditioned house."

"Jet-lagged? Girl, if you don't. We in the same time zone!"

I stop responding to him, and before I remember how small the space is, he's bounded over to the bed and spun my laptop to face him.

"What are you even looking at," he says like he's not already looking at it. "Knights of Naema."

A moment ago, I was ready to snatch the device back, but I'm suddenly curious what he'll think.

"Don't sound so mystified," I tell him.

He's scrolling, and the farther he goes down, the higher his brow curves.

"So. You started your fan club over somewhere else?"

"I didn't start it, stupid. Somebody linked it in my LOVE comments."

"You can't resist, can you?"

"I can't resist what, Courtney?"

"You're like a pretty bird with a mirror, you can't look away."

I roll my eyes, but I snap the laptop shut.

"I mean, you ain't gotta close it on my account," he says, hands up like he's surrendering.

"We have an errand, remember?"

"Wherever you lead, my liege," Courtney says, and bows his blond coif, one hand across his torso, the other toward the door.

"I can't with you."

Courtney is a pathetic liar.

As soon as we were in the car, An Errand became A Few, and when my face fell at the news, he hit the lock and backed out of the garage at breakneck speed.

"Can you silence that?" he has the nerve to ask when we're on the road, and my phone has been buzzing up a storm.

"It is on silent. It's vibrating."

"Right, but you can turn that off?"

I can feel him occasionally glancing at me as I hold my finger against the Home button on my phone so that I unlock it just enough to read previews of the messages.

I miss you too much alreadyyyyyy, Jamie says.

Way to let us know you landed safely, Gavin says, and then, *Hey, I love you.*

Are you gonna talk to Priam? You know he's devastated, right?

Jamie again.

"Lemme guess, you downloaded the Knights of Naema app so you don't miss a single oath of obsession."

I take a relaxed breath and ignore my salty cousin.

"Oh, Pretty Bird," he carries on. "The whole point of leaving your little Portland bubble was to get *away* from the celebrity. Commune with us little people."

"You're gonna tell me the purpose of my trip now," I say through a sigh.

"I mean, Aunt Simone did."

And I can't help snapping my head to the side, but I refuse to interrogate him, which is clearly what he's trying to bait me into doing. I'm pretty sure my irises have been replaced by cartoon plumes of smoke but that doesn't mean I'm gonna confess how pissed off I am.

"What, like I don't know my mom tells y'all everything, too? That's just how family works, cuzzo."

"Clearly I'm gonna have to come right out and say it: living and staying in Portland doesn't make me any less family, and it doesn't make you any kind of authority on how one works. We good?"

"Sheba's big mad," Courtney says, and I have no idea what tf that's supposed to mean, so I roll my eyes. "Oop, your vibrator's going off again."

"I'm sorry you don't have friends who'd check on you if you'd just broken up with your boyfriend, Courtney."

Which I really wish I hadn't said, because (a) I didn't say it for sympathy, nor do I appreciate any, and (b) I don't perform sadness, not even for my followers, so even if I *were* posting on LOVE, I wouldn't have mentioned it. It was intended as a Shame On You that sort of backfired. I may or may not be off my game.

I blame the heat.

"You and Priam called it quits, for real?" And the worst part is how much softer Courtney's voice has become. Like any minute, he's gonna reach over and massage my shoulder. At which point, I would literally tuck and roll out of his hideous vehicle and take my chances with traffic and skin grafting.

"Fine, Courtney," I say, and swipe up on my phone to turn on Do Not Disturb. "Totally silent. Happy?"

"The surge of serotonin I just got, you don't even know."

He pulls into a lot and parks, but when he turns off the car and opens the door, I hiss.

"Oh my gawd," Courtney says and then falls forward laughing as he catches himself on his knees. "What is wrong with you!"

"The heeeeat! I'm melting!"

"Get out the car," he yells while I laugh, and a white woman passing on the sidewalk looks at us confusedly, because she's not accustomed to the sound of human laughter.

"Close the door and lemme stay in the car!"

"It's gonna get hot in there, too, c'mon! The store has a/c, Naema, dang!"

I groan, and then double-time unlatch my seat belt, throw the door open, and rush to get inside the shop.

"You know opening day of the reunion's a picnic, right? You 'bout to suffer."

"I'm staying home," I say as he reaches around to open the door for me and we're hit with a wall of cool air. "Or here. I'll just live in this store. Tell Little Bit I love her."

"Will you *please* get out the way." But instead of walking around me, Courtney pushes my back and guides me to the counter. "Babcock family reunion," he tells the blue-polo-wearing clerk, then flashes a handsome smile.

"Babcock?" I ask when the clerk disappears to get whatever we're here to collect. "This is Mommy's side of the family, that's Johnson, I thought."

"I'm surprised you didn't think it was Bradshaw, since clearly the world revolves around you in particular."

"How do you survive with that much jealousy inside? It's so sad."

"Our grandparents' last name is Johnson, but this is the Babcock reunion. So everybody descended from Grandma's parents. We do it big down here or we don't do it at all."

I nod and mouth understanding.

"But I'm not the authority on how family works, though."

I elbow him as the clerk returns with the first of several boxes. As soon as Courtney cracks one open and inspects the baseball jerseys with the family name across the back, I wanna pull out my phone and post it.

"I'm gonna look a*dor*able in that hoe."

Courtney snorts and looks at me, shaking his head. "Alright, Pretty Bird. C'mon. We got other stops."

He pays the fee, and not only do I have to go back out in the heat, but I must do so while carrying one of the boxes. I chuck it quickly in the bed of the truck portion of Courtney's ridiculous hybrid before leaping back into what has in very short measure become a sweltering coffin.

"Gimme the keys," I cry, as Courtney sneers at me, transporting my box from the bed into the back seat.

"Really, Naema?"

"Well, what do you even have a pickup for! Turn on the car."

"Shoulda left the windows down," he says as he climbs in and starts the car and a/c at last.

"What would that have accomplished, Courtney? I thought you were smart."

"If you wasn't my cousin, Naema, I'm for real."

See, what I have failed to mention is that in a devastating plot twist, the debilitating heat of this southwestern burg is not content to just roast you. Instead it includes an alarming amount of wind. It's as windy as Portland in December, if in December Portland is beset with the devil's morning breath. Which, if you can believe it, is responsible for the fact that when Courtney and I arrive at the next destination, and while I wander around with heatstroke as he tends to the errand, I accidentally leave my finger on Home too long and open my phone, thereby opening a text that has just arrived.

"Crap."

Talk to Priam, Gavin instructs me with the authority of someone who mistakenly thinks me obedient.

And of course, once open, Gavin can see that I've seen it.

At which point, he calls me.

"Crap!" I didn't realize my own level of Really Don't Wanna Be Bothered until one of my best friends is calling and I seriously do not want to answer it. Like Upside-Down Portland will seep through the speaker and infect my vacation, if a family reunion can be considered one.

The calls ends, and then he's texting me again.

I lock my phone just as Courtney finishes with the extremely enthused riverboat tours manager and comes over to me, gums smacking.

"They've had us booked for a solid year, and when they found out Great-Gram Lorraine, the matriarch herself, is about to be ninety-one years old?"

He's pretty self-satisfied. I can tell because he's doing what I'd be willing to bet is supposed to be a hustler stroll, but looks like the beginning of some hip wedding procession choreography just awkward enough to go viral.

"What? What about it?"

He stops like it's a dance break, and stares at me like I'm supposed to already be impressed with whatever he's done.

"What, Courtney? I'm hot."

"Your boy got a whole photographer thrown in, at *their* expense." He lets his tongue hang out while he chuckles.

"Which is basically a cute way of saying they'll be using us for free publicity."

His eyebrows come crashing down, and his eyelids fall to half-mast.

"Petty, Pretty Bird. Very petty."

I fall in step with him as we head back to his hideous beast of a wannabe Transformer. Gawd, I miss my Fiat. When we get back in, heading back to the house at last, I look at my phone once.

"That's getting real old, fyi," Courtney says, glancing at it while trying to pretend he's disinterested in my phone.

"Mind your business," I snap.

"Didn't you mute your notifications?"

"Why you worried?"

"Because it's corny. If you don't wanna talk to folks, *turn off your phone*." He further emphasizes his words by slapping one palm with the back of the other hand as he says them.

"Heavens! Sincerest apologies, Courtney, but I—like many others—use my phone for a variety of tasks and cannot turn it off just because my boyfriend and our friends have begun bothering you."

"Don't you mean ex-boyfriend?"

"See, this is why I don't tell you anything."

"Because I remember? Seat belt."

"I know how to ride in a car, Courtney, even one as unfortunate-looking as yours. You boss Carmen around, not me."

"But you put that seat belt on, didn't you?"

"I cannot stand you," I say, and turn off Do Not Disturb to spite him.

"Sit then."

"Who's corny?"

He flicks the music on, which drowns out the next several messages to bubble up on my lock screen.

So you'll read Gavin's texts but not mine?? Jamie asks.

Look, I know we've been butting heads lately, but if you wanna talk anything over, you know I'm here, Gavin says. *And I won't share it with Priam.*

And then there's one from Priam himself. Finally.

Can we talk soon?

I sigh, and I want to say it isn't like a swoon. But it is. Or like an ache. It's only been a day and it already aches. I'm about to unlock my phone and reply to Priam when all three messages assemble into a group notification, which hides the previews and just shows how many there are, because my mom is a VIP contact, and she just texted me.

911.

"Crap." I flick the music off, and call her phone, so freaked out that I absentmindedly put it on Speaker. Which is probably why Courtney doesn't object to my interrupting his flow.

"Ny?"

As soon as I hear her voice, I straighten in my seat, and hold the phone closer to my mouth. No idea.

"Mommy! What happened? Where are you?"

"I'm at home—"

"Where's Dad?"

"He's somewhere around here." It sounds like she's looking around.

"What *happened*?"

"Ny, is everything okay?"

"What?! You texted 911, Mommy! Do you know what 911 means?"

"Yes, Naema, it means call me back."

Courtney snorts.

"No! No, it doesn't! 911 doesn't mean call me back, Mommy, and it *really* doesn't mean that when a pregnant lady dials it!"

"Oh, I'm sorry, darling, that's all I meant." She sighs, like she just lowered herself gingerly into her favorite oversized love seat and hoisted her Seriously Not That Pregnant Yet legs onto the matching ottoman. "Are you busy? Are you by yourself? I hope you're not down there being antisocial."

"Hey, Auntie," Courtney calls in his best Killmonger.

"Is that my baby boy?"

I can't roll my eyes hard enough as the smile carves into his stupid face, and also at the completely ridiculous way folks act about nieces and nephews. What is the big deal, honestly. They're not your kids.

"Keep it in your pants," I mutter.

"Don't be jealous, Ny," she coos, making it worse. The bug-eyed, open-mouthed, silent guffaw Courtney's giving me has me caught between laughing and throat-chopping him, but suddenly it disappears, and he's speaking with a straight face.

"It's normal, Auntie Simone. I went through it when Carmen came along, and my mom and I read this great book on transitioning from being an only child together. I'll ask her for the title, if you want."

"Courtney!" she says, incredulously, and at least she's not so far gone in hormone soup that she can't see through him. "That is so considerate!"

"Mommy! Are you crying?!"

"Hush, Ny," she says through a laugh, and I can literally hear her wiping her eyes. "He's always been such a precious heart. Oh, don't let me forget to give you a few messages before we hang up. People keep trying to get ahold of you today, a professor and a producer."

"Producer?" I ignore the academic because I'm 100 percent certain it's just Heather Vesper-Holmes again.

"You fancy now," Precious Heart mutters, perfect eyebrow cocked.

"I can't remember her name—"

"Was it Leona Fowl?" I blurt. I meant to follow up with her, but maybe she just needed a minute to coddle her ego before realizing every point I made in my first email was dead-on. "The film producer?"

"Well, it wasn't a film producer, I know that. It's somebody from one of the primetime investigative shows, and it's national! I can't remember their name. I took down the number, I can text it to you, but Ny, it's so exciting, they want to finally hear all about how you were one of the victims, and how hard it's been for you, and how much hurt *you've* gone through, too!"

I don't move. And not just because I've perfectly positioned and angled all of the vents to the right of Courtney's steering wheel to wash over me in a nonstop stream of too-cold air. I notice after a moment that my eyes are roaming; it probably looks like I'm tracking one of the birds flying in loop de loops because apparently they, too, can get heatstroke. But I'm thinking.

"Ny?" Mommy's voice breaks the arctic air between me and the speaker.

"I'm thinking."

"About what?" she asks like she's surprised that I would need to do that.

Or like she doesn't have a single alarm bell ringing in her head. Like the description she just gave isn't mildly infuriating. The idea that my story has appeal as long as I got hurt, that maybe folks will fawn over me again if only I'm willing to lay bare my trauma, and really lean into the devastation of being Stoned, of losing my melody for six hours, of not knowing if I was ever coming back.

Of counting thoughts because I didn't have any other way of keeping time. Counting, and crying despite not having eyes, screaming despite not having a voice, and then pulling myself together and starting the count again because I couldn't tell how many times I'd said the same number.

If we're gonna valorize my pain, if I get to regain my right to be beautiful and brutally honest by bleeding, do we also get to talk about their part in it? Are we gonna discuss Upside-Down Portland? The betrayals, the lack of empathy, the fickleness of the fame they assigned to my kind that made coming out of the stone just another stage of it? Because I doubt it.

In a way, the Knights of Naema are the only good thing to come out of any of this. Courtney's misgivings aside, at least none of them needs to see me bleed. None of them is asking me to get teary-eyed and weak before they'll give me back my place.

"Ny? Courtney, is your cousin still there?"

"I mean, technically?" I can feel Courtney watching me when he should be watching the road. "Is it normal for her to stop talking and keep moving her eyes around like she's possessed?"

Mommy laughs. "She's thinking. She's just like her father, they're strategists. I can never keep up!"

I don't want some forty-minute chop shop episode of All Of Your Children Will Eventually Be Kidnapped. I want Leona Fowl. I want a direct response to that Tavia Philips propaganda. I think I can hook her if I just tell her the real up front. Except I'm not sure how to do that without telling the world that there's such a thing as networks, which. Takes me right back to Powell's, and the donna. She'd say that a few sirens might have decided to come out in the open, but a lot of them haven't. Most. Telling everyone that there are totally ordinary people in the Black community doing the work of keeping those identities secret because they don't trust society doesn't seem like a good idea for anybody. And that includes the elderly Black woman who oversees it.

But there's still the true story of my Stoning.

That Tavia Philips gave the command.

"Ny, I'll text you the number, okay?"

"No need," I say. "I've got a line on someone else. I don't want an interview. I want a movie." My mom squeals on the other side of the phone. I expect either a similar or an intentionally opposite response from Courtney, but when I glance at him, he's studying me.

"Okay, I'm gonna get your father to make me some food, I'm famished."

"You're not." I'm still locking eyes with my cousin.

"Love you, love you, love you, Ny," she blathers on, adding kissy noises. "I wanna hear everything soon!"

"Bye, Mommy," I say, and push the phone toward stern-faced Courtney until he says goodbye, and then I hang up. "So, what's up with you," I ask, in a singsong voice, so he knows I already know.

"That's what I was gonna ask you. That was like watching a supervillain hatch a plan."

"'Kay."

"Look. It was all over your face, so."

"It's honestly fine. I mean Mommy said strategist but you made the leap straight to supervillain, I mean."

"All I'm saying is your energy got real dark, cuzzo."

"Are we making 'cuzzo' a thing? Is this your version of a dad talk?" I know I'm winning because he starts shaking his head, but there's no nod afterward. "Listen, I'm really very sorry that I took a moment of serious thought before deciding if I wanted to talk to a producer about doing a segment on me, Courtney—"

"Okay."

"In the future, I'll not look so solemn and supervillain-y when considering business opportunities? I'm not sure what else I can do. Cuzzo."

"Right."

When we both fall quiet, and without his extremely loud and extremely regional rap, the sound of the air conditioner is almost hilarious. I've turned his car into a wind tunnel, yet I regret nothing, especially when we stop at the last light before his neighborhood. The heat is wafting off the pavement and creating a mirage so tall the other cars are driving through it.

Like the Walking Water from Tavia's movie. The way they turned Renaissance faire lore into part of Effie's story.

The same way they gutted mine by creating Nina.

At least the story I'm going to tell will be true.

At least they'll know, at last, who the real villain is.

Chapter XIII

Knights of Naema Post

STATEMENT OF PURPOSE

NaemasNobleman [Metadata: posts (53)] *This is about loyalty.*

This is about making a truly safe space to celebrate our favorite Eloko. A place that won't stretch and a conviction that won't waver to make space for anyone or anything else, and a membership that refuses to judge her by some new and evolving standard that tries to take away a magic she was born to.

Naema is #ElokoFirst.

We are here because no one gets to take that away from her.

We are the Knights of Naema.

Chapter XIV

NAEMA

I Gets My Way: The Naema Bradshaw Story.

Subtitle: How to Ensnare a Film Producer.

When Courtney and I got back to the house, and before his entire family could descend on us for what was clearly going to be an evening-long meeting to assess reunion readiness in anticipation of opening day, I begged off to Carmen's room to rest. And promptly emailed Leona Fowl.

Tavia Philips is the real villain.

How's that for a killer opening? Controversial. (I guess.) Concise. I know *I'd* be intrigued.

I followed it up with some privileged and therefore legitimizing content: some more prom footage that hadn't been posted or streamed anywhere; a casual confession about the network television interest I'd received.

Because, you know.

Folks wanna hear from me, girl, do not hesitate.

I didn't tell her about *the* network or that Tavia and I have more history than the Nina story line showed. I'm exiled, but. I won't betray the donna. No matter how quick folks are to betray me.

At the end of the email—and maybe just because I wanna underline the whole I Am Not Nina sentiment—I linked the Knights of Naema forum. Which also served the dual function of subtly setting the standard.

This isn't the story of a fallen Eloko yearning for redemption. It's the story of an attacked Eloko refusing to be demonized.

To be honest, I think the end of the email goes harder than the beginning. Either way, it got the job done.

Some people would be deterred by the fact that Leona Fowl hadn't replied to my first attempt at contact. I knew she'd come calling now. It was a matter of time and, not to be all Oracle or anything, but. I knew it wouldn't take long. I'm charming, and clever, and convincing—and despite the deluge of praise and rabid bandwagoning, there's still at least *some* evidence that other people can see through Tavia Philips.

So the next day, I'm happy to pass the time between sending the email and getting one back from movie producer Leona Fowl by helping set up the Babcock Family BBQ. Which takes a lot, and which I can personally verify *will* feed five thousand. I know this because I make sure to help arrange the food, as it is the best way to score a permanent gig beneath the park's one wooden picnic canopy and stay close to one of the tower fans. The weather hasn't ceased being sticky and offensive, not that you'd know by watching Aunt Carla Ann pinball back and forth across the park area we've reserved, and occasionally *literally jog to her car* to double back to the house for something.

Couldn't be me. I have not acclimated enough to do any of that, sorry not sorry. Like, I'm two seconds away from going inside the throne room that's been erected for Great-Gram Lorraine when she arrives. It's a canopied mesh enclosure with an actual recliner someone brought for her—which *sounds* borderline ratchet but is actually the sweetest—and it's surrounded by personal fans. The fact that they're not on yet is the *only* reason I don't hunker down in there.

The swarm of hungry locusts better known as the descendants of Lorraine and Clarence Babcock (and a few assorted baes and besties) begins to arrive, and I'm getting what I would never admit is nervously excited for my first big family BBQ. Courtney says serving food ensures it'll probably be the largest turnout of the four-day extravaganza, so if I make it through this, I'm golden. I've got my name tag, I've got my Babcock jersey, I've got my phone vibrating my butt every few minutes, which I assume is just Jamie or Gavin, or hopefully Priam. Whoever it is refuses to calm their tits, so eventually I pull off the clear gloves all the food-prep helpers are wearing and retrieve the device from the back pocket of my jean shorts.

"Yuuuuuussssss," I whisper when I've opened a message from a number I don't have in my contacts, but that my phone has labeled Maybe: Leona Fowl. I lightly twerk for a moment or two, and read her message.

Naema! Leona Fowl here! Beyond excited to hear from you. Free to talk if you are? xx

Hell yes, I'm free! I mean, I'm actually not, and should really not let Courtney see me checking my phone anyway because, for a seventeen-year-old, he's surprisingly obnoxious in his whole Anti-Phone Or Social Media convictions. Weirdo.

But BBQs are supposed to be chill, right, so I'm sure I can steal a moment in the near future. Which is to say, I am *going* to have a phone call with a film producer today, periodt.

Satisfied that I am a playmaker, a mogul in the making if you will, I check that my ponytail's still swinging through the back of my baseball cap, with a few strands loose around my face because I do not ever pull my hair all the way back. Beauty tip: always give the breeze—and the boys—something to twirl. I'm pretty sure I gave that exact advice in a livestream once, and I noticed a lot more effort in hairstyles at school that week, so. You're welcome.

"Why do you look so happy?" Courtney's giving somebody a hand lugging the coolers into place, but when they set this one down, he drops onto the top, his sweat-soaked hair in distinct spirals of bleached blond.

"This is just my face," I say, but I also snatch the towel from around his shoulders and roughly wipe the glisten from his.

"Leave the skin, please."

"Shut up."

"Is it that difficult to admit you're happy outside Portland?" He snatches the towel back from me when I'm done and slaps it back over one shoulder. "That it's just better down here, where folks are real?"

"Yes, Courtney. That's what it is. Do you need a medic, you sound super out of shape, cuzzo."

"Oh, we say 'cuzzo' now? And I don't see you doing any heavy lifting in this heat, girl."

"No, I've just been arranging hot food because I guess cold cuts and ice tea are too bougie for the Babcocks."

"Who serves cold cuts at a reunion, Naema, if you don't!" He acts like he might stand and then collapses between his knees, laughing. "You don't make no kinna sense, I swear."

I push my finger into his already re-slickened forehead and am preparing to get back to work when he yells.

"Ay, Clay!"

Our cousin Clarence is almost back with two big bags of ice, but he nods at Courtney.

"Sheba said why we ain't serve cold food for the reunion!"

The two of them bust a gut, Clarence barely making it back to the slab of asphalt under the canopy before he drops the ice.

A little dramatic.

And again. Who tf is *Sheba*.

"That's all right, cuz, we're gonna show you how to get down."

"Mkay." I turn around and get back to work unpacking the disposable cutlery, but before Courtney can follow Clay back to wherever they came from, I grab him. "What is this Sheba crap?"

"Sheba? It's called a nickname, Pretty Bird." He's smiling like he knows it's not.

"It's not a nickname if I've never heard it, Courtney. When you only use it behind someone's back, it's just called name-calling."

"And I clearly just said it where you could hear me, Sheba. Family's gonna poke fun. Don't take it so seriously."

I love the way he keeps driving home the fact that I'm not used to being surrounded by family, and do not know their ways, without neglecting to imply that I'm also an uppity Eloko who he makes fun of.

Except I quickly learn it's not just Courtney and Clarence. It's a whole Babcock thing.

"Is that Sheba?" someone calls from the parking lot. "Oh my *God*!"

Like everybody didn't already know I'm in town. Like Aunt

Carla Ann hasn't told everybody they're gonna see me at the reunion this week.

Stop.

I ignore them when Carmen beckons me, and instead join a group of girls between my age and hers in the grass to learn her latest dance team routine and hopefully sweat out my irritation. As well as life-sustaining nutrients, I assume.

That's when it starts.

At first I don't even notice something's happening. I'm used to the idea of a ghost-wind lodged in my core by now, and that there's a chorus of whispered voices I can't make out. But something's different now, because it's not like I can make out what they're saying . . . yet I know things.

I'm standing in the grass while Carmen and Co. dance around me, laughing and singing along with the music someone's started blaring. They're all so loud I shouldn't be able to hear whispers in the first place.

But when I look at each of them, the piece of wind that stayed behind throbs faintly in my chest, and I know who each of the dancing girls is.

Like I know precisely how we're related.

Whispering aside—as much as you can compartmentalize the *transient ghost spirits that became whispering voices inside you*—I need to know if I'm imagining this. Because the knowing isn't chaotic or cluttered at all, despite being so sudden. It's like recall, except . . . did I know this before? Did someone tell me at some point, and I just can't remember?

I discard my baseball cap like my brain needs to breathe, and as I step away from the dance, and Carmen claims it despite the sweat—I realize. It for sure isn't just my own memory. Looking around the park, I know exactly how I'm related to *every* face I see. There are Babcocks of every surname, shade, shape, and height, and even though the safe bet at a reunion this size is to greet each other as Cousin, I don't need to. I know anyone who qualifies, whether by blood or adoption, whether legal or spiritual. I know my family.

"How's your mom doing?" someone asks without introducing herself to me.

Her name's Patrice, seventh-born, daughter of Gerald, second-born, son of Clarence and Lorraine Babcock.

Patrice was born in 1985, making her a few years younger than my mom, who would be her first cousin. Making her my first cousin once removed.

This is wild. The way the ghost-wind got lodged in my chest and became whispers, the way the accompanying throb doesn't last long enough to possibly transmit that information to me in words. Like it's just to alert me that now I know.

She's got what I now recognize as big Babcock eyes, and she's tall like her aunts. Carissa, third-born, and Tina, fifth-born, daughters of Great-Grandpa Clarence and Great-Gram Lorraine, got their dad's height, so it's weird that Patrice's height gets attributed to *them* and not *him*, but.

Family's weird.

Says the girl hearing voices. I mean, it's pretty widely known that aural hallucinations are a sign of something very serious, but I know there's nothing wrong with me. I may not have the benefit of a question-answering, Eloko-protecting collective, but I know when something gives me calm.

Especially after everything that's gone down in Portland.

This feeling, the one I get whenever the ghost throbs in me or when now the Carol Of The Voices tells me something new, is the closest thing to peace I've had since before junior prom. There's something familiar about it, about the idea that being Eloko is familial, and the voices are telling me family things.

It makes sense.

"Mommy's good," I answer my cousin Patrice like none of that happened. "Pregnant again," I say, even though a second pregnancy doesn't impress much in these parts, but Patrice only has one child so far herself, I now know. "Didi can dance."

"Oh yeah." She looks like she wants to get back to wherever she was leading the conversation, but mentioning someone's kid causes an obligatory search. She's gotta find her thirteen-year-old and lay proud eyes on her before we go any further. Or apparently she can multitask. "She and Little Bit are always at it, you can't keep those girls still. Or apart. But that's what family's for."

For dancing?

"It's good to have your cousins, they're your first best friends. It's good for them to be so close."

I shrug because I'm genuinely amused now. Why ever did I move my family all the way up to Portland? Oh, that's right, I'm seventeen, and had no say in a decision made before I was born.

"My first best friends were just my best friends," I say, trying not to giggle because that might give away that I'm being obtuse on purpose. "But I guess in about ten years, maybe me and my little sister or brother will be best friends, and that'll be almost as good as cousins."

Patrice recoils, and it's not even about my snark. "Simone don't know if she's having a boy or girl?"

"Oh yeah, in Portland, no one finds out ahead of time," I say, because I can make up whatever I want about my city, and no one'll know better. They don't visit us any more than we visit them. "And that's not really the part we care about anyway."

I don't say Eloko, but she cuts her eyes at me, and mhms. She gets it.

"Lemme set aside a few hot links so they're not gone before Daddy gets ready to eat," she mutters, waving back at someone before ditching me for the food I helped Aunt Carla Ann shop for and then helped her husband, Uncle Deric, get on the grill.

I do notice I'm getting quite a bit of side-eye for someone everyone's been dying to see. Not to mention for a spoiled brat who's been extremely helpful leading up to opening day. When Courtney jogs past me with a water bottle that looks freshly fished out of the cooler, I snatch it out of his hand so he'll stop.

"So, how many of these people live in or around the area, would you say?" I ask, snapping the cap and drinking half the bottle in one go while he protests.

"I don't know," he whines, looking back toward the coolers like they're desperately far away. "A bunch of 'em?" He reaches for what's left of the water, but I swing my arm away from him and guzzle the rest.

"Right." I smack my lips to really signal that the water is gone. "So I'm the prodigal cousin Sheba—"

"Oh, you tryna own that now?"

"—who thinks she's too good to come from her Portland throne, but these locals just roll up to a function they didn't help organize, eat up the food though half of them probably didn't send in the contributions Aunt Carla Ann has been sending polite reminders about for the past six months—"

"Yeah, no, about four people pay for these things, to be really real." He looks around the crowded park and nods, like everything's in order.

"—and two of them are my parents, but that's cool."

"I mean. Basically. Some folks do help, but it's my mom who makes sure we even have these anymore. They show up and that's the only part she cares about, so it's good."

"Mhm." And I decide I've been exceptionally well behaved.

I have earned a phone call.

"You finna replace that water you drank or nah?" Courtney calls after me, as I take off for the outskirts of the BBQ for some privacy, and to call Leona Fowl.

On the other side of the park, I'm giving myself a minute to get all the way to neutral, to light and delightful, before I push the call button. When I speak to her for the first time, I plan to channel the bubbly and carefree Naema of my LOVE account. I plan to make it clear that, yes, Tavia Philips came for me, but I remain unimpressed. So while I walk, I breathe evenly, stretch my neck, and take in the natural beauty around me. Despite their varied cooling devices, away from the concentration of Babcocks and their dancing and laughter and Necessary Hot Food, the air is actually slightly cooler. Which probably means the sun is starting to set.

Listen. It's not that the sunsets in the Southwest aren't ridiculously, unfairly gorgeous. They're glamorous, I'm the first to admit that, and for a few moments every day, I think maybe people living down here makes sense. It's just that immediately following that consideration, a legion of bloodsucking insects descends upon me, specifically, and I remember they have spiders the size of parking meters, and I know in my heart that this place is cursed.

Not to mention the sounds. When I'm far enough away from milling humans, I start to hear the various clicks and snaps. The mysterious, horrifying, taunting sounds from beasts I cannot identify because the Pacific Northwest is bleary and wet—not nearly as much as it gets credit for, but fine—but guess what.

Zero scorpions.

Oregon also isn't home to thirteen of the eighteen species of rattlesnake, if you can believe it.

So there are differences.

I'd told Courtney to watch the clock to make sure this shindig wraps before the sun goes down. I probably don't need to tell you he laughed at me. I'm still gonna need a ride home when it gets dark, cuzzo. Mess around if you want to. After this phone call, I'm out.

"Naema!" Leona says as soon as she answers, and her voice is not at all what I'm expecting. She's from LA so I guess I assumed it'd be airy and sort of valley. Instead she has a nice rasp, but she also sounds like she's eternally on her way out the door. "Thanks for making time to speak with me today, and I apologize for not replying to your first email, which I totally intended to do, and was incredibly thoughtful, not that I'm surprised."

Ew.

I'm not one to judge too quickly, but producer or not, I immediately do not like this chick. Plus, beside the whole I'm Super Disingenuous thing, she's the one who wanted to speak to me, right? So why does her rushed monologuing make me feel like I need to be considerate of *her* precious time? Do not appreciate.

"So I was going to start by assuring you that it was *al*ways our intention to tell the story of the Stoned—is that term offensive, by the way, you let me know what you'd prefer to be called—and while . . . Naema? Are you there?"

"I'm here," I say, but make sure it's carried by an obvious exhale.

"Oh. Did you hear my question?" Something rustles on her end, like she's doing a dozen things at once.

"I did. I assumed it was rhetorical, since you didn't leave space for an answer. Perhaps we should speak later, when things for you are less hectic."

That does the trick.

"No! I'm so sorry. I should back up. Thank you for calling me, I'm really pleased to speak to you. How's your day?"

"Lovely to speak to you as well, Leona. My day has been fine, thank you, but I'm at a family reunion so I'd really rather only make time for this if you seem present."

There's a gaping sound, like she's openmouthed.

"And Stoned doesn't offend me, but I can't speak for anyone else. You were saying?"

"Yes. Right." Her tone adjusts some, and whatever she thinks "present" means, she's speaking more softly. As in literally quieter. As though she's trying to prove to me that she's calmed down. "It was always our intention to tell the story of the Stoned, in particular those kids in Triton Park"—okay *that* feels insensitive—"but that understandably is gonna take some time, and we don't want to do it without all three of the kids—"

"Four."

"That's right, excuse me. And Effie Freeman is essential to that; she'd have to be part of it in some capacity, and Tavia's saying that's not possible right now. I get that the girl's gone underground, but this is such an important story, and you'd think she'd want to help the families as much as she can."

I know her name was listed in the credits of the Tavia Philips movie but something about the way she's talking makes it really clear. Leona Fowl knows Tavia. And has spoken to her. And trusts her, I'm sure. Or whatever it's called when you find someone, at the very least, profitable.

"But I think *your* story is of equal importance, and I think I can convince my team of that, especially if we could fill in some of the blanks and omissions from the first film."

I sort of hate that she's using that word to describe what was absolutely not some serious, art-house fare. It was the epitome of my dad's business mantra: You Can Build Something Fast, Or You Can Build It Right. I don't care how many views it gets or how many streaming records it sets, like, three true things happened in the whole movie: Tavia and Effie went to some protest; Tavia revealed Effie at prom; Tavia awakened Effie's victims. Nice and neat with some mean girl Nina moments tossed in, and sprinkled with Effie's Renaissance Faire Life.

It's not a film. It's a very long commercial for siren synthesizers, and a mind-boggling endorsement of Tavia Philips.

"And so I suppose your choice to erase me into Nina was strategic? So that you could also then reveal the *true* story of the only Eloko Effie Stoned?"

And that's when her slip starts showing. She did not appreciate my question, and when she answers, it is not at all subtle.

"I think it was more a decision to guard you from any additional criticism over allegedly exposing a siren. Especially being from the same community."

I don't know Leona Fowl well, but I know she's not Black. So this attempt to put me in my place, which is apparently below her at least as far as authority goes, is extremely rich. Because being that Tavia's a siren and I'm Eloko, there's only one community she could mean, and she is therefore swerving wildly outside her lane right now.

She must be mistaking my rage-regulating pause for her own shell shock a moment ago, so she continues.

"And that's another reason I think it's time to talk about the events at prom from your perspective, and working closely with our writers so we really capture what being Stoned is like. And what it's like after. Do you summer in the Southwest often?" she asks, and the correlation is implied. Am I only here because I can't stand to be in Portland?

We have a very big problem, Leona Fowl and I, and it is that she thinks *she's* in the driver's seat here. An assumption from which I will have to gently dissuade her.

"Ms. Fowl, I feel like I should tell you that this really isn't going well."

She shuts all the way up, and I'm not even getting started.

"You seem to be under a few ridiculous impressions. One of which is that I'm interested in your supposed protection. Or that you have any to offer me. Portraying a one-dimensional Black girl as a jealous mean girl who outs a siren isn't to your credit, for one thing. It actually felt more like stripping away my Elokoness so as not to sully it when you threw me under the bus."

"I'm so sorry you feel that way, Naema, but I certainly had nothing to do with the script—"

"Secondly, you seem to think I want to tell a story centered on the Awakening, or what it was like being Stoned. I thought I made myself pretty clear in my correspondences: I don't. There are plenty of people offering to tell my story if I'm contrite or broken or bleeding enough, and lemme save you some trouble: I'm not. I'm pissed."

Leona stumbles in another attempt to speak, her pretty rasp masking the way her voice starts to break.

"See, what you took out of the story so Tavia could shine is that *I'm. magic.* And not just because Tavia and I are from The Same Community. Because I'm me."

"Naema, can we start over," and there's an undeniable trill in her voice. "I may have been saying this all wrong. I certainly didn't mean to reduce your story to the Stoning; I might've been thinking more about it because of what's been posted on the Knights of Naema site you showed me."

"You're Eloko."

We both fall quiet for a moment, and I almost miss what she said about the Knights. Because Leona Fowl is Eloko.

"That's . . . interesting. I guess."

And it's a first. This woman I immediately did not like—or trust—is Eloko. I don't know what to make of that, or what to say, but I don't apologize. Something tells me she's betting on it increasing my trust level—which, to be fair, I'm a little surprised to find is not the case, at least not as far as I can tell in this moment. Because if she's Eloko, then: "Exactly how much did you work on Tavia's movie?"

"I had some involvement," Leona says, carefully, because Eloko or not, disingenuous seems to be her thing. "Is that an issue?"

She doesn't see the way my lips purse. "Why would it be? Anyway. I've got to get back to my family."

"Is there anything you need from me at this point, Naema?"

she asks, to prolong the conversation. No doubt she's hoping for some indication of whether or not I'm on board. And despite that this is something *I* set in motion, now I have questions.

About whether Tavia got a say. About whether Leona is why Nina wasn't Eloko. About whether or not she believes Tavia is who they said she is.

About whether she can grasp the story I need to tell.

"I need you to answer a question. Honestly." I don't care if the implication offends her.

"Shoot."

"What would you think if I told you Tavia Philips is the reason I got Stoned? That it wasn't Effie's fault."

She only needs a moment. "I'd say that's something I definitely wanna hear more about."

For once, she gives the right answer.

Good.

"Then we should talk again," I say.

"I would love that. And Naema. Before you go," she says, and there's something different about her voice now, or just about the way I'm hearing it. It still sounds like it's supposed to be apologetic, and nervous, but . . . intentionally. Maybe I'm suspicious because of the way she's letting her trill slip when I already know what she is. Whatever the reason, I feel the ghost behind my sternum throb, and I know: this is just how she usually operates. Her trill is how Leona Fowl gets the job done. I'm certain. She might be Eloko, but she's a producer first.

When she asks her last question, it's a doozy.

"I was just wondering, how did you know Tavia was a siren?"

The sun is low, and away from the lights Aunt Carla Ann strung up around the BBQ area, the corner of the park where I've been standing is quickly darkening. That might be why Courtney's coming over to me, and when I lift my chin, he thinks it's at him.

It isn't.

I can't even explain it. It's like I'm making room for the ghost-wind to dislodge itself. To spread out, and when it does, what before felt like a breeze passing through becomes a tornado inside me. It's wind so strong that the voices aren't caroling anymore. This is like a bellow. Now that I've given it free rein to move, it's churning my guts, upsetting my stomach. Something is very wrong.

"I didn't," I say, smooth and easy, despite the grimace I have to fight back. "I thought Effie was the one."

"Huh," which sounds involuntary. She's gonna have to up her game if she wants to do this with me. "Really? I thought"—and there's rustling again, like she's poring over documents—"someone said they overheard you and Tavia talking, after the livestream stopped. I don't know." She says the last bit to suggest that she's confused, but she's fooling no one. "Or maybe it was in some of the footage you sent?"

"Huh," I mimic her. "I don't see how it would be, since I didn't know. And I'm not sure who could've thought they overheard that. It was chaos, as you could probably see from the footage. I don't think there was anyone else in the courtyard when I stopped filming, except the other victims. And we couldn't hear from inside the stone."

"Okay," she concedes.

But Leona Fowl just tried to play me. And I have a good idea who she spoke to. The only other person I know for sure saw me turn to gray.

I hang up, and whether or not Courtney was planning to chastise me over my phone call, when he gets to me, his brows crunch together.

"You good?"

"My stomach hurts," I say, because there's no pretending I'm not visibly upset. "I haven't eaten yet."

"Are you serious? You really are new to this. You don't ever wait this long to make a plate if you want something other than hot dogs," he says as we walk. "If only there were some authority on family and family-related events who could take you under their wing."

There's a bit of commotion around the canopies when we get back, and instead of going to the food, I wander closer to the throne room.

"You ready, Gramma Lorraine?" That's Wilbur, first-born, son to Carissa, third-born, daughter to Clarence and Lorraine. He's behind the tripod, with the camera trained on the matriarch who at last is seated on her recliner, surrounded by fans, enclosed in sheer drapery, and clearly not interested in any of this.

"I don't know what y'all want me to talk about," comes her deep, velvety voice.

"Mama, we're gonna record you talking about our genealogy so we'll always have it," Carissa reminds her in what seems like an unnecessarily loud voice. Maybe it's for her own benefit, since the svelte, still tall Carissa is turning seventy herself this year.

Lorraine doesn't seem hard of hearing. Not that anyone cares, but she seems annoyed.

"Well," she says through a sigh of resignation like she's used to being ordered around. "Where y'all want me to start then?"

I peek around the equipment and the small congregation outside the opening of her tent to see her willowy white hair and soft, spotted brown skin. It's the weirdest thing, but I'm not sure whether I've seen her already today, and the picture that accompanies all the bits of history that just collected in my mind match her perfectly, or if the picture came to mind first, and it's the real live Lorraine matching *it*.

"Introduce yourself," Carissa's saying, "and tell us what year you and Daddy were born."

"All right, well, I'm Lorraine Babcock, and— Wait, Cece, what now?"

"Lorraine Babcock, born Milo, 1930."

When Wilbur and his mom turn and look at me quizzically, I just stare back.

"What?" I ask when they keep right on looking. But I get the feeling that they either heard and interpreted the Whispered Wind Voices, too, or I accidentally repeated something out loud.

"How'd you know that?" Wilbur asks.

So I said it out loud. Delightful.

Wilbur's wiping a palm over his bare scalp while he and his mom stare at me. He's not bald since he's clinging to the tufts of dark coils that shroud his ears, and while he waits for my reply, he scrunches his nose to reposition his glasses without taking his hands off the camera. This man is only fifty years old.

"You said Milo something," Courtney says from beside me.

"Milo's my maiden name, Cece," Great-Gram Lorraine offers, smiling like she hasn't heard it in a while. She bends with some effort, trying to catch me in her gaze, and I step around the others so she can see me better. "Why don't y'all ask Sheba to tell it, I bet she knows."

She knows who I am. I don't know why that makes me blush, but I can feel myself swelling. I almost float to the folding chair beside my great-grandma, I've inflated so much. When I take a seat, her soft hand pats my arm, and she pushes her chin at me, to signal that I should begin.

Whatever it is I'm supposed to say.

I make the mistake of glancing back toward the camera and find a few more family members have gathered, several of them looking at me with a mix of expectation and skepticism. And just a hint of She Don't Know Us. Just a light dusting of This Uppity Portland Cousin over their expressions, but I see it. And I hear the family tree, as though it's being recited by several people at once, their voices overlapping, but somehow so clear. I don't have to concentrate; it slips into order on its own.

"G'head, baby," Great-Gram Lorraine says, and when I look back at her, I can't help thinking of the donna.

"Lorraine Milo, born 1930, to Wilbur and Mary Milo. Clarence Babcock, born 1927, to Gerald and Mildred Babcock."

Her eyes glisten, and I have to pause or everyone will hear the catch in my breath. I use the time to translate the lists of facts into story.

"You married Great-Gran Clarence in 1947, and had Lorna, Gerald, and Carissa, one after the other in 1948, 1949, and 1950."

She nods, laughing with an open grin, and at first I think she's going to say something, but she doesn't. She just motions for Carissa to give her something to wipe her eyes.

"Then it took three years to have Mary Lorraine, my grandma, in 1953. She was named after your mom and yourself. And then you had Tina in 1955."

"Is that right?" I hear Patrice ask, but she's hushed.

Please. I'm not finished, cuzzo.

"Your oldest, Lorna, had five children of her own, and Gerald had seven. Edna," I say, searching for her face because I know she's here, "is his first-born, and I saw her son, Clay, earlier." I call him by the nickname I heard Courtney use, because in this family, birth names don't mean much. "Patrice is Gerald's youngest. Carissa had four sons, starting with Wilbur in 1970. Grandma Mary Lorraine had five, including my mom, Simone. And Tina had six."

When it's clear I've covered all of Great-Gram's kids, she starts a delicate clap, like over time maybe she's forgotten exactly how. Her palms pat together too lightly, but people get the picture, and soon everyone's clapping along.

"I didn't know your mom kept track of all that stuff," Patrice says, because of course she does. Even though they were close in age, my mom always said that her cousin was immature because she was the youngest of her siblings, born when her eldest sister was already fifteen, and babied by everyone. At least until their Aunt Tina gave birth to Lorna when she was almost fifty.

Late In Life Lorna is my first cousin once removed, same as Edna and Patrice and a million others, but she's only three years older than I am.

The more I look around at the faces on the other side of the sheer tent and behind cameraman Wilbur, the more history pops to mind. I can't get over it. There's the wind, the whispers, and then the knowledge is just there, right on the tip of my tongue, no struggle or concentration necessary.

"Why do y'all think I made you send all those belongings up to Simone and her husband?" Great-Gram Lorraine is saying. She takes my hand, and does something like squeezing it. "So Sheba could know. Having an Eloko in the family means someone will remember. Everything."

For a moment we just look at each other, and she's right. The longer I look at her, the more I know. I didn't know being Eloko was like this—but she did. So when my performance makes the greats and aunties and cousins start sharing what details they know about their immediate families, I stay beside her.

Great-Gram leans close.

"Sheba," she says, and it doesn't sound like name-calling when she says it. "You're listening to them, aren't you?"

"To who?" I ask, but not as quietly as she's speaking, otherwise she won't hear.

"Your Ancestors."

At the mention, they return. The voices that are close without being frightening, that begin without ever startling me, that whisper to me about who we all are.

Great-Gram's eyes light up. "You are." She smiles with something like relief. "Good girl."

"That's what the wind is?" I ask. "The rushing sound that turned into whispers?"

"If you listen, they'll speak more clearly. They don't bother unless you're listening," she tells me.

"Great-Gram Lorraine, are you Eloko, too?"

"No, not me, baby." But she smiles about it in a way that doesn't match the slights I've felt from other family members. "You're the first one in my family for a long time, but I was glad your mom wanted to try. Eloko are ancestral gifts."

"I don't think the rest of the family feels that way."

"They do. But Eloko don't act right anymore. Especially where you're from."

There's nothing worse than an unintentional old lady burn.

"Don't feel bad, Sheba," she goes on, petting my hand with her delicate touch. "There's a difference between having a child and rearing one, believe me, and the latter is much more about the child and less about being famous for having them."

"Is that why I've never heard the Ancestors before now? Because I've been in Portland? Or because I wasn't around family?"

"It's not that you're near family. I'm sure you've got plenty of family back home, too. It's because you got quiet. Or something forced you to."

Lovely. So it really does all come back to Tavia Philips, whether I want it to or not. Whether it's the devastating quiet of being Stoned, or the quiet I never knew existed until the chaos made

Portland unbearable and I finally got on a plane, it started with junior prom.

"Somebody's gonna take me home, right?" Great-Gram asks suddenly.

"Oh. Are you ready to go?"

"Oh yeah. I don't stay out after sunset. These bugs'll eat me up out here."

I smile, and know that when I do, I look very much like her.

"I'll take you home," I say, wondering if she'll agree with me on Courtney's ugly car, too.

Chapter XV

NAEMA

I should've asked Great-Gram Lorraine *why* the Ancestors speak to Eloko—or are supposed to. So much happened at the BBQ, though, and not just an unexpectedly confrontational conversation with Leona Fowl. I let the wind loose inside me, and I found out whose voices they are. Besides which, for weeks I've been wondering what being Eloko means besides a melody and a bell charm and a place at the top of the social food chain; when someone finally told me I was right to wonder, that there *was* something more, I needed a minute to process it before I got to the How Come.

I've been feeling the wind at odd times, too many to see a pattern, to be honest. But the times the swell has been strong enough to nearly make me sick stand out.

When I felt like two parts of my identity—being Black and being Eloko—were being pitted against each other.

When Priam promised that Portland would always love me best. Because I'm Eloko. Like he couldn't see how my Elokoness was under attack.

When Leona Fowl asked how I knew Tavia was a siren. When no one outside the network's supposed to know I did.

Every time, I knew something was off—like, *way* off—and then the Ancestors flared up. Which totally makes them sound like a medical condition, I realize. But their wind, or voices, were like a gut punch of confirmation, too strong to miss. Which, if Eloko mythos is all about Ancestral Wisdom, makes total sense.

The thing they aren't, apparently, is a Magic 8 Ball. The whispers brought family photos and lineage to my mind in an instant, yet they can't be bothered to tell me what to do about the things they Gut Punch Agree on. Which is honestly fine, because as much as I like old folks, I *can* think for myself. I mean. I'm still Darren Bradshaw's daughter.

We can talk, I texted Priam while Courtney and I chauffeured Great-Gram Lorraine home. *Wanna come visit?*

His reply was exactly the categorically ecstatic *Yes* you'd expect it to be.

"So all y'all got Last-Minute Plane Tickets money?" Courtney asked when I told him I needed to borrow his keys today. "What do *his* parents do?"

"His dad's a cop," I answered, despite being bored. Or pretending to be, anyway. I really hadn't thought anything of asking Priam to fly down on a whim, and I wasn't surprised when he said he would.

It never occurred to me until now that every Eloko family I know in Portland seems to live pretty comfortably. Obviously, not everybody's Bradshaw comfortable, but disposable-income comfortable. It's like even just having an Eloko kid gets you a better rate on your mortgage and credit card, and maybe being seen favorably by the entire city means unconscious favor, like more frequent promotions and, I don't know, grace periods or something.

None of which is magic, so much as good ole-fashioned privilege.

Have I mentioned Professor Vesper-Holmes gets on my nerves?

Anyway, Priam being able to hop a flight because I said we could talk and being Eloko potentially directly impacting a family's economic flexibility is why I'm back at the airport first thing the next morning. Also because despite having another family reunion event to help with, something tells me it wouldn't be *nice* to make Priam Uber to me. And I'm all about making sure people think I'm that, remember.

He comes out of the automatic doors, and even when a hot

gust of wind rearranges his hair, he just shrugs as if the strap of his messenger bag threatened to make a move, too. He takes in the assembly line of vehicles waiting for their travelers, the drivers eyeing the stalking security guard and ignoring the blare of the airport intercom that warns against idling in this area. Now a seasoned traveler, I feel equipped to declare airports and the act of being in or just outside them fresh hell, but that's beside the point.

People are buzzing all around him, shouting into phones, and gesturing wildly to rides stuck farther back in the procession, but Priam stands still. He can't see me yet—he thankfully has no idea what Courtney's car looks like—so I watch him. The way his face is both blank and tense. The way even the bustle of the airport can't distract him. He's waiting. For me.

He *is* pretty.

I can almost hear his melody. I can't, literally. It's always a delicate sound, like a shop's welcome when a customer arrives, and the airport and the traffic drown it out before it reaches me. But I know it by heart, and I can tell a couple of people hear it, because they perk up and look around, like maybe they've just thought of something. It's one of the differences between Portland and here; that people aren't constantly preoccupied with Eloko presence. Here, even when people see my bell, it seems to take a moment to register what it means. Sometimes they ask, or I'll catch someone sneaking a picture of my necklace and then typing as though googling or texting someone to confirm.

Anyway. Priam doesn't wear his bell; he keeps it loose in his pocket most of the time, so the travelers who get close enough to hear his melody don't seem to figure out that the boy beside them is the source.

I pull Courtney's ugly truck into a recently vacant stretch of curb and honk, but it's Little Bit who calls his name like her prince has finally come. Something tells me it wasn't just Courtney who watched my LOVE streams and posts, because this girl is swooning like a long-held dream has come to life.

"Priam!" She has to call again, and this time she hangs the top half of her body out the passenger window and waves most of it.

I don't know if she expects him to recognize her or what, but at least it works. It's only a moment more before he sees me behind the wheel.

He almost smiles, but it doesn't quite take.

"Little Bit, can Priam sit up front?" I ask her as he approaches, and then I whisper, "It'll make staring a whole lot easier."

When her eyes flick down but her cheeks perk up, it's the Black girl equivalent of blushing, but she hops out and repositions herself directly behind my seat where the looking is good. Priam takes her place and I almost lean over to kiss him, playing it off by stretching the opposite way, too, before pulling away from the curb.

"Hi," he says, and looks me over while I drive. So I'm pretty sure he noticed.

"Hey. Priam, this is my baby cousin, Carmen," I introduce them, careful not to use her nickname. Which is apparently not good enough because she quick-punches the back of my seat.

"You can just say cousin," she says through gritted teeth, and then, "Hi, Priam, I'm Carmen, I'm Naema's cousin." I can hear the full mouth grin, and roll my eyes. Adorbs.

"Hi, Carmen." At least he's smiling now, too.

"Where's your luggage?" she asks, and it's such an immediate follow-up she may as well have pounced on him.

"Little Bit, do you have your seat belt on?"

She catches my eye in the rearview mirror and bulges her bright eyes at me before mouthing, *Whyyyy.* When I snort, Priam catches wind and looks between us.

"I'm just here till tonight, so. No luggage." Then he twists in his seat and grins at her. "Little Bit, huh? I like it."

In the rearview, I bulge my eyes back, and then roll them when she can't contain a smile.

Today's perfect for Priam's visit because the Babcock Family Reunion is split up for separate group activities, which means I won't have to parade a white boy around the entire tribe at once. He wouldn't be the only one, but he'd be the one with Sheba, the

Eloko cousin from the Pacific Northwest, and something tells me that would be a whole thing, even if they were just doing it to get under my skin.

Courtney, it turns out, deserves as much credit for organizing this whole shindig as his mom. I discover this when he informs me that he is—and now we are—responsible for shepherding a herd of young Babcocks to something called an Indoor Action Sports Playground, which, if we're being honest, just sounds like word salad or a poor translation. But apparently it really is a thing. It also happens to be a big deal in this town, and despite my misgivings, when the kids find out they're taking a Ninja Warrior class, they go wackadoodle. It also happens to afford me a solid hour of freedom (to stay within eyesight), and since Courtney isn't *not* going to partake in walking handstands, Priam and I have it to ourselves.

"I missed you," Priam says when I've taken a seat. He hasn't. Instead he looks like he waited as long as he could, and ran out of composure just before sitting down.

"I miss you, too, Priam."

"What does that mean?"

"Are you going to sit? We need to talk while everybody's preoccupied."

"What does it mean that I said 'missed' and you said 'miss'?"

"I don't know," I say through a sigh. "I guess that I understand it's still going?"

He chews the inside of his lip, puts his hand on the back of the chair he's still refusing to inhabit. "Why?"

"Because the entire time we were together, you had a weird fixation with someone I don't like? And you never explained, despite having plenty of opportunities? And it made me look like a jealous girlfriend, which please. I feel like I said all this already, Priam. And anyway, talking about this isn't why you're here."

"Yes," he says with surprising insistence, but he finally sits down. "It is."

"Okay, then it's not why I asked you to come." I lean to the side so I can see my cousins, who are all following the instructor's lead in their warm-up stretch, except of course for Courtney, who is waving him off and tickling his sister and the others when the adult isn't looking. "Sorry. It's good we have some privacy, but I also feel like Courtney probably doesn't count as supervision."

I realize I'm laughing, and Priam is decidedly not, so I reel it in. I don't even get an opportunity to be annoyed at having to batten down my spirits so as not to offend before he softens.

"You do seem better down here." He leans forward so he can take hold of the tendrils I've purposely left out of my ponytail. (See? Beauty tip for the win.) "You look really happy again."

"Yeah." I gaze into his dark eyes. I can't say I've missed them, since I have an endless supply of pictures. I may be good at not answering his texts; I'm less good at going without seeing him altogether. But it's different, having him in front of me. I realize what I've missed is the feeling of *him* admiring *me*. The way I know he loves the things I love about myself. The way he smiles at my snark and never tells me to tone it down. Never tells me to be nice. Never says I'm too pretty for my own good, the way even my own parents have on occasion, like it's the only thing making my personality palatable.

He never thinks palatable is something I need to be.

"I *am* happy. I'm glad I came." I haven't been wearing it every day like I do back home, but now I take hold of my necklace so I won't take Priam's hand. "I'm not glad about us." There's no harm in confessing that to him.

"Neither am I." He shuffles around in his seat like he wishes the table weren't between us. "So can we get back to normal now?"

"I think normal's gonna be new from now on," I say, because there's a lot I want to tell him, once the big thing is out of the way. Before he has an opportunity to wonder, I ask, "What did you tell Leona Fowl?"

"Wait, the producer? Why?"

"What did you tell her you heard? At prom? Between Tavia and me?"

"I just," he starts, which is enough to confirm that—just as I concluded—he's the one she spoke to. Despite the fact that I'm the one who reached out to her, she—for some reason—found it beneficial to speak to Priam before she spoke to me.

I'm sure there's a super compelling, perfectly unproblematic reason for why that would be. I'm sure it had nothing to do with the other aspects of Priam's identity making him trustworthy enough to vet me to someone who's a total stranger to us both. I'm sure it's just because he showcases in the prom footage I showed her, and maybe even in the unchopped livestream footage where I captured Gorgon Effie streaking around the courtyard. Maybe she saw him in a blur, and knew he hadn't been Stoned, and—What? Why would that mean she spoke to him first when she knows we're *both* Eloko.

That isn't a question, because there's no good answer.

Priam's brows are knitted and tense, and he's recalling. But then they ease, and he looks at me, sharp as the point his hair comes to just above his mole. "Is that why you wanted me to visit? To talk about your movie?"

"Not to talk about the movie I didn't get a chance to tell you about because some producer already had, to talk about what you told a strange woman about something you don't understand. And something you never brought up to me."

"Wait, first of all, Leona's Eloko," he says, both hands slightly off the table. "So—"

"So what? You don't know her. *We* don't know her."

His head jerks back like I've slapped him. "So since when is another Eloko a stranger? Like, a *stranger* stranger?"

I could say since nary an Eloko came to my defense in Portland, but I'm trying to stay on message here, so instead I tell him, "Since she's also a movie producer who's more interested in her project than the people it's about."

"I'm just. I don't know, that doesn't sound right coming from you."

"Coming from me?"

"Yes, Naema, coming from you. Being Eloko's all that matters to you, it's the most important part of who we are, so why—"

"That's not true."

"How? How is that not true?" He waits, and he looks genuinely confused.

"Ask Upside-Down Portland." Which understandably doesn't lessen his confusion.

I guess this *is* the message now. There's no avoiding it.

"Did you not notice how it doesn't get to be, for me? Portland hasn't treated me like I'm Eloko first since Tavia became a celebrity herself, and I get that *you* don't understand why that is, or how those two things are related, but." I roll my eyes and exhale like I'm done. "Figure it out."

Priam's quiet for a moment, and then he asks, "Isn't it a good thing if a known siren can be a celebrity? Doesn't that mean Portland's getting something right?"

"Okay, I'm about to explain something that's actually super basic, and I mean basic to the point that I really thought it didn't need explaining. I thought we were all on the same page, which is actually my bad. I get it now. Because despite what I knew, I still thought being Eloko meant we transcended all of this. That's what I thought. I thought they saw all of me when they poured out their adoration."

I'm talking a mile a minute, and I have to stop again, roll my head between my shoulders, and then press my chin to my chest to stretch my neck. If it looks like I'm preparing for a marathon, it's because that's what this feels like. And it's not even the conversation I thought we needed to have. It's literally the foundation without which that convo can't even happen.

"If it's gonna upset you, we don't have to talk about it," Priam offers.

"Yes, we do, you're just gonna have to accept that it upsets me, and figure out whether it should upset you, too."

This just keeps getting worse. The breakup was about something else, but there's no scenario in which I can be with someone who doesn't see what I don't get a choice in seeing. In experiencing.

"Okay," he says. "Then tell me."

"I've been Portland Famous my whole life, right? And I'm a

Black girl. So by your logic, Portland has always been getting race right. I mean, no shade, because that's what I thought, too. Except, as we know, it's *new* that a known, unapologetic siren who isn't wearing a silencing collar can be a celebrity. So either they were cool with me because I'm Eloko, which means they've been overlooking that I'm also a Black girl, which means they've never been getting it right with me—or I'm totally safe because they just hate sirens in particular. And since sirens are exclusively Black women—right? Do you see the problem?"

"Yeah . . ."

"So like, neither of those possibilities is acceptable. And neither is holding only enough space for one Black girl to shine at a time. Tavia's not a litmus test for Portland's wokeness, she's just the new exception." I shake my head. "Portland's idea of Eloko is *not* the most important part of me. Not anymore."

I want to tell him what being Eloko is really like. About the Ancestors, and the wind, and the fact that it isn't all about performance or entertaining fans.

But I can't. Because I've just said so much. And it wasn't a relief. It didn't make me feel lighter. It didn't set me free. If anything, it feels worse. Because these are things I never say. These are things that having a carefree livestream, and an adorable Fiat, and an Eloko boyfriend, and my necklace charm on perpetual display keep me from having to say.

Which means I don't even know if it's coming out right. I don't know if I'm making myself clear, if I'm saying anything linear or in a way that someone outside it can even understand. After a life in the Portland Eloko Bubble—whether it was real or not—this is the heaviest, most uncomfortable, most joy-crushing reality to face, and that's without even wondering what it means that I'm only facing it because of something Tavia did, that I high-key hate her for.

I don't even know if I'm doing it right.

What if the donna could hear me, and she said I was wrong? That I didn't know how to describe the predicament of being a Black girl because I didn't know how to be one. Because I'd never really had to be one.

"Ny?" Priam is looking at me with borderline panic in his eyes.

Which is probably because of how quickly I've been breathing. Over the past few moments, I've been sucking in chestfuls of air, and I thought I was doing a pretty good job of having what I can only imagine is The Most Discreet Panic Attack. I've never had one before, but the fact that I'm simultaneously light-headed *and* feel like my head is filled to capacity, that my chest is burning so bad I feel like I could scream *and* am also unnervingly quiet—I'm relatively certain that's what this is.

When the wind starts to swirl, it cyclones into a chorus.

This will pass.

This terrifying feeling—like I'm a fish outside the water—is not going to last.

I nod, as though the Ancestors are outside me and will see. Like they're sitting with a worried Priam who's clasping one of my hands in both of his, and looking like he's gonna get a professional involved at any moment.

"It's all right," I say, but I'm echoing their voices. Luckily, it calms Priam as well. "It's all right."

"Should we go outside? Do you need some air?"

"I'm good now." I take in a deep breath to prove to him I can. There's still something I need to know. "I need you to tell me what you told Leona Fowl happened at prom. Between Tavia and me."

"She asked me for the story between you and Tavia."

"And you told her . . ."

"I told her you've never liked Tavia, that you guys have never been friends, because she thinks her thing is more, I don't know, *authentic* than yours."

"Oh my gawd."

"Which, yeah, made a lot more sense after prom night, since you obviously knew what she was before the rest of us."

Balls.

He did hear us.

"Priam."

I want to curl up and die. Or throttle the boy sitting across from me. Of course Leona Fowl thought she had license to come out of her lane. She thinks she got some intimate insight from the person I'm closest to. Because she did.

"I didn't think you'd have a problem with me telling her, she said *you* came to *her,* and you shared a bunch of stuff with her—"

"Yeah, prom videos!"

"And some new forum you're part of since you left LOVE—"

"I'm not *part*—" I immediately lower my voice again, searching the facility for evidence that anyone is paying attention to us. They're not, of course, nor could they possibly hear our conversation over the victorious bellows coming from Courtney and the cousins. "She obviously wanted to give you the impression I'd confide in her, and clearly she succeeded."

His face falls, and he looks at the table between us.

"I didn't wanna be another person who betrayed you, Naema. I swear."

"Then why didn't you tell me you were still in the courtyard?" I try to sound earnest instead of angry, and when the wind picks up in my chest momentarily, I take a calming breath and ask one more question: "Why were you?"

"I wasn't gonna leave you." Priam answers like the question makes zero sense.

"Even with Effie zipping around turning people to stone? It would've been understandable. It was chaos."

"I just made sure not to look at her. That's what set her off. I mean. Until you."

I'm not abrupt about it, but I release his hands and withdraw.

"I'm sorry, Ny. I'm sorry I didn't tell you that I saw her give Effie the command," he says, careful now, like he doesn't want to say her name, or like he's not sure I can stand to hear it. "But I didn't think I was keeping a secret. Why would I think you'd want to talk about it? She hurt you."

It's too bad I watched that stupid movie, and all those response videos and entertainment panels; I know exactly what everybody else would say.

"I deserved it, remember?"

"No, you didn't." His dark eyes are overshadowed when his brows crash down above them. "Not after you kept her secret that whole time. You wouldn't even let me parade our relationship around school because of her, which I totally didn't understand. But it made sense after that night. You were a good friend to her."

"We weren't friends," I blurt. "We never were."

"Okay, well. You were something, otherwise why protect her?"

I don't know how to answer that, and not just to Priam. No one's ever asked me why I shielded for Tavia. Even in the unspoken way it always seemed I was being treated like an outsider. No one questioned whether I was inside enough to do her that service.

"Because it was right. It was the right thing to do. No matter who she was."

"Right. So maybe you weren't friends, Ny, but you were still good to her."

"As long as you don't tell Gavin. I don't want him thinking I've taken his instructions about being nice to heart."

For a moment he just smiles, and I can almost see the relief seeping out of him. This is without question the most difficult conversation we've ever had. It goes against every tenet of our relationship and culture, and I don't think I'm being dramatic. I think there's no way he'll ever want to have a serious and sustained conversation again—and then it's Priam who starts it up again.

"Can I ask you something, Ny?" When I nod, he says, "Why didn't you tell me about the nucleus thing? The . . . network?"

I freeze up. Even knowing he overheard Tavia and me talking in the courtyard that night, I still feel a slight panic at hearing someone outside the network bring it up.

"Because you broke up with me over me keeping a secret from you, right? And you made me feel really crappy about it. About being fixated on Tavia, but. Aren't you? Haven't you always been? Isn't the network a whole Tavia-related secret you kept from me?"

"That's . . ." I need an inoffensive way to say Totally Unrelated WTF Are You Talking About, but it doesn't come.

"I'm not trying to pick a fight, I just wanna know why your secrets are okay, but mine are worth breaking up over."

"Because mine are about a community you're not a part of that needs protecting, Priam," I tell him. "You're here because I needed to tell you that you can never speak about it again. Never."

I don't know how I'm expecting him to respond, but he's quiet. It isn't brooding, or sulking, which is actually a bit surprising. Instead there's an expression that's almost like recognition.

"My dad knew, too." He's looking off to the side, and then he runs his hand through his hair before leaning into his forearms on the table. "About what she is. I don't know. I guess it makes me wonder what kind of person I am if my girlfriend, my ex, *and* my own dad didn't trust me with that."

"It's not about you," I tell him. "And the network isn't just about me or Tavia. That's why you can't talk about it. To anyone. Not even another Eloko. For sure, never to Leona Fowl."

He hesitates. "And that's really the only reason I'm here? So you could tell me something you could've texted?"

"I mean. I'm not gonna write about it where it can be screenshot and shared," I cluck, before realizing how it sounds. Priam doesn't miss a beat.

"You mean that *I* might screenshot and share. Because it's not just Leona Fowl or Portland you don't trust anymore, it's me, too."

"If you're dead set on being offended, Premium, I don't know what to say. I trust me. That's all anyone should expect for a while, and I don't feel bad about that."

He draws in a deep breath and looks away again, but when I think he's going to pout, instead he stands.

"Do you want something to drink?" he asks, before rephrasing. "Can I get you something to drink?" And then he sort of smiles. "Only so many hours to feel like your boyfriend again."

"I'll come with you," I tell him, and when he offers me his hand, I take it. I let myself enjoy that he's here, regardless of why, and I don't hesitate to wrap my other hand around his forearm like I used to.

I hadn't noticed what my cousin wore today until now. I'm sitting between Priam's legs, him on a tabletop, and me on a bench in front of him, watching my cousins enjoy a free play after their lesson. Priam's been alternating between petting my hair and rubbing my shoulders, occasionally laughing at something one of the kids does.

I must've seen the siren synthesizer masking the bottom half of Little Bit's face, and I must've heard the autotuned version of her voice every time she speaks. There's music blaring through the facility, and a sea of kid voices, but I realize my gaze has been trained on her for some time.

And then I realize that I'm not the only one.

A little white girl has been absorbed into a cluster of my little cousins, the group of them taking turns flipping off of a trampoline platform into a basin of chunky foam blocks. The non-Babcock tween is completely comfortable, egging on Little Bit with the rest of them when she makes her dying call during another dramatic, acrobatic descent.

The tween's mom is another story. I know who she is because she's been standing with another parent, speaking behind cupped hands like lip-readers are a concern, and taking indecisive steps toward her daughter, and then turning back. Finally the other adult goads her enough that she quicksteps to the trampoline area and reaches toward her child, careful to withdraw her hand whenever one of my excitable cousins almost makes accidental contact.

"Corey," the mom finally shouts over the noise, and her daughter whirls around. Instead of interrupting her play, the tween starts bouncing around like a cartoon bomb with a lit fuse. She's demanding her mother watch her flip and despite the fact that it looks very possible the kid is gonna explode otherwise, the mom reaches through the throng of children and yanks Corey away.

Kids are thankfully just kids sometimes, and my cousins make space for the little girl to be retrieved before recongealing. They don't know or worry over why she's been taken away; sometimes parents just do that.

But I've been watching the mom, and the way she scared-scowls at Little Bit in particular. Like she doesn't get that a synthesizer's just a toy, and wearing one basically ensures that the little Black girl beneath it is *not* a siren—otherwise she wouldn't need it.

Finally the woman feels my gaze, and looks over at me.

"Little Bit," I call while we're still watching each other, and I put my trill in my voice to make sure it catches my cousin's attention.

She barrels into me, trailed by a couple of others, and the smell of kid sweat almost makes me wave them off.

"Lemme hold your synthesizer while you play," I say.

"Okay!"

Easy. She yanks it indelicately, wrenching it around her face the way kids do with things they didn't personally pay money for, mussing her ponytail made of braids.

"Here," she chirps, gives me a very sweaty kiss on the cheek, and then bounds off.

Across the room, Corey's mom and her friend still watch while trying to act like they aren't. The mom puts her hand over her heart and shakes her head, like she's relieved but still shaken up, and the other parent gives her a quick hug.

Give me a break, and then take a seat.

"Did you hear that little girl's name?" Courtney asks when he drops on the table next to Priam, greeting him with a series of hand slaps they clearly have not discussed beforehand.

"Yep." I can't stop watching Corey's mom, especially now that it's obvious she's avoiding my eyes. For what. What does she think I am? "There's a lesson in there, I swear."

"In a little girl named Corey?" Priam asks. "What's wrong with that? Names don't have a gender."

"That's what I'm always telling her, man," Courtney says, and I almost laugh.

"Here," and I chuck the sweaty, twisted synthesizer into his lap. "Maybe don't let Little Bit wear this out in public. Those parents almost had a heart attack."

"And I'm supposed to care why."

"Because you don't want people looking at your little sister the way they did. Just take it, Courtney."

"They don't need to see a synthesizer to act a fool," he scoffs.

"You can think whatever you want, but maybe remember she's a little girl and just do what I ask."

"Dang, calm down, Sheba." He balls up the contraption and shoves it into his pocket.

"Pro tip: telling people to calm down almost never results in them calming down, or you keeping your hairline," I say as I shove out of my seat and go keep a closer eye on my little cousins.

The day fades too quickly. I try to dig my nails into it and keep the hours from ticking by, but with Priam around, and the constant eventfulness of Family Reunion Week, time slips away from me.

We're back at the airport, and I told Little Bit I wanted to go alone this time. I don't want to share our goodbye, and after Priam and I park so I can walk him in, at first all I want to do is hug him. But there's something else.

"This is gonna sound weird," I start, and while I pause to decide whether I really want to ask at all, he moves my hair behind my ear.

"Okay. Be weird."

"Do you ever hear . . . voices? Not like that. Familial voices."

"Familial . . ."

"Your Ancestors. It's an Eloko thing."

"Well, I'm an Eloko," he says through a laugh.

"That's why I'm asking you, butthead."

"I mean. I don't think so? Why?"

But instead of answering, I just shake my head, and pull him into me.

"Don't forget," I say into his neck, and then pull back and watch his brows relax with acknowledgment. "You can't ever mention it. Not even to other Eloko."

"I get it, Ny. I won't." He rubs my arms, and then wraps me up in his again. "But I already told her you knew Tavia was a siren. What do I tell her if she brings it up again?"

"Tell her you can't be sure. You were eavesdropping, in a high school courtyard, with a gorgon on the loose. You were scared of Effie."

"But I wasn't."

"Great." I roll my eyes. "She'll believe you were. Or tell her I dumped you, and you were mad at me. You were trying to get back at me."

His hold on me loosens.

"I really don't care what you tell her, Priam, as long as it isn't true. You could always just never speak to her again, but that's not really up to me, is it."

"I don't have a reason to. Do you still? What are you gonna say?"

I straighten, lift my chin so I am looking squarely into his dark eyes. "I'm gonna tell her that Tavia Philips made her sister turn me to stone."

"Ny—"

"Yes?" I wait. I could cross my arms or cock my eyebrow, but my unflinching gaze is enough.

"I watched the movie." He shakes his head, like that's not what he meant to say. "I mean, I know that doesn't matter, it's just. She didn't tell anyone. About homecoming."

I don't answer him. I already know that.

"The thing I was afraid would make the world afraid of me. Of us. When I accidentally hurt her . . . she didn't tell."

"Isn't that darling," I say through a sigh, and before he can go on, "but what she did to *me* wasn't an accident, Priam. You know that as well as I do."

He glances down, and I touch his chin so he'll look me in the eye.

"I'm going to tell Leona Fowl what Tavia did to me, Priam. Do you have a problem with that?"

I'm sure someone would say it isn't fair, asking him that question when I know how much he wants us back together. But this should be an easy choice, relationship in the balance or not. He knows what happened, and he knows what I've gone through for her. He knows about the network and that I refuse to expose it. I have a right to my own story, and this is the safest story I can tell. And if it takes Tavia down a few pegs, I fail to see how that's unfair. Her being a siren doesn't give her carte blanche on terrorizing someone else.

Victims can have victims, and the world needs to be reminded.

"No," he tells me. "I don't have a problem with that."

"Good. Because it's only really up to me."

Chapter XVI

Knights of Naema—Members Only

SilverSchalem [gold/45]: #Justice4Naema

SilverSchalem: I didn't take these, but I am posting them with permission. I know a lot of us won't want to see these, which is why I've tagged them NSFW—but we SHOULD see them. Because we should never forget what was done to our girl. [upvotes: 115]

Anon [no shield]: Just as a point of clarification: permission from the photographer? Or are you in contact with Naema herself?? [upvotes: 5]

SilverSchalem: ETA: Permission from the photographer. Thanks for pointing that out. I'm not in contact with Naema herself. I wish. [upvotes: 1]

Anon: Understood. I'm actually glad you didn't mean her. As important as this documentation is, I wouldn't want her having to see herself Stoned. She's been through more than enough. [upvotes: 60]

NaemasNobleman [silver/39]: #Justice4Naema

HelmedDefender [bronze/15]: #Justice4Naema

Lancelot [bronze/9]: Even in gray, she's still beautiful . . . [downvotes: 125]

SilverSchalem: Downvoting.

Greaves [silver/40]: I get what you're saying, but we're not celebrating an attack.

Lancelot: Not my intention, I just meant the way you can still see her through the stone, she's still an Eloko goddess no matter what that snake did to her. [upvotes: 4; downvotes: 25]

SilverSchalem: Totally get what you're trying to say, but it does diminish the brutality of what was done to her if we comment positively on this. That's not what it's for.

Anon: I wouldn't put it past the siren being involved. [upvotes: 43]

WyteKnight [silver/28]: Nobody can tell me this wasn't a vendetta. [upvotes: 45]

Nutting4Naema [no shield]: Sirens are trash but they don't have this kind of power.

NaemasNobleman: Why are you so sure you know what they can do? We don't even know how many there are. [upvotes: 120]

Anon: And you can't ignore the timing and the victim. All the others were decoys to get to Naema. [upvotes: 99]

WyteKnight: Zero dispute here. It came directly after the livestream. [upvotes: 100]

Anon: Not a coincidence. [upvotes: 40]

TheCavalry [bronze/9]: Our girl's such a rockstar. You can still see the collar she wore, in the stone. She has every right to stand her ground and make a statement about the dangers sirens pose. [upvotes: 120]

NaemasNobleman: And some siren comes and proves her point. They're dangerous, period. [upvotes: 145]

SilverSchalem: And now the siren's supposed to be a hero, like Naema's suffering and her rights don't matter. [upvotes: 120]

Anon: Beyond tired of that siren being praised. [upvotes: 35]

Lancelot: #Justice4Naema [upvotes: 5]

Lancelot: #Justice4Naema [upvotes: 1]

Lancelot: #Justice4Naema

Chapter XVII

NAEMA

I call myself Sheba503 when I finally make an account on the Knights forum.

I'd been meaning to investigate the Members Only subforums anyway, and it occurred to me that our dear producer friend, Leona Fowl, claimed to have mentioned my Stoning because of something she'd seen on the site—and yet I've seen nothing of the sort. Nor immediately do I when I've returned to the solitude of Little Bit's room, whose full bed feels much fuller when I'm not sharing it with a nine-year-old cousin, no matter how adorable she is.

After the cousin outing, the young ones decided to have a slumber party, which means Little Bit, Didi, and the rest are sleeping at my cousin Patrice's house. Apparently they didn't get enough of trampolines because the plan is to sleep on the outdoor one in her backyard, under the stars. Carnivorous southwestern bugs, scorpions, and snakes be damned, I guess.

In Little Bit's bed, I starfish, sheets askew. I've been down here long enough not to be considered a guest anymore, which means Aunt Carla Ann's thermostat is no longer hovering around a comfy cozy 65 F. I've got the bedroom window open, with an oscillating tower fan running on high, but it's still barely enough to cut through the humidity.

I wasn't nervous perusing the latest posts in the main area, but when I return to the subforum that requires a membership, I hesitate. I'm not sure what to hope for, what could warrant this extra, if ineffective, layer of security—and the things that leap to mind aren't great. The site's Community Commitment To Avoiding Child Pornography Charges is all well and good, but this is my body we're talking about, and if there's anything worth hiding behind a second access point, I'd like to know how it exists and where it came from.

The last thing I want to find out is that the only group of admirers who *don't* have to attach some sort of disclaimer or criticism to their adoration, who *don't* see my time in the stone as some sort of redemption arc, are actually smut-peddling incels.

When I land in the subforum, I'm not prepared for what I find.

In Little Bit's room, the only light is coming from the laptop screen balancing on my lap, and yet I swear the bedroom around me dims. Whatever ambient sound I'd grown accustomed to quiets.

All I see is gray.

That's not a trick of my subconscious, either. I'm not post-traumatically slipping back into my prom night memory.

I am seeing myself. Imprisoned in gray.

Literally.

That's me in the photo, standing in the courtyard of Beckett High, stone eyes wide, mouth slightly open.

Stoned.

The expression on my face must be the one I had when I heard Tavia give the command, and when I saw Effie's gorgon eyes train on me, her gargantuan tail coiled endlessly beneath her body.

Someone stood in front of me before Tavia returned, and they took this picture.

They took several.

Close.

My eyelashes.

The siren-silencing collar, and my collarbone, and the rise of my breasts.

My hand and my phone, which wouldn't survive the stone grip and would have to be replaced.

The gray is porous, and it's . . . beautiful. If looking at beautiful statues makes bile hurtle up your esophagus, and burn the back of your throat.

It's a foggy morning kind of gray, with flecks of white, and sudden flourishes of something like periwinkle.

Worse, it's me. It's what I look like when my skin isn't skin anymore, and my hair isn't soft and healthy, despite being relaxed. The beautiful and unexpected hints and transitions of color spell out my face, and my form—but I'm not there. I wasn't standing there, still as stone.

I remember those six hours, and there may have been silence, but there was no peace.

Nothing about these pictures is true.

On Little Bit's bed, I'm cold now. There's a sickly kind of chill that doesn't match the temperature in this room or in the night outside the window. Because I was only Stoned for six hours, but whoever took these pictures knew where to find me. Which probably means they watched my livestream that night, and that they're subscribers, or were before my deactivation. More than that, it means they're probably Portland-local, or within six hours' driving distance at the most.

I don't know why that frightens me, and maybe "scared" is too strong a word. The Knights of Naema haven't given me any reason to think that proximity should worry me. The photo is even captioned #Justice4Naema.

Still. No one asked me whether or not I wanted pictures of my darkest moments plastered on the internet, even behind a flimsy authorization wall, even for the sake of remembrance.

I read their uncharacteristically serious discussion below the photos, and my breath hitches.

I'm conflicted, and part of the reason for that is the way the Knights know the truth. They've figured it out, even if to an outsider their discussion would sound like a paranoid conspiracy theory.

They know Tavia had something to do with what happened to me. And they know the heroine worship she's getting isn't fair.

There's something else, too. Something new framing a few of the Knights' avatars, in gold or silver or bronze. There's what looks like a shield on the bottom right of the frame, and a number. The highest belongs to the Knight who started this subforum, interestingly, and I can click a + or - under the avatars if I want to contribute, apparently.

I leave the new shields and ranks alone, but I've got my Sheba503 cloak on, so after a moment's hesitation I *do* upvote the comment about Tavia being responsible for what happened to me.

It doesn't change the other hitch I'm feeling, the queasy confliction. I don't know if that's the Ancestors trying to rise up inside and tell me how they feel, but I resist. I push it back down by liking another comment, the one about my Stoning not being coincidental, because I don't want to hear that I can't have *any* support. I don't wanna hear—or feel!—that this is an intrusion. That no considerate admirer would do this.

I don't want to catalogue the myriad possible red flags.

After everything I finally said, that I said it to Priam, and the fact that the cost of saying it was so immediately apparent—and foreign . . . I don't wanna wonder how much of it applies to the Knights.

Because those pictures *do* serve a purpose, unlike the movie and the articles and the infotainment discussions and faux academic research. At least now I know what the world has seen. The static, immobile, hardened shell. The stone that looked like me exactly, not like a replica or a wonky wax statue, but like *I* was changed. It's worse than I thought back when I was trapped, because I was gone, and I forgot that there was something left in my place.

They could see me, or a facsimile, anyway. Something was there, my shock and unmaskable fear entirely readable on a frozen face. A form of me was standing there, the whole time. My punishment, public and humiliating. She left me there, exactly where I'd been when I recorded her, exactly where my viewers would know to find me, could gawk at my comeuppance, and she went about her business for six hours. Everyone who's attacked me since, belittled or diminished me—they all know what was done to me, and they did it anyway.

I wish I hadn't seen the photographs. I wish they didn't exist, and that just makes me angrier. She isn't going to take away the comfort of this community when she's had hers all along. When

I got expelled from hers, and she gets to stay no matter what she does, because she's The Whole Point.

Thank gawd for the Knights. I thought saying Tavia Philips Stoned me was gonna sound like slander—and it probably would've, coming from me. Claiming that *she* hurt *me* would sound like retaliation, I was aware, given that her story got told first, and with the benefit of an emotion manipulating score, and tasteful merch, and a publicity strategy that was better executed than the movie itself.

It matters that someone else—quite a few of them—thought Tavia was the villain from jump.

I can't resist. I make a modest post, and I don't blather on about being a first-timer or tell them what it means to me in excruciating detail; I just say, *I'm so glad this forum exists. It means a lot.*

And when I get my first upvote, I smile like a true Pretty Bird.

Why did only Priam get an invite? Jamie texts, and to her credit, she waited until the visit was done to do so. He's been home a day now, and at least I can tell by her questioning that he didn't immediately go back and blab everything I told him he can't talk about.

Jamie's feelings are really hurt, Gavin informs me like he's taking that previous, heat-induced phone mishap to heart and thinks I'll read his message but maybe not hers. He is now not only my conscience, but also my liaison.

I'm opening everybody's texts now anyway. I miss my friends. I miss light and carefree. I miss the way the worst thing that happens in our group is Jamie thinking I'm playing favorites.

I thought you wanted me and Priam to make up . . . I say via group text, and then I lock my phone. I go back to my quiet time in Aunt Carla Ann's backyard, with my hand wrapped around the chain. In the shade of the back porch, the links had been cool but eventually the heat from my hand transferred. It's not quite refreshing anymore, but it's better than swampy.

"What's up, Pretty Bird?" Courtney finds me, and drops into the bench swing beside me, setting it in motion. "You look real unsocial out here," he says, tugging on his blond coils like the shape got flattened and he's plumping it back up, no mirror required. He nods at me. "Cross-legged, straight-faced. Quiet enough that Little Bit gave up and went inside. She's watching TV, Sheba. That kid never watches television except as a last resort."

"There's something wrong with quiet now? Is it very uppity of me?"

"Everything all right?" he finally asks.

I nod, slow and steady, the way we swing.

"'Cause you can talk to me if it's not." He clears his throat and it's obviously more serious than he intended to play this, so he nudges the porch with his foot and sends us swinging with a bit more gusto. "I kinda wanted to talk to you anyway."

"Oh yeah?" And it sounds exactly as enthused at the prospect as I feel.

"Yeah. Just about Little Bit and like. Just how much she looks up to you, you know?"

He tilts his head as though to elicit my formal agreement, but I don't budge. I'm watching the sky burn. I swear they live under a completely different sky down here, and this one bleeds and burns and combusts. It brings the drama, consistently. Today, there are clouds and they started out fat and side by side, like the biscuits on Aunt Carla Ann's chicken pot pie casserole. When the sun started to set, it's like they deflated, losing their form along with the day's heat—only it looks a lot more destructive. But like. In a gratifying, calming way. Now the clouds are a thin duvet above our heads, still all the wild and reckless colors of flame, but accompanied by the smell of impending storm. I plan to stay right here on this back porch until it breaks.

"Naema."

"Little Bit looks up to me, and that somehow resulted in you interrupting my alone time. Did you know I have a whole suite to myself back home?"

"Yes."

"It's bigger than it was when you were there. And the amazing thing about that suite is that people don't barge in. Or knock while simultaneously opening the door."

"Great, you're used to more privacy than we are."

"Mhm." I haven't taken my eyes off the sky, and it isn't because I'm trying to snub Courtney. I just really cannot get over how perfectly it reflects . . . well, everything. I'm not much of an artist, but if I had to paint an autobiographical sky that captures where I'm at right now—with Upside-Down Portland, with Leona Fowl, with discovering the Ancestors, with my boyfriend knowing about the network, and the Knights having a subforum with pictures of Stone Naema and as much as I decided it's not gonna be a big deal, I keep getting the feeling that it's a big deal—this is the sky I would choose.

"Can we be serious for a sec?" he asks, a little too delicately.

"How exactly am I giving you the impression that I'm not serious, Courtney? Is my disinterest too jovial?"

"Oh my God," he mutters under his breath. "I try to be nice to you—"

"Maybe that's where you're running into trouble."

"Okay." He's getting exasperated for some reason. Like, what does Family Whisperer And Literal Golden Boy Courtney have to be exasperated about. Honestly. "You don't seem to have an issue with folks being nice to you, Sheba, let's not lie."

My head snaps in his direction.

"Oh, now you'll look at me," he mutters again.

"Wasn't that the point? Getting my attention?"

"I mean, I was kinda just telling the truth, you do really like attention as long as it's the kind you want." He says the whole thing through a face-contorting grimace, like it's just the undeniable facts and they can't be helped.

"Being accustomed to attention and *need*ing it are two different things—"

"Why do you get all formal and tert when you tryna cut somebody down—"

"Did you say 'tert'? Because it's terse. The word you're looking for is terse."

"And the function of language is communication, so if you know exactly what I meant, I guess I did it right."

I stop and narrow my eyes at him. "You got real formal just then, Courtney."

He pauses. "You get on my nerves."

"That's not very nice."

"You don't need it."

"You're right, I don't. So whatever you came out here to say, just say it."

"Why'd you make Little Bit take off her siren toy?"

I feel my brow come crashing down. "I told you—"

"Right, 'cause some white lady was clutching at her pearls or something—"

"And looking at *your* little sister in a way I didn't like."

"The rest of us get looked at like that sometimes, Naema." And we both stop. "I'm not tryna say anything by it, I'm just letting you know. We don't go around on tiptoe. *I* don't, anyway. And I don't want my sister doing it, either."

"'Cause you don't codeswitch."

"What?"

"No, I forgot. Nobody codeswitches but Naema. That's why you think I'm putting on airs on my livestream, or maybe down here, I don't know, because it's weird for me to speak differently to white folks than I do to my cousin, I guess. *I* invented codeswitching." I've been talking with my hands, and now enthusiastically shrug, my arms comically high. "Courtney's always his Blackest self, and does nothing for comfort or self-protection!"

"Why are you like this, that's not even what I'm saying, but if you wanna talk about codeswitching, I don't think calling yourself Eloko first is that."

I'm actually laughing now, because it's ridiculous. This is ridiculous. For someone who's spent the majority of my visit thus far trying to put me in my place or haze me, or what*ever* he calls it, Courtney is real certain of his moral high ground. The thing he isn't is informed. But I don't need to tell him what I've been going through, everything I'm processing, *any*thing I've come to realize. Not when he's still convinced he's better than I am.

"I wonder why I would embrace being Eloko. Why would I lean into that, do you think? When really all it entailed most of my life is popularity and a bell." I tilt my head at him, one side, then the other, and I probably actually look like a bird at this point.

Between my gestures and rhetorical questions, he can't make eye contact with me, so it's working. "Good. Be embarrassed. But that doesn't mean I'm letting you off the hook."

"Okay—"

"Yeah, it is okay," I say, and then I watch him cross his arms over his chest. "Because have you ever heard of an Eloko being strip-searched at school for being too giddy? Have you ever heard of an Eloko being body-slammed by a school liaison officer?"

His eyes creep back toward my face, even though they never quite make it.

"Why exactly am I getting judged for identifying with something that can shield *me*? Or do only sirens get protection."

He looks up, and Courtney and I are eye to eye again, at last.

"I'm not apologizing for finding armor. And real sirens have people like me," I say, because the way he was completely unfazed by my mention of siren protection makes me think Courtney already knows. Even if he's not allowed to tell me. "So before you let Little Bit pretend to be one, remember that they have something she doesn't."

I don't like the way he looks at me now. He turns on the porch swing and puts his arm along the back, like he's putting it around me. Like he's about to say something very stupid, but he thinks he's onto something.

"Okay. But is your real issue with that toy that she can admire you *and* a siren . . ."

Told ya.

My legs unwind and shoot out, my feet slamming down on the porch and stopping our motion.

I could say that I don't have a problem with sirens, that disliking Tavia can't make that true, that it shouldn't even be a question, but again. I shouldn't have to.

"Gosh, Courtney, why would I have a problem with that?"

"Don't get mad—"

"Why? Why not? Why shouldn't I get *mad*? Isn't that my character? I'm Nina. I'm the mean, bitchy, angry Black girl, and you know what's super cute about that? It's that under the circumstances—

you know, of being treated like it's my fault I was born Eloko, and it's a discredit to my Blackness, and oh yeah, of *having been turned to fucking stone, Courtney,* and then having my attacker made America's Sweetheart, and needing to work with somebody I know better than to trust to get the *real* story told—I am a pantheon of pleasantness! I am a gee-dee whimsical sprite, full of mirth and mischief!"

"Okay—" he tries to diffuse the situation.

Diffuse me.

And I am not having it. Because I'm seeing it, thanks to the Knights of Naema. Not because I was Stoned, and what it was like wherever I was. That should've been what haunted me, but now I can see the statue I became. I've got a picture in my mind now, forever, of exactly what was done to me.

I have to stand up because there is a very good chance I am about to blast off. It's not even just that I'm right. There's this surge inside me, like an entire village of people surrounds me—and every voice is in agreement. It's a swell of conviction like I've never felt, and I almost can't contain it. I step out from under the covering of the porch, and spin around to face my cousin. All I wanted was to admire the fiery sky in peace, but now it can blaze behind me for him to see.

"Look," he begins.

"No, Courtney. You asked, so I'm gonna say my piece. Do you know how wildly, ruthlessly, homicidally *pissed* I would have to get to convey even a fraction of the anger I'm owed? And, speaking of a siren, do you know how many people thought I was a mean girl before that movie came out? Two. Tavia and Effie. And do you know why they thought that? *Because we didn't get along.* Which is allowed!"

I'm laughing again, arms thrown wide this time like otherwise I can't release it all.

"I am allowed not to get along with someone, Courtney!" I inform him, and the swell from the myriad voices concurring is still going strong. "Two people can not totally love each other, whether there are an equal number of us or not. Do you know what it means when they can't? When it doesn't matter who we like or want to be or want to be around? It means we're not free. Everything can't always be bigger than me."

"Ny," Courtney whispers.

"I dare you to say calm down."

"I'm not *that* stupid," he says, and then his forehead creases and he gestures with his head for me to come back to the swing. "I was gonna tell you to get under the porch," he says. "The rain's coming any minute."

"I don't care," I answer, but a thunderous clap overhead drowns me out. And then it's raining like it has never *not* rained, or like someone's getting paid to make it look that way. It's like this town got turned into a movie set, too, only they're shooting for Seattle or San Francisco, where supposedly the rain comes down in inescapable sheets. The fact that the water's warm is the final insult.

Courtney's face is scrunched up. "Tried to warn you," he says.

Awesome.

It is very difficult to maintain a steely gaze and power pose when you're standing under a fuggin' waterfall, and after a moment, I relent and step back under the porch.

"I'm gonna go inside," I say, calmly because I can't compete with this storm. Courtney stands up and looks like he wants to hug me. Thankfully I'm soaking wet.

"Sorry for intruding on your alone time, by the way. I'll make up the pullout for Little Bit."

"You don't have to do that. She'll be disappointed."

"Disappointed happens," he answers. "She's more resilient than you think."

"Hey. Be nice."

"Heh." His head snaps back in an amused nod. "My mom's gonna kill you for tracking water through the house." And he slaps my shoulder before we head inside.

I take a shower because even though folks dance in the rain, I'm pretty sure it's filthy and shouldn't be left on your hair. But washing mine, relaxed or not, means I have to actually do something to it before I can go to bed. Of everything that's happened lately, I'm beginning to regret standing where the rain could get me. I'm willing to concede that it would've been easier to get back under the porch.

Aunt Carla Ann gives me a soft hood that connects to her blow-dryer, and after brushing and braiding my hair, I put it on. In Little Bit's vanity, I look like a nutcracker, but it frees up my hands and my attention to focus on more important things. Which means I can grab my laptop and lose myself on Knights of Naema for a half hour, careful not to slip back into the subforum. Tonight's visit is all about bad poetry, upvoting the non-gross pictures they've shared of me, and taking part in the polls, since you know. I know myself slightly better than the Knights do.

Despite my maybe misgivings last time, it's immediate relief. Even better this time. Purple isn't my favorite color—I honestly have no idea why it's the site's theme—but it's growing on me. But the best thing is that someone's a legit artist, and they've shared their portfolio, which—to no one's surprise, given where he's posting it—is entirely made up of portraits of me. There's charcoal, and chalk, and acrylic pieces, and even a time-lapse video of him creating one from start to finish.

I watch that on a loop for a while. I marvel and it's really not just because I'm a Pretty Bird. It's the way I begin as faint pencil strokes, and slowly am revealed, like I've been on the canvas all along, and he's letting me out. My favorite thing is how he hasn't even chosen a picture to replicate for this one; it's an original. Sort of, anyway.

I don't look mean in his portrait, or nice. I don't look angry, or . . . whatever the opposite of that would actually be. It can't be happy. It can't be anything you can be at the same time, and I can attest to the possibility of being both those things at once. Just since coming down here.

In the portrait, I look like me. Like the Naema I remember being a year ago, before junior prom. Like the Naema I thought was coming back until everything I had to tell Priam, until realizing my movie plan is still gonna work, but it's not gonna be nearly as enjoyable as I'd hoped. But it's going to happen, and when I go home, Upside-Down Portland is gonna get set right side up again. I'm not losing myself over Tavia Philips, or anyone else.

Thank you so much, I tell the artist as Sheba503. *It's very appreciated.*

I'm smiling. It isn't super explicit, but I feel like it's phrased in a way that suggests who I am. Especially given the avatar I chose for my profile.

Or not.

Thanks, man, the original poster replies.

Okayyy.

Not a man, and I throw in a wink emoji. And even though it's not exactly what I was planning to do with my first comment, I suddenly really want him to know it's me. I want the Knights to know it's me. So I finish with, *and I've never been a muse before.*

I try to contain the escalating giddiness, anticipating his next reply. Maybe it's because I haven't posted on LOVE in what feels like forever. Courtney might say I'm missing my fan base, but what never gets mentioned is that it's also a community I'm used to having. I wouldn't mind feeling that again. By the time the artist comments again, I'm fully biting my bottom lip.

Okay . . . so that makes you THE Naema, I'm guessing?

I speed-type. *THE one, yes,* and I toss in one more wink emoji, because two can't possibly count as abuse. *I had no idea you Knights existed, but I've been *lightly* stalking about, and am officially a fan.*

There's a longer pause this time, and before the guy returns, another post materializes at the top of the page. A poll.

Does Anyone Believe That Sheba503 Is THE Naema?

Uh, what.

Fine.

I cast my vote, and roll my eyes. And the opinions start flooding in.

Verification suggestions.

Mentions of my profile photo, which someone has *finally* figured out isn't one they've ever seen, or can find.

Where does the real Naema live?

Right, like I'm gonna give them my address. They're harmless, but when I realized one of them is in or near Portland, I was glad the city's a lot bigger than many people realize. And that Beckett's an Eloko beacon, so they can't assume I even live in the school district just because I attend.

Which doesn't even matter, because according to another member, that information wouldn't be proof enough.

Obviously, we know where she lives, and I sincerely hope this person means In General. *We can get your portrait to the real Naema, if you want.*

Which. Makes it sound like he meant Specifically.

My core is swept through with a cool wind. The voices have never seemed to have a temperature before, but this one absolutely gives me the chills. And I get that they're the Ancestors, but that also means they're probably even more paranoid about the internet age than living old folks, which is saying something. I'm a whole Interwebs Personality. I mean, I'm not the hugest, but I've done a meet-up or two with a few of my LOVE followers. Granted, they were also my peers, and not grown men, but. I don't technically know that the Knights are, either. And I'm not gonna jump to conclusions, like people haven't claimed to have all sorts of information for clout.

I don't know. That feels like a breach, doesn't it? I don't think IRL contact is cool . . . the artist says because he's a normal human being with boundaries. As I suspected.

I totally get why it seems that way, but there's actually a way influencers drop clues nowadays. It's their form of invitation. Naema did it all the time on LOVE, and she meets with people when they figure it out.

Is a lie. I mean, not the meet-ups I was just mentioning; the whole Congratulations On Decoding My Posts, Come Into My House.

C'mon.

I didn't know that, the artist answers. Like he believes. *I wasn't on LOVE.*

Okay, but there's nothing stopping him from verifying that claim, since LOVE still exists and all.

Np, dude. PM me and I'll explain.

What.

How did dude go from reasonable person with an understanding of physical boundaries to gullible potential stalker in the space of like, three comments? It's like watching someone get radicalized in real time. In that, that's exactly what it is.

The cool wind is still there, and yeah. That wasn't exactly a winning display. But I've been on the internet long enough to know that the only way to fight it is by playing by the same rules. This radicalizer—the dramatically named NaemasNobleman who I actually saw on my first visit—is a nobody. Proving I'm the real deal immediately gives me more influence. I can shut this whole She *Wants* You To Find Her thing down, so I read the other verification suggestions.

Post a ***new*** *picture.*

Easy enough. Given what was just said, I don't want to show too much of my cousin's bedroom, so I make the frame tight. I also don't want the flash and the close proximity to make this verification picture any less flattering than it has to be, so I depend on the light from the laptop. It's grainy, but it's kinda artistic, and very obviously me.

"Hello, All The Knights But One," I mutter as I post. Hopefully they don't think the quality and weird angle is—

And of course someone does.

Photoshopped. That was quick.

NyNative is the commenter's name, and he's got more to say.

Where are you even supposed to be in that photo? Where's that huge bedroom from your LOVE posts?

"Calm down, son," I say, and then comment, *I'm actually out of town atm. Not in my own room, sincerest apologies!*

Haha, Naema always says that.

"Yeah," I say through a smile, upvoting the support. Which is not coming from NyNative, whatever that name's supposed to mean. *You're right, I do.* Okay, that wink emoji was definitely my last.

Welp, we've got ourselves a phony, NyNative comments.

"Uh . . . excuse?"

The REAL Naema ***is*** *in PDX right now. Saw her and the boyfriend on Burnside last night.*

"No. You didn't." My eyes are almost crossing. Why is this so frustrating? Who is this dude? And how is he on my fansite, and doesn't even know what I look like. Because I'm extremely sure he didn't see me on—

Unless he saw Priam with someone else, and just assumed it was me.

Who would Priam have been with?

Okay, what I'm not gonna do is spiral out into paranoia because some rando thinks he saw me and my boyfriend—*ex*-boyfriend—in Portland last night. Because seeing Priam with someone doesn't even mean anything, because Priam can have friends. Who from a distance might be mistaken for a significant other.

Thanks, NyNative.

This was fun.

Chapter XVIII

Knights of Naema Post

TO ARMS

Lancelot [silver/41] [metadata: posts (30)] [upvotes: 215]

Last year, somebody wrote an article about an Eloko behaving badly, which was obviously about our girl. Maybe I'm the only one who noticed, but that was the beginning of a campaign against Naema. For the past year, someone—everyone—has been trying to demote her, trying to bring into question her identity as an Eloko, and they've used the basest tactic available: race. Ironic, coming from the self-proclaimed progressive Portland crowd.

We're the only ones who seem to take Naema at her word. That's she's #ElokoFirst. That she *decides, not someone else.*

If we're going to call ourselves Knights, at some point we have to actually do the work.

We have to defend her.

The media, the movie, the LOVE platform—they've done a good job putting her down and shutting her up. Yes, she's the Eloko goddess, but she's also just a girl. She shouldn't have to face them all down on her own.

We need to launch a campaign of our own.

#Justice4Naema needs to mean something.

Well, Knights? Who's with me?

Chapter XIX

NAEMA

The biggest adjustment has been the quiet. At first that's all I thought it was. It happened as soon as I left Portland, and I didn't exactly mean it literally then, but. Now it's impossible to ignore.

Eloko life is something very particular in Portland. It's loud. And yes, it's attentive and adoring, but it can also be cloying and cluttered. The cost of being the center of attention is that everyone has a take, and once they think you've done something wrong, trust me. That is much less fun.

I didn't even notice it before. When the noise is constant, it feels natural. How would I know there was an alternative? How would any of us? And now that I have a clearer head, that's exactly what I want to know. What exactly Professor Vesper-Holmes thinks she knows.

So I go have a look.

The first thing to acknowledge, she writes on the blog that appears on her personal website, *is the local disinterest in this work.*

Pout face. Portland isn't clamoring for your Eloko Ain't Even All That study?

Actually, that's sort of news to me; that isn't how it felt. Unless they were only okay with demoting Eloko as long as I was the only one.

I'm constantly asked why I'm studying Eloko, and archiving what we know of them, what mythos we have on record, and what their magic actually entails. I'd be lying if I said that question didn't confuse me.

It may seem to go without saying, but in scholarship, nothing does:

the role and reception of Eloko in Portland is a local phenomenon. This is the second thing to acknowledge, and it understandably impacts and informs the first. It may be because the population is so much higher here—a fact which might be appreciated partly for the way it seems to reflect well on the city itself—but whatever the reason, Eloko are at the top of the social stratosphere. Whatever else they are, Portland Eloko are adored because they are Eloko.

*Elsewhere, Eloko are beloved, certainly. But so are mermaids, and sprites, and the memory of oracles. Indeed, the unwaning obsession and glorification—*which feels like a strong word, but that's just me—*Eloko enjoy in this city is not universal.* (She isn't wrong about that.)

It's because of this unyielding fixation that I first began to wonder—why? What dictates the adoration? How have Eloko earned it? How have we decided that this privilege is deserved, especially when there are others with magic whom we do not adore?

I'm asking these questions because I think there's something very wrong with refusing to. Perhaps for someone else, questions only arise about the less privileged, or when someone is at a distinct disadvantage. Personally, I think privilege should attract the most scrutiny, not the least. The only reason for the sometimes vehement disapproval of my work I face is a fear of what we'll find—or in this case, perhaps it's a fear of what we won't.

I breathe deep and just stare at my laptop screen.

I'm waiting for . . . something. Rage, I guess.

A week ago, I'd probably have been royally pissed. A year ago, there's no probably about it. I would've declared Professor Vesper-Holmes unfit to carry out even ethnographic research on Eloko on the grounds that she's not one of us. But that was before I met Leona Fowl, who is.

I wonder if her research has revealed the Ancestors to the professor. If she's tried to get in touch with nonlocal Eloko the way she tried to get in touch with me. And if she has, I wonder whether they've known about the wind all along.

And—if she does know about it—why doesn't she think it constitutes magic?

Never Left PDX Naema wouldn't even be able to focus on these questions after that whole NyNative Saw Priam With Someone

Else bombshell last night, that's the first thing. There's this extensive bandwidth I didn't know I was missing before I came down here. If that's not evidence of the magical and potentially medicinal qualities of the Ancestors, I don't know what is.

That being said, I *do* want to know the deal with Priam. So despite the fact that I didn't text Jamie last night about it, now I type a few practice messages that I also immediately delete. Things like, "Hey, did you and the boys hang out on Burnside recently?" and "What's Priam been up to lately?" Neither of which sound anything like me, so I just cut to the chase.

Is Priam hanging out with someone new?

Send.

Immediate dots. Good ole Jamie.

Like, dating hang out? God no, why would you even think that.

See, what I love about Jamie is that despite her recent pouting, she doesn't require pretense. There's no need for buildup, no reason to ease into it with halfhearted salutations or small talk, or even give her context. Question, answer. Done.

But it doesn't exactly satisfy. And being Jamie, she knows that, too, so the dots begin again before I've given a reply.

Ny, he came back more in love than ever. He said it was like meeting you for the first time all over again.

Aw.

I sort of feel like that, too. I write, and then, *About me, not Priam.* [emoji]

I smile at the message, and then snort back a laugh when she responds in kind.

I miss you so much it's stupid, she says.

Same, I write back. *But I'm having fun down here. I'm on my way to prison as we speak.*

And . . . that's fun?! Wait, are you serious? Wtf?

I roll my eyes, like I've ever visited a prison before, or like when Courtney told me about the day's excursion involving security clearance, I didn't internally balk. I sort of thought the prevailing notion was that if you get sent to jail, you accept that most folks aren't gonna visit. I mean, *I* didn't get in trouble, why would I go to jail, too. But for some reason, Jamie's incredulous reaction makes me think it's more about disbelieving I could possibly *know* anyone in lockup, or be willing to admit it.

Anyway. It turns out I do. I mean, technically I *don't,* since I have no memory of the last time I saw my cousin Kyrie. He's in his early twenties, and the son of my Uncle Lorrance, Mommy's eldest brother. Well, her only brother. Some people think he's named after their mom, Mary Lorraine, but he's actually named after their eldest sister, Lorraine, who died in her crib a few months after she was born. Grandma Mary and Grandpa Tobias didn't have another baby for several years, and when they did, she was glad it was a boy. She thought naming another girl after a dead sister would be troubling, but I guess boy-ifying the name was totes different.

I know all of this because Uncle Lorrance has just arrived, and as soon as he walked by me to get in the van, the story started bubbling up in my brain, from start to finish, but also somehow all at once. Being Eloko around family is like riding shotgun with the auntie who spikes all her drinks and is very loose with the tea.

Which, by the way, is Aunt Toni.

She isn't actually coming today, but we got the full range of I Must Have Misunderstood The Email Instructions headshaking and I'm Really Trying To Reach Back In My Recollections eye-roaming. Because it turns out, if ever your family reunion involves a day trip to the local prison facility to visit a cousin and you don't want to go, simply ignore the many informative emails from Aunt Carla Ann explaining the pre-visit application process. It takes up to sixty days, includes a background check, and, it turns out, you can't just show up the day of because It's A Family Thing. Not to worry: a gaped mouth, tilted head, and a few exasperated gestures of This Just Isn't Fair later, and the rented commercial van carrying the rest of us will pull away, leaving you free to carry on with the rest of your day. Though fair warning: ain't nobody fooled.

Luckily for me, my parents did the requisite paperwork and paid the fee for all three of us, in case we made it to the reunion this year—which is interesting, since we never do. I didn't know three months ago that Upside-Down Portland would have me down in the desert, and yet here I sit with about ten others, including Courtney, Aunt Carla Ann, and Uncle Deric. If nothing else, this trip is giving me major ammo against any future Not Babcock Enough slights.

"I'm gonna get up there on my own, though," Aunt Toni promises everybody's backs while they work on getting Great-Gram onto the lift and into place beside me.

"All right, Toni," Uncle Deric says without turning to give her his attention. He consistently serves We Have Been In-Laws For What Seems Like Forever around her, and I love it.

"I mean, they wasn't gonna let me in anyway," she carries on, laughing overloud and raising her arm to jangle her half dozen bangles. Consequently, she also ends up jiggling her supersized to-go cup, which actually gets a few people to turn and cast a side-eye her way.

Coming up behind her, Courtney catches my eye and mouths, Drunk! before taking her by the shoulders and saying, "'Scuse me, Auntie, can I get around you?"

"You going, Courtney?" Aunt Toni steps to the side, but wraps an arm around her nephew and has to look up at him.

"Got to. You know I'm down with Kyrie."

"Mhm." There's a whole lecture in that sound, and in her comedically long sip. Whatever is in that cup tastes very good. "Well, just make sure you don't go *down* with Kyrie—"

"Is this new?"

"What? The vest?" Aunt Toni takes stock of her own garish ensemble at Courtney's diplomatic interruption. "Honey, yes, did I not show you this one?"

"'Cause I know you be going to those trunk shows, Auntie."

"I do," she says, and they laugh. Okay, he's good.

"You really do. And it came like this, or you added the crystals?"

"You know I always gotta doctor it up." She's still admiring herself, doing half turns, throwing one leg to the side, forcing Courtney to step back.

"Okay!"

"You know."

"Go 'head, Auntie." And then he looks up at me with a ridiculously huge openmouthed grin and thrusts a thumbs-up into the air, none of which Aunt Toni interprets as poking fun at her, and not only because she's taking long sips again. She makes me seem overly sensitive by comparison, for sure.

Courtney comes by his masterful charisma naturally, though. While Aunt Carla Ann lets her sister watch Little Bit, nobody in their right mind would get in a car Aunt Toni's driving. Luckily a few years ago, Aunt Carla Ann—and my mom, apparently—convinced Aunt Toni to get a car service, so not only does she not drive, she feels fancy about it. No fuss, no need for confrontationally direct conversations about a family member's excessive drinking, I guess.

Once Great-Gram Lorraine is in place, we leave Aunt Toni on the sidewalk and get on our way. It's really not a long drive, and I'm not sure why I assumed it would be. I guess prisons aren't all Alcatraz or Château d'If, separated from the rest of society by a moat of water. This one's like thirty minutes from where we started, and between eavesdropping on the grown-ups talking about Aunt Toni and laughing with Courtney, I don't realize that I sort of ghosted on Jamie.

"You hear that?" Great-Gram Lorraine asks me as we're pulling into the visitor parking section of the prison compound.

I look back down at my phone to find that Jamie's sent several messages. I'm impressed my ninety-one-year-old great-grandmother heard the combination ping and vibration.

"Good ear, Great-Gram."

"What's that?"

Never mind. "We're here!" I tell her instead, and everyone in the van starts looking out the windows and turning in their seats like we just got to an amusement park instead of a medium-security federal correctional facility.

"Great-Gram?" I say, and I lean close while we're looking for parking to accommodate the size of our van. "Can I ask you something about the Ancestors?"

"Of course," she almost whispers back.

Her brown skin is too soft, I can tell by looking at it. It's beautiful and perfumed with a face lotion she's been using since she was raising her children, but it's paper thin, and she has more freckles than she used to; the delicate black dots are sprinkled under her eyes and across her nose. I'm not always a huge fan of people, but there's something about the elderly that consistently humbles me. Like the network donna. I can't help but approach them with what some might call an uncharacteristic reverence—and now that I know about the Ancestors, I'm wondering if that's part of who I am as an Eloko.

"It's just. You said their voices would get more clear?"

"I said they would if you're listening."

"Right. Does that mean I always have to agree?" I ask, but she doesn't answer. I mean. When she answers, it's like she didn't hear my question.

"Everybody started to think Eloko are good at speaking, because you're charming and all. But it was oracles who were good at speaking. Eloko are supposed to be good at listening."

It feels like anything I say in response to that would be wrong, so I just nod and know that I'm gonna meditate on her words whether I want to or not. Try to fit it into some sort of direct response to my question. Figure out if Great-Gram is a master of old lady burns, and it's a personal criticism I'm meant to decipher.

I'm still deep in thought and not entirely paying attention when we're parked and pile out of the van, and then Courtney pulls me aside.

"You might as well get comfortable out here," he tells me. I must look confused, because he says, "We gotta go in shifts," like that totally clears it up.

"Who's gotta go in shifts? Who said?"

Courtney's eyes dart around. "The Department of Corrections."

"Well, how come?" I ask through a laugh. Thinking about the Ancestors is more distracting than the Ancestors themselves.

"I don't know, Sheba! That's just the rule here. He can't have more than three visitors at a time, but they'll let us do four, and we can stay a few more hours, which is good 'cause it means he stays out of his cell all day."

"Wait, why will they let us do that?"

"Becauuuse," he says, and rolls his eyes for some reason. "He has a visitor from out of state."

"So. Since I'm here? We can go in four at a time *and* we can stay all day?"

"I know you're not gonna try and score on this," he says, tipping his head all the way back so he's looking down his nose at me.

"I'm just repeating what you're telling me, I like to get all the facts straight."

"Imma need you to be on your best behavior though today for real." He's making prayer hands.

"I'm giving him full Sheba. The works." It's my turn to lift my chin.

"Please don't."

"I'm giving Pacific Northwest humble brags," I pop one shoulder, "I'm giving coastal elite foodie demands," and then the other one.

"You're *real* lucky you're from out of town, cuzzo. We get to bring outside food. The alternative are these big vending machines and a microwave. You would be disappointed."

"I wasn't do— What do *you* usually eat?"

"That!"

"You think you're better than me, Courtney? You don't think Sheba can eat prison vending machine microwave food?"

"I do not."

I scoff, but can't think of anything else to say before the adults start talking. Apparently Great-Gram Lorraine is going in the first shift, with Uncle Lorrance and a couple others. Another group'll go in after that, and then Uncle Lorrance, Courtney, Clay, and I will go in, while the bus takes Great-Gram Lorraine and the others home. We're staying for the duration.

"So what, we just wait out here in the heat through two shifts?" I ask Courtney quietly.

"They're not gonna be in there long, trust." His face sobers. Usually he looks on the verge of or the tail-end of a laugh, but he's suddenly surprisingly straight-faced. "Especially coming like this? The pressure's off, they know he's gonna have more visitors, and they know I'm gonna stay the whole time. Thirty minutes each. Watch. We'll be in there in an hour, tops."

"Okay . . . but like, can we keep the van running? Because I don't think I can make it out here for even an hour. It's a blacktop parking lot, with some sprigs somebody *just* decided to plant last week." I gesture toward the closest sapling. "I can't."

"Who's gonna ask my dad for the keys? And explain why we need them?"

"Who has been the savior of this entire affair, Courtney?" I ask, tapping my chin and foot at the same time. "Who—" and I reach out and grab his shirt when he tries to turn away, "who among us has the sway, nay, the gravitas for such a task?"

"Hey, Court." And when we both turn, Courtney's shirt still in my grip, Uncle Deric is jogging back toward us across the heat-reflecting pavement, keys jingling between his fingers. "Hey, man, keep the van running so your cousin doesn't melt out here, all right?"

I turn back to face Courtney with my mouth wide open.

"That ain't have anything to do with y—"

"Thank you, Uncle Deric!" I call, making sure my trill twinkles between my words, and Courtney just shakes his head.

By the time the first two shifts are done, it's just shy of a full hour. I felt so guilty after running the van's a/c for a mere twenty minutes that Courtney, Clay, and I turned off the ignition and rejoined the others in the heat. Now I'm hustling to get into the facility before the rest of the family has even saddled back up. Except once inside, it's a game of hurry up and wait.

"Take off all jewelry, belts, buckles," the first guard I encounter past the sign-in area is saying. And they don't appear to be saying it to anyone in particular. Hands behind their backs and eyes crawling up the wall opposite them, they sound like they've said this, just *like* this, for a very long time, and they really cannot be bothered to slow down or wait until they have your attention.

I turn around in almost two full rotations, looking for written instructions, or a restart button for the guard, but by then Courtney,

Clay, and Uncle Lorrance have started disassembling themselves, and clearly not for the first time. I follow suit, removing my bracelets, studs, bobby pins, and placing them in one of the lockers lining the wall.

Courtney taps my bell, like he doesn't want to speak out loud.

"Oh." I look down, and take my charm between my fingers. "This, too?"

And he nods, once.

It's not a big deal. I've worn it sporadically since getting here, but. That was by choice. I've also never been in a place like this, and the two things—being in this prison and not wanting to give up my Eloko charm when I've been super casual about it as of late—seem related.

Uncle Lorrance is taking his wedding ring off, and that feels pretty extreme, but he's putting it in the little tray alongside his wallet and belt like it's nothing. So obviously a necklace is fair game.

I unlatch my necklace and put it in the small tray designated to me, the bell clinking against it and then the chain pooling around it protectively. I put my phone next to it and close it all inside the locker for safekeeping, before taking a deep breath. All that matters is that I'm ready to see Cousin Kyrie.

Except that's not what happens next. There's a whole 'nother process, because apparently none of this has been the security check, just sign-in and disrobing. Now I'm directed into another room, and my cousins and uncle continue down the hall past it.

Wtf is going on.

My hand is at my collarbone before I remember my charm is gone. Left in the locker for safekeeping, instead of here, where I need it, keeping me safe.

Because apparently, that's what it does.

The room I'm in now is just like the locker room, except there are no storage units. There are two rows of plastic chairs, and the chairs have metal connectors between them. I don't sit down because I'm not sure what's supposed to happen in here, and no one followed me inside to explain it to me. The only noise is a truly annoying whirring sound, like a bathroom fan that's on its last leg. It whirs and then intermittently it whines, and then when it's good and ready, it goes back to the whirring. It will become unbearable very shortly, I'm quite sure.

Everything—here, the locker room, the sign-in foyer—is this muted green color, which I think is supposed to be calming, but instead is overbearing in its insistence on being calming. Not to mention that, coupled with the economic seating selections, clearly chosen for function over any potential inhabitant's comfort, it kinda feels more like a friendly holding cell than a lounge.

Why am I *here*?

How long do I wait for someone to come find me and take me to visitation?

I wrap my hands around my elbows and hug my arms tight against my abdomen before I figure out I'm shivering. It's not cold, and it's not Ancestor breath either, so.

It's the noise, honestly. If the noise would stop, I think I'd relax. I keep getting tricked by the transition between the sounds, thinking or hoping it's going to stop altogether, but it always comes back around.

I wanna pop my head back out into the hallway and ask what the deal is, but I won't. I just assume that's not the desired behavior, and the last thing I want is to be denied visitation, or worse, have my cousins and Uncle Lorrance denied visitation with Kyrie because of me. These visits clearly mean a lot to Courtney. So even when I catch sight of the black orbs clearly concealing cameras on both ends of the room, I don't react.

Courtney coulda warned me about this nerve-racking interlude. Honestly.

As soon as I take a seat, a guard steps in, holding a clipboard. They close the door behind them.

I stand up again. It just feels appropriate.

"Naema Bradshaw?" they ask, only they pronounce it "Nay-muh." It may be the first time I've heard someone mispronounce my name.

I say my name correctly, and then grimace a little. Probably shouldn't have done that.

The guard flicks their eyes up at me, and catches the tail end of my grimace, so I can't help smiling a bit. They do not.

Okay.

"Date of birth?"

We went over this at sign-in, but—again—I'm not gonna say that, so I just tell them.

"Speak up," they say, and they're speaking louder, too, as if to show me how.

I'm in the middle of repeating myself when I catch sight of what looks almost like plugs in the guard's ears. Which makes no sense, so maybe they're hearing aids? In which case, it might help for me to step a bit closer, which I try to do discreetly.

"Step back." There's an inflection at the end that keeps it from sounding aggressive but the firmness ensures that it's definitely authoritative.

"I'm sorry," I say through a charming smile, a breath slipping free, an intentional exhale meant to convey an almost self-deprecating whimsy. "I didn't want you to have trouble hearing me."

"I can hear you fine, you need to stand back unless I direct you to approach."

So I step back. And I stand up straighter.

"It says you're from Portland, Oregon?"

"Yes." I answer without any embellishment, nonverbal or otherwise.

The next question is asked with the guard's eyes glued to their clipboard, but their voice doesn't hesitate or break.

"Are you or have you ever suspected yourself to be a siren, or afflicted with related abilities or aspirations?"

"Wait." I yank my head back and blink a half dozen times, like they started actually throwing things at me and I am too confused to raise my hands and fend them off.

There's so much to unpack. And I know some of it has to do with that gawd-awful movie. You cannot tell me, a security question reconfirming that I'm native to Portland being followed up by a question about whether I'm a siren has nothing to do with Tavia's mediocre biopic. Not exactly the impact they were going for, I'm sure, but—as has been made *perfectly* clear—the whole world is not Portland, and Portland is not the whole world. It *is* all Upside Down.

But it's worse than that. They didn't even just ask if I'm a siren, they asked if I have ever *suspected* myself of being one! Because now apparently we have the Thought Police, which on top of being laughable and absurd, forces me to begrudgingly reference the plagiarist George Orwell.

"Ms. Bradshaw, you are required to answer the question prior to entry."

"But I'm already inside." *Best behavior. Best. Behavior.* That's not even the Ancestors. That's just me not wanting to get tased.

"Prior to entry into the visitation area," the guard says, like they are running out of patience.

I am not accustomed to this, and I'm not talking about prisons and clearances and redundant questioning. I'm talking about the way nothing I do fazes them. It isn't even like I do it consciously, but I am used to having *some* effect on people when I interact with them, whether they like it or not, and almost always to my benefit. I don't know how they're warding off my charms, but between the fact that this person is probably genuinely unfriendly just as a personality trait and the broken bathroom fan filling the room with incessant cacophony—

Which is when I realize why the plugs. Why the Black girl segregated for further questioning. Why the fan.

They're not just gonna *ask* whether or not I and every Black woman visiting are sirens. They're going to operate on the assumption that we *are*. *That's* why the abrupt isolation and destabilizing confusion of being left in the room alone and without instruction.

The funny thing is, if it weren't for the noise, the guard would've heard my Eloko melody when they joined me in the room. Assuming they know anything about us, they'd know exactly what I am and what I'm not, and that I'm not a security threat, at all. If they knew anything about Portland besides whatever fearmongers fabricated out of Tavia's being from there, they'd know it's a hotbed for Eloko, not sirens.

Not that sirens are particularly known for infiltrating prisons and then inciting riots or revolutions, or whatever is the concern here. Just saying.

"Can you repeat the question?" I ask the guard, mostly because I hope to make them feel as ridiculous as the words they repeat verbatim. In the absence of feeling free to openly mock people, I think of it as a public service to inspire at least a kernel of doubt in them and in the validity of their position. The supposed security question is stupid enough that saying it again should do the trick.

Except that the guard takes frequent pauses as though for the sake of delayed comprehension.

"Are you . . . or have you ever suspected yourself . . . to be a siren, . . . or afflicted with related abilities . . . or aspirations?"

"Okay," I say, before flashing my most livestream-able smile. "I think I've got it all, here goes." I clear my throat. "I am not a siren; I've never suspected"—I giggle—"myself of being a siren. I, um." I let my eyebrows break and my cheekbones soar, because, as I've mentioned, it's the Black girl equivalent of blushing, and it's much easier to fake. "Lemme see, I . . . don't *think* you can have siren abilities without being a siren? Aaand, I've never as*pired* to be a siren, but I don't think that'd make much difference." I close it all off with a seemingly nervous titter, and I feel the Ancestors swell like a chorus of *Yes, Child*. Which is a nice surprise. It's good to know they like me even after I ignore them.

It doesn't matter whether all of it lands or not. The one thing it isn't is angry, or abrasive, or confrontational. That, I'm not at liberty to be, not while there's a melody dampening noise being funneled into the room, and not while my Eloko bell is locked away out of view.

The guard studies me for a moment and then grunts, and I definitely detect some level of amusement. Whether because they bought my performance or because they just enjoyed it, it doesn't matter. It's the right response, so I can smile for real now, and lace my hands behind my back while I wait for them to tell me I can get on with the visit—which they do, promising someone will come back to escort me to the right place.

I nod, still smiling, as they go, leaving the door open behind them. As soon as they're gone, my smile disappears, and I wait.

This is a joke. An unfunny, terrorizing joke.

Because imagine I *was* a siren. At the very least, I'm pretty sure I'd be sufficiently intimidated. The guard didn't do anything to really confirm or conclude it, and they couldn't have; there's no blood test or physical examination that would tell someone whether or not you're a siren. There's no inflammation of the vocal cords, or brain scan that gives it away, and that's part of the reason networks are able to shield them; because they look just like us. So confirming and protecting the facility against a siren threat—and again, I've never once heard of there being one—wasn't even the point.

The point was to let us know they're on guard. They're ready to engage. Always. They will, at the slightest provocation, and there's a built-in defense for any potential, and probable, overreaction. Because there's no way to know a girl *isn't* a siren, just like there's no way to tell when one is. They just have to say they believed it.

What keeps snagging my brain is how an attack set for sirens could so easily debilitate an Eloko. As long as she's also a Black girl. Which means, at the end of the day, that's who this is all designed to confront. Whether she's a nine-year-old sweetheart like Little Bit, or a ninety-one-year-old great-grandmother with good mobility days and bad ones, like today, when Great-Gram Lorraine must've gone through this whole ordeal, forced to answer questions about siren aspirations from her wheelchair.

The Ancestors speak, and I must be listening, because it's so clear I say it out loud myself.

"We're all in the same boat."

Courtney and the others aren't waiting at the end of the hall for me. When I'm shown to the cafeteria-sized visitation area, not only are they already there, it's clear they have been for a while.

At a table off to the side, Clay, Uncle Lorrance, and Kyrie are deep in conversation, and Courtney's coming back from the microwave with a plate of homemade food for Kyrie, which he swaps for another one in need of heating before heading back. If he had any foresight, he would've brought at least two plates at a time so he could be heating the second while he delivered the first, but he's not as clever as he thinks, so now he's gotta wait for the microwave to be free again.

I hurry to his side. The room is too wide to cross on my own at the moment.

"You coulda warned me," I say, pinching the tender, exposed meat at the back of his arm.

"Hey," he yelps, snatching his arm out of my reach, and then apparently realizing for the first time that it's me. "Sheba, where the hell were you?" He puts the offended arm around me now, having transferred the plate of food to the other hand.

"I had to go for the siren check that nobody told me about." I pinch him at the waist now.

"Will you stop," he says, taking back his arm and elbowing me to a safe distance. "What siren check? I didn't understand why they sent you to a different room, but I for real was not expecting it to take that long."

"You could've come looking for me."

"For real? In prison? Sheba?"

"So much for chivalry and solidarity, but whatever." I wrap my arms around myself and find that I'm close enough to him again for my elbows to rest against his side.

"You okay?"

"I'm whatever. Just. Don't bring Little Bit here."

"Oh, that wasn't gonna happen anyway, but just till she's older."

"Yeah, well." The microwave is free and we step up to use it. "Maybe until they stop profiling."

"Naema, look around this room. I don't think that's gonna happen anytime soon."

The food is ready, and I return with Courtney to his table.

"Ayyy," Kyrie says when he sees me, and he stands. He's about Courtney's height, with his dark brown hair in a nice neat fade, and he's clean-shaven so I can see how strikingly similar he looks to our Great-Uncle Gerald at that age. The Ancestors speak and I've got a picture of Gerald at twenty-four in mind. It sends a rush of warmth through me, just to know that Kyrie's got the same square chin, and the same chestnut skin. In my image of our great-uncle, however, he's rocking a flamboyantly retro butterfly collar, and Kyrie's wearing a neat tan button-down with a white belt and slacks in the exact same shade of tan, just like the other inmates.

"How are you?" I say into his neck when my cousin wraps me in a bear hug. I almost choke on the words, I'm so caught off guard by the sincerity and warmth in the embrace. I mean, I think I'm a good hugger, but Kyrie is better. There's the slight rock, which runs in the family, but there's also the pressure and the way it eases up just a little before reengaging. Like he was gonna let you go, but can't. It feels like a legit massage, and I am more relaxed than I have any business being given where we are and what just happened.

I don't remember Kyrie very well, but there's a choir of voices reminding me that I *know* him, and that he isn't forgotten. I don't exactly know what he did, or how long he's locked up, and I'm not curious. I'm just glad I get to see him, so I hug him back, Johnson-style.

Chapter XX

That evening, no one's ready to go back home. Between Courtney, Clay, his sibling yet another Lorraine, and me, no one wants to go back inside a set of walls just yet. Instead we drive out to the desert, and I realize that everything I thought I knew about it is a lie.

Fine, not everything. Weatherwise, I was pretty dead-on, so movies and television aren't entirely useless. But I could have sworn the desert that Wile E. Coyote runs around in is brown on brown on brown. I was not prepared for the colors, and the foliage; the yellows, whites, and greens. The mountain range that begins and ends in a circular formation in front of me, that looks like it just recently sprang forth from the ground, and also might be a human-made monument. The castle-city remains of a bygone dynasty of giants.

I certainly wasn't ready for the way the sunset washes over the stone in the most unnatural-looking shade of red.

Like. What does Portland even do. Does the sunset even *try*?

"What're you thinking about?" Courtney asks me as I stare up at the mountains, transfixed.

"Nothing, mind your business."

Instead, he pretends to wipe a tear from my eye, and I shove him from where we're sitting on the open door of his car. *Now* I'm thinking about how it's just absolutely terrible looking, and its manufacture is inexcusable.

"I feel so strongly about the wrongness of this car, Courtney."

"You've mentioned."

"Why did you buy it, though? Like, how come?"

Clay and Lorraine both laugh, so I know it's not just me.

"Whatever. I wanted something with more character than a truck, but I still need to haul my bike and gear and stuff when I go hiking or camping. Plus, look." He gestures at me on the door. "Built-in seating. You're welcome."

"You know all cars have that, right?" I ask.

"Roasted," Lorraine says, and shakes their head. They look like Clay's twin, except I know the two are a couple years apart. Their hair is in a similar, coily flattop, but Lorraine's tips are dyed green and they're wearing a color-block snapback that covers all but the front fringe they've intentionally left visible. They have a stud piercing underneath the right corner of their mouth, and another one on the opposite side of their nose, neither of which seems to go without being remarked on whenever the older family members are around. Which makes it even more passive-aggressive when they inevitably conclude, "But Lorraine's grown, so." Because Lorraine, or Lo, as their brother is allowed to call them, has to be about twenty-five.

As an aside, I do not think my Babcock elders were built for Portland, if a very subdued hair color and facial piercings get their blood pressure up. How very '90s, I assume.

"You tell Sheba you tried to get the whole family to do a hike to close out the reunion?" Clay says over his sibling's laughter. Apparently the idea is ludicrous, and I can't help smiling. "Thought Great-Aunt Tina and Cousin Wilbur an'em was gonna follow you out here to their deaths."

"My dude, it is the dead of summer," Lorraine piggybacks on their brother's clown. "You're lucky I'm out here *now*. Youths, man."

"Why Wilbur make fifty look so old?" Clay derails, and the two are laughing so hard it's almost impossible to understand him now. "I thought he was finna keel over at the doggone picnic!"

"Where did his hair go in such a hurry, though?"

"Lo!" Clay collapses against his sibling, and they give up on words.

"My parents totally would've hiked with us," I admit, nudging Courtney with my shoulder. The relentless teasing is easier to appreciate when it's doled out indiscriminately, but I still feel the need to side with him. Maybe because of our visit with Kyrie today, and the way Courtney doesn't seem to notice or want recognition for everything he does for his family. In his experience, they've always been there, but it doesn't make him complacent; he adores them still. In a way, he's the personification of the Ancestor phenomenon I've been experiencing. He's the same warmth and reverence.

Which makes me think he must've been pretty hurt all those years ago when I never came down and stayed with him like he did with me. And I only came this time because I needed to get away. Which he's never brought up. No one has, actually. They tease and roast me about plenty of things, but not what sent me running toward a place I didn't give a second thought before.

"You know how weird you look without your phone in your face?"

"That's what I get for having good thoughts about you, Courtney." I had completely forgotten about my phone. I turned it on Do Not Disturb before locking it up for our visit, and never turned the feature off. "And why don't you have a nickname?"

"Why don't who have a nickname?" Clay's head swivels like he has the dexterity of an owl. He and Lorraine have wandered toward the mountain range, squatting to study whatever ungodly things live between the surprisingly diverse plant life, and occasionally pretending they're shooting a desert music video. I just assume that's what they were doing; Lorraine kept starfishing standing up, and Clay would immediately drop into a squat, and they'd just hold for a moment. Siblings don't make sense.

"Did Short-ney say he ain't have a nickname?" Lorraine squawks, eyes big, like a shocking secret is forthcoming. But I'm pretty sure the secret is Short-ney.

"You was a Little Bit?" I ask, exaggerating my swoon and grabbing at his cheeks.

"Yes, Naema." I have never seen his face so blank, even with me pinching it. "Because I was once a child."

"But like a toddler-sized child," Clay interjects.

"And before that a fun-sized toddler," Lorraine adds, their finger in the air like this is a Point Of Order.

The two of them are like Great-Grandpa Clarence and his older brother, Frederick, born in 1925. A rush of whispers swells into a moving image of the pair, and they are wearing the highest waisted pants I have ever seen in my entire life, Great-Grand-Uncle Frederick falling forward on a folding chair, and his brother collapsing in tearful laughter on his back.

I pull my lips into my mouth to keep from joining the memory or my cousins in laughter, but it's only barely working, and I have to go hard in the opposite direction, furrowing my forehead and looking Very Serious at Courtney instead.

"I hate you." And he stalks off toward the trail, yelling back, "Nobody follow me!"

Clay and Lorraine must be used to this more adorably petulant side of Courtney, for which they possibly definitely are always responsible, because the two head off after the bobbing blond mushroom, who is kicking at desert flora as he goes. I stay on the truck bed because despite the breathtaking view, I have no desire to be bitten by a snake and die in the desert, or to be stung by a scorpion and die in the desert, or—you understand.

I only pull out my phone because Courtney brought it up, but when I do, when I unlock it and am assaulted by big red bubbles in the corner of nearly every messaging or social media app I own, I realize how long I've been unplugged. In the space of eight hours or so, I've accumulated so many notifications I almost forget I haven't uploaded any content all summer. It's like the good old days, only more redundant because everything's from the same four people.

Priam has filled our private chat with a million pictures, like we're still a normal couple who refuses to miss a moment of each other's day. He got a latte at some point. Broke in his latest Adidas. He met a puppy at Macleay Park, and I'm assuming the owner served as videographer for the footage of him declaring the thing his best friend. He knows I'm not a dog person, but it's head knowledge; it has never truly settled in his heart despite the fact that I never swoon like you're supposed to. I'm sure if he posted this video anywhere, he'd get an immediate invitation to be the first Teen Bachelor, which sounds just awful enough to work.

The puppy *is* the same pale brown as my beloved Fiat, which Priam wisely points out, and that accounts for why I swoon a *lit*tle.

Jamie has finally decided to ask what made me question Priam's dating life. Which momentarily sends me back to all of his messages and pictures, in case I missed some snippet of an arm or shadow or evidence that he was with someone new today. There's nothing, and I feel ridiculous for putting so much stock in the opinion of a super-argumentative Knight who couldn't even tell my picture wasn't Photoshopped.

Gavin wants advice about Girlfriend, who apparently still exists and is Starting To Feel More Like A Fan Than A Girlfriend. Le gasp, Gavin. Much incredulous. Very plot twist. I can't roll my eyes hard enough, but Gavin Shinn falls in love like rain on Portland. It's not *actually* constant, but every time it starts up again, it sure feels like it.

Mommy began the day informing me she had no updates regarding the baby, to no one's surprise. Children need longer than three months to gestate, if health class is to be believed. She then proceeded to tell me every time she felt a flutter in her abdomen she's sure is The Baby and she knows because She's Very Attuned To Her Body And Always Has Been. Which apparently means I, too, must be attuned to it.

There are four pictures, just from today, of her uncovered stomach, reflected in various mirrors around the house.

If she weren't so small, it really would just look like she had a big lunch, but it's fine. She's excited.

That's everybody, but there are still so many emails and voice mails and missed calls, and finally I realize it's all Leona Fowl.

"Hi, Naema," her unmistakable rasp blares through my phone, a crackling distortion laced throughout like she really wants to talk to me but she also really had to go swimming, maybe? "This is L."

Everybody's got a nickname.

"Just wanted to let you know I'm ready if you are. I got your message about your family reunion ending tomorrow evening, and I cannot wait to catch up once you're free." And she says, "Naema." Dramatic pause. "This is gonna be big."

And then I get still. It *is* big.

Setting the record straight about Tavia Philips is a big deal. Defending myself for once, whether I should have to or not, is a big deal. Refusing to be the easy villain is a big deal. Getting to do all that without creating collateral damage is the biggest deal. For once it's gonna be about me and Tavia. Two girls and what happened between us, without all the rest. I'm over having to protect folks just because. And while we're at it, I'm sick of female rappers not getting to beef as is customary in the game because the conversation inevitably becomes about women tearing each other down. I'm sick of being chastised, of having to uphold the humanity of so many intersections that I'm not allowed to just dis*like* someone. And I would've been fine to go on doing that in our own little corner of the world, but apparently we make diss movies now.

She got hers. I get mine.

"Hey, Naema."

Oh. Okay, this one's from Leona, too.

"I've forwarded you some information. I'm over the moon excited about getting this chance to work together—"

I actually look at my phone, and though it's inanimate, I feel like it just shrugs because despite the fact that it's not tomorrow evening, Leona's still talking. And there's suddenly a lot of We and Together, and mentions of Our Window Of Opportunity. It's almost like she's hoping that by verbally aligning us as a partnership I won't remember that it's *my* story, and she's just one producer out of who knows how many. I mean, I don't know any others. I just naturally bristle at someone who thinks I don't see what they're doing. It's this quirk I have.

I delete her message, but there are three more just like it. She's equally in a rush, equally super chill and casual like she's not bordering on troubling insistence.

Delete delete delete.

What I'm *not* expecting to find in my inbox are new travel itineraries, since I haven't bought my return ticket home, and—that doesn't really matter because they aren't mine.

Leona Fowl has forwarded me confirmation of her flights to and from my safe space in the Southwest. And she arrives first thing tomorrow morning.

Despite knowing that tomorrow is the closing day of the Babcock family reunion, which means the professionally photographed riverboat excursion, which means all hands on deck, reunion jerseys and all. There's no way I'm missing that, I don't care how much initiative Ms. Fowl thinks she's showing by popping down uninvited. I didn't even like her that much over the phone.

"How the hell does she even know where I am?" I ask Courtney as he, Clay, and Lorraine return to the car. "Like, where, specifically? Because I didn't mention it."

The three exchange blinks, and Courtney opens his mouth.

"I *know* Priam wouldn't have told her, I was *real* clear."

A swirl starts and of course the Ancestors have something to say, but let me guess. Stranger Danger! Or maybe, why so suspicious of her trying to win you over when you *want* her commitment? Am I right? Or maybe this cool wind is just another form of Be Nice, Naema.

I'm full up on that.

"What do you wanna bet my pregnant-brained mom gave her your address?" I ask Courtney like this has been a dialogue.

This time his forehead creases, his face transitioning through a few expressions before his lips part again.

"A fast-talking, raspy-voiced chick shows up promising the most glamorous of runner-up TV movies, so sure, send her after your child, that sounds fine." Before Courtney can interrupt, I say, "Oh, but she's Eloko, so she *must* be trustworthy."

It's totally quiet when I'm done, and none of my cousins look like they have anything to say, though all three of them continue staring at me.

"What."

"Nothing," Courtney says, shrugging his shoulders. "You just haven't said anything about the snake under the door, which is really impressive, considering—"

I don't hear the rest of whatever he's saying because I'm screaming at the top of my lungs, and also suddenly on my feet somehow, standing in the bed of the truck, before I realize he's lying.

"Sheba," Clay says, and he's laughing with the other two, but he knows me pretty well by now so he offers me his back so I can be carried from the truck bed to the passenger door without touching the desert floor. Which of course I shall never trust again. "Sheba, Sheba, Sheba."

The double-decker riverboat is not air-conditioned, and I'll be honest: the Naema who arrived a week and a half ago would have been personally offended by that. That the proprietors felt being on the water would be enough to quench the heat, or that sightseeing from afar the desert you just drove through to get to the boat would be distraction enough. The problem is that I have either acclimated to the weather down here, or I'm imagining there really is an occasional and uplifting coolness. It sweeps around the outer decks and through the open doors and windows, swirling into the lounge on the lower deck. It carries music, conversation, and laughter, and maybe it's not coming off the water at all. Younger kids race along the same path, and it might just be their breeze I feel. Either way. It's a beautiful day.

Clay and Lorraine were supposed to be leading a two-step tutorial, but to absolutely no one's surprise, they quickly derailed into a competitive b-boy dance-off. That, too, becomes a tutorial when Little Bit, Didi, and the others try to mimic them.

Patrice is hovering around the pies, making sure there'll be some pecan left whenever Great-Uncle Gerald decides he'll have some. Which means she's policing slice sizes, offering to serve people, and then giving them what she wants to give them regardless of what they asked for. The adults give her side-eye and make sure she gives them what they came for, but any kids just have to live with being bamboozled and double back whenever she finally sits down.

Wilbur's got his tripod out on the upper deck right now, capturing the wake of our boat, and the hilly terrain on either side of the river. He got plenty of footage of the professional photographer getting footage of Great-Gram Lorraine surrounded by several of her kids and grandkids, thank heavens. I know I for one can't wait to watch that random dude's back again and again and for years to come. I'm sure the layers will reveal their true depth with each watch.

But I'm a huge hypocrite because I've been taking video all day, too. Yes, of the water, and the hills, and the older second cousins cutting one another off because nobody can agree on how something from thirty years ago really went down. I've gotten the dancing, and the younger kids, and Courtney at the dominos table, which is officially gambling-free. That wasn't the cruise's decision, as I assumed. Apparently, there have been scuffles in the past.

In my defense, I've been sending the videos to my mom and the squad back home. Plus, I mean. I want to remember it, too. I've never experienced anything like this week; not that I can remember anyway. Even once the Ancestors have my familial knowledge up to date on precisely who everyone is, and who they resemble, or who they take after in mannerisms despite the century between them, there's still just this . . . energy. Being around family, especially this much family at once, is indescribable. And, judging by the way they all look at one another, and the fact that they're all here, that's not just an Eloko thing. It makes me wish we could have a reunion in Portland, too. There's so much I'd love to show the Babcocks, so many parts of my life they've never seen. And it'd be nice to laugh at their confusion over the ways of the Pacific Northwest, so they can be humbled a little. It's all fun and games until *you're* the fish out of water.

Leona Fowl's been sending me Check-In texts periodically, like she doesn't want me to forget she's in town. I haven't seen her yet, and I've restricted myself to sending emoticon replies so as to keep her from thoroughly intruding before her designated time. Nobody picked her up at the airport, and she took a cab to her hotel, which was also intentional on my part. She's either got a serious lack of discernment even by the standards of a non-Eloko, or she's super passive-aggressive, because despite my refusal to leap at her arrival, she still lets me know once she's had lunch on the premises, going so far as to assure me she'll stay there in case I need her. Despite me responding to her emailed itinerary with a reminder that I'd be busy till the early evening at the earliest, and no I couldn't make any adjustments. Upon my fourth insistence, she *totally* understood. And also just in case, here's her room number and the name of the hotel again, and where the in-house restaurant is located both from the vantage point of the elevators and from the front entrance.

'Kay.

"Are you over the Babcocks yet?" Courtney sidles up to me at the rail, but he turns his back to it like the view isn't spectacular, resting his elbows on the bar and watching the activity on the boat instead. "Ready to get back to the Eloko coven, and away from here?"

"First of all, we're not witches."

"Says you."

"Yes, Short-ney, says me."

"See," he wags his finger in the air and scowls like something stinks, "this is why I don't tell you anything."

"Well, you didn't, remember?"

He scoffs, and turns to face the river.

"And no," I say. "I am not over the Babcocks. Yet."

He doesn't say anything, but I can feel him smiling next to me.

"I'm gonna need you to be less of a cinnamon roll when we meet this producer for dinner tonight—"

"First of all, I have no idea what that means."

"—I need her to think we're *both* fierce."

"And secondly, I'm tryna get put on, Sheba, just a heads-up."

"Okay."

"Imma be *in* the movie before this dinner is over."

"It'll be in my contract. Courtney has to be in every scene, hidden somewhere in the scenery."

"Dope."

"I gotchu." We knock knuckles, and nod, like it's a done deal.

But he's still glancing at me, and he waves Clay off when he calls for him, so I know something's up.

"What, Courtney?" I ask, enunciating and rolling my eyes.

"You good, though?"

I start to snap at him, but he's serious. "Me? Yeah, Courtney, I'm fine. Why?"

He shakes his head.

"You're a mother hen, I swear."

"So Kyrie tells me."

"I'm used to people wanting to be around me all the time, like, they feed off my presence, which—don't roll your eyes, it's not a Sheba thing, it just comes with the Eloko territory! *Any*way. I was just gonna say, nobody ever actually checks on me."

"What, not even Priam?"

"No, I guess Priam does. Did."

"Did. You still pretending you're not together?"

It's my turn to turn my back on the river. "I don't know. He might not be pretending." I don't know why, but I'm surprised by how seriously Courtney seems to be taking this. He's not facing the family or the river anymore; he's giving me his undivided attention.

"Why do you say that?"

"I don't know," I tell him, because I'm done being transparent for the moment. "Just something someone told me."

"Hm." He looks over my face, like I've given him a lot to think about. "Well. Make sure they know what they're talking about before you take their word for anything."

"Huh. That's quite a vote of confidence for a dude you met for one day."

Courtney looks sheepish, and then turns so I can only see his profile. Something's weird, but he looks done being transparent, too, for now.

"Let's go eat," I say, nudging him.

"If we can decipher Patrice's riddles three," he deadpans,

and I laugh, snaking my arm through his and pulling him from the rail.

~

There are speeches before the day is done, and folks have gotten into the wine coolers by then, so. I'm ready to reconsider my stance on the Babcock family by the time Wilbur gets the microphone away from his Aunt Tina. She's the youngest of Clarence and Lorraine's children, born in 1955, but I have to remind myself she's still in her mid-sixties. Sure she's wearing a pair of jeggings, and what I'm now realizing is an Aunt Toni number of bangles paired with an ambitious collection of chunky statement necklaces that no one said *couldn't* be layered, but that's not even the best part. She started out thanking everyone for showing up to this reunion—which I had to remind myself she did *not* organize despite her weird insinuation—and then graduated to thanking the family for supporting her and her second shot at love. In case anyone wasn't following, she went ahead and shouted out her Second Husband, First In Her Heart—her words!—and their Late In Life Blessing Of A Daughter. The cherry on top is either that the husband in question is inexplicably not in attendance, or that they've been married for like, twenty years. As in, none of this happened yesterday, and this is in fact *not* her wedding reception, or first anniversary.

Family reunions are undefeated.

This is the best thing ever, and if I livestreamed it, I promise you it would do numbers. Great-Aunt Tina and her Youthful If That Means Over The Top pedicure/toe ring situation would land the family a reality show all on her own.

Folks are snickering, talking among themselves, and randomly calling out for her to wrap it up, so I'm thinking none of it is exactly shocking behavior. Maybe the family reunion isn't really over until someone makes a drunken and meandering speech on a riverboat at sunset.

Priceless.

And then it's over. The cruise is ended, the boat is docked, and folks are getting the elderly Babcocks situated and ready to return home. Carpools are taking off, and the goodbyes don't seem to rise to the occasion until I remember most of them live within a couple hours of here. Apparently this is just goodbye until somebody has a birthday. I try to imagine a birthday party not being an extravagant big-ticket gift I've known about for six months, and my friends decorating my bedroom suite, and locker, and car. A million messages across social media, but only a handful from people who actually know me. And, no, this is not the part where the final ghost of Christmas Past gets through to Ebenezer Scrooge, and I realize my whole life is vanity. A million messages and home renovation as a birthday gift are nice, thank you. And so is a Babcock birthday party, I'm guessing.

Maybe next year. I'm already mentally working out my freshman-year schedule at UP, looking for gaps and holidays that'll let me swing down for a visit, and it's not *not* because the end of the reunion suddenly has me wondering if the Ancestors will follow me home. Whether I get to keep this, or whether part of being Eloko requires more than living with heirlooms and hand-me-downs. Maybe it's like jumping a car, and the charge I couldn't make on my own will at least keep.

I can't even speak about it yet, to Courtney or my friends. How do you describe something so personal and also so . . . historic. The swell of centuries before you, voices that speak pictures and memories, a sense that pieces of me have already existed, making me somehow more myself. Naema Bradshaw has always been confident, no one would dispute that, but that's what I want to call this energy the Ancestors bring. Portland might turn on me, a movie might strip me of everything but negativity, but I am who I'm supposed to be.

I *am* magic. Without question.

Anyway.

It's time to shake off the feels for now. Courtney and I ride back to the house ahead of Aunt Carla Ann and Uncle Deric, who'll be charioting folks and food and equipment around town all night, and I undo the Babcock Reunion transformation.

I take a leisurely shower to get back in the spirit of Naema

Time; I take down my ponytail and plug in my curling wand; I swap out my Babcock baseball jersey for a floral romper and sandals, and I am not shy with the baby oil.

Poor Courtney thinks we're headed out the door until I giggle and pull out my makeup case before climbing onto the bathroom counter.

"She made a reservation!" he exclaims.

"To have dinner. With me. Which means the dinner begins when I arrive," and I apply my primer.

"Do you even want this movie?"

"It's about setting the tone, cuzzo." I lean closer to the mirror, and perfectly anticipating Courtney's next exclamation, simultaneously smile at my reflection and say, "Pretty Bird," before winking at him.

"Imma go eat a pre-dinner. Cannot believe you."

"Drama," I say through a breath, and then call after him, "I'm basically ready," before spending an unhurried thirty minutes beating my face. It's wonderful to get back to some semblance of normalcy, and the heat having burned off—for the most part—means it doesn't feel like a complete exercise in futility to put on the works.

When Courtney returns with a mostly eaten sourdough roll, I'm applying my setting spray. "See? All done."

"You look exactly the same," he deadpans.

"Aw. Liar," I reply through a swoon.

"That was not a compliment."

Despite his lack of appreciation for the art of cosmetics, when I walk through the unnecessarily fancy restaurant where Leona Fowl has made our reservation, and face her for the first time, I am That Bish and everybody knows it. I mean, I take some personal, non-makeup-related credit for that, but people are shallow; they like clear, simple cues interpreted at a glance, and a full face, a power strut, and bouncy hair says Flawless. Fight society, not me. I didn't make the rules, I just win at the game.

One hand is Absentmindedly Fiddling With My Bell Charm when Leona greets me by standing and shaking the other. Yes, I realize she's Eloko, but there's no harm in reminding her that I am, too.

"Naema, at last," she says, and she's That Bish, too. I should've guessed. She's wearing her Serious Career Girl brunette hair in California-appropriate beach waves, and the highlights are respectable and almost pass for natural. Her lips have been plumped—again, respectably—and they're sporting an almost imperceptibly coral gloss, beautifully accentuated by her flawless cheek contouring and the bombest of cheekbone highlight. Her peach-beige skin is smooth and taut, and I can just see her jog-hiking the canyons. Probably with a surprisingly big dog at her side.

I see Leona came to win as well. I like a challenge.

Our melodies mingle for a moment and the diners and wait-staff in the vicinity light up a little as they look around, smiling but unsure.

"And you must be Courtney," she says to demonstrate her attentiveness, and she shakes his hand.

"Shall we?" I invite her to sit at the table *she* reserved, and anyone else might not notice the slight tick in her eyebrow.

"Of course," she says, in an impressively gracious tone. "I took the liberty of ordering a few hors d'oeuvres; please feel free to help yourselves."

Which is when I notice the small plate in front of her, already blemished with an orange-yellow sauce that probably belongs to the soft-boiled egg and truffle butter dish.

How dare.

"I hope we didn't keep you waiting," I offer, knowing we did, and that I meant to. "You must've been hungry."

Courtney glances at me as he helps himself to the clams, as if to ask who's winning. I blink slowly, and begin to study the menu so that he knows I am.

"Oh, you're fine," Leona assures me. "I'm never disappointed with my own company," and her laugh is light and convincing as she takes a sip of wine.

Fine, maybe we're even.

"I was surprised to hear you were coming down," I tell her. "I was expecting another phone call. It almost feels like we're rushing."

"Oh, I'm nothing if not proactive," she says, and if she's perturbed at the suggestion, she does a decent job hiding it. "And everyone on the team thought it was important for us to meet face to face, especially after what you told me. I wanted to be sure you understand how important this is."

She's gonna tell me how important *my* story is. I bristle at the audacity, which Courtney seems to notice from across the table. To my surprise, he's able to sober me with a discreet glance and the lowering of his chin.

"I'm *relatively* aware of how important it is to tell the world what really happened to me," and I give my own delicate laugh. But I tuck my chin toward my chest and recoil when she dabs the corner of her mouth with the cloth napkin, turning to me like she's about to impart some serious wisdom.

Who is this woman.

"I mean this in the most respectful way possible, Naema," she begins, and it does not thrill me. "But if what you told me is true, it's about a lot more than what happened to you."

. . . What.

My poker face slips, and when I look at Courtney, the incredulousness is visible. I can feel it dripping down my face. I am very rarely this bothered by any one individual, but Leona Fowl is stunning in her pursuit of the title.

"I came down because this is something we need to move on, and it's got nothing to do with ratings or riding the popularity of Tavia and Effie's movie—"

I snort in Imma Let You Finish, But It Absolutely Has Something To Do With Those Things.

"—it's about public safety."

"'Scuse me?" I blurt out.

I want to kick myself for being so flappable, it's just that everything she says is more ridiculous than the thing before. Worse, she's got an almost sociopathic lack of shame. If she knows this is bs, *I* can't tell.

"It's about the safety of Eloko, period. I'm just sorry you had to be the one to find out how sirens really feel about us." Leona's wearing this earnest expression, and has reached across the table to squeeze my hand, which she is able to do because I'm too stunned to resist.

I just keep looking at Courtney, like he'll make it make sense, except his eyebrows are as furrowed as mine, and he's stopped eating mid-chew.

"How did you get from Tavia Stoned Me," I ask, quietly, "to sirens hate Eloko? Exactly?"

"Can you honestly say they don't?"

"No, see, that's not how this works. You posited something completely without basis, and when I ask you to defend it, you can't say it's up to me to prove a negative. I'm a teenager, Ms. Fowl, I'm not stupid."

"I have no doubt about your intelligence," she says.

"Because I'm Eloko."

Her lips rest together.

"I'm just confused at your absolute conviction, given that I told you what Tavia did when we spoke last, and you didn't seem to think it was a public safety issue then."

"I've had time to process it," she responds.

"Hey, didn't you make a movie with Tavia?" Courtney interjects for the first time. "I mean. She didn't turn *you* to stone? I assume."

"I had a very cordial working relationship with Ms. Philips over the course of the production." Leona shakes her head while she speaks. "But I think you're both old enough to know that people aren't always at liberty to act on their prejudices."

"Stop," I blurt again, but she doesn't.

"That's just real life."

"This is . . ." I shake my own head, eyes squeezed shut like the absurdity is physically crowding me. "Such a bad look. So bad. You're aware that sirens are exclusively Black women."

"I am, but—"

"And you're saying Black women are out to get you."

"Naema, that is *not* what I'm saying. We aren't talking about all Black women, we're talking about the ones who are sirens."

"You want to tell the world that sirens are out to get Eloko, many of whom look like you," I say, gesturing over the hors d'oeuvres at her. "Because me and a girl I go to high school with got into it?" When she tries to speak, I talk over her. "And you don't think the world is gonna hear Black women. Period. Because I can tell you that as soon as I left Portland, where everyone expects to see Eloko, and checks our jewelry before anything else, folks treated me differently!"

I feel my cousin watching me, and I sincerely hope he doesn't come around the table and try to hug me or anything, because I do not put it past him and this is not the time. It's bad enough that the Ancestors are warming the inside of my chest. They're underlining what I'm saying to Leona, emphatically reverberating my words back to me.

"The first thing people think when they see me is not Eloko, surprisingly enough. And the safety measures they set up specifically against sirens? They're wide enough to grab anyone who could possibly *be* one. Which means whom, Ms. Fowl?"

"Naema, I hear—"

"Which means Black women," I answer for her. "Any of us. All of us."

The table falls quiet as I stare into her eyes, neither of us willing to lose the battle.

"So no, we won't be telling that story." And I pick up the menu again, though I have no intention of staying long enough to order.

Unfortunately, when Leona starts talking again, it's like she heard nothing I said.

"I understand it's a lot to process," she says, calmly, like I'm a sleep-deprived toddler she's trying to negotiate with.

"It would be a lot to process if it were true," I snap, my side-eye lethal. "It's not. It's a super irresponsible fantasy you're trying to weave so you can sell a movie. And you think you can sell it without backlash if I'm the face of it."

"And if you heard it from the Knights of Naema?" she asks, in only slightly muted exasperation.

"What a strange and strangely childish change in approach," I say, almost before she's finished. At last, a crack shows in her façade, and I want her to know I see it. "And a very ineffective one, I must say. But you're desperate, or you wouldn't have asked.

What, were you hoping I believed them because they're fans of mine? That I'd believe anything they say, and then just hope against hope that they somehow jump to your same outlandish, self-centering conclusion?" I make a mocking pout. "Ms. Fowl. Ma'am."

The pink almost drains from her face, and her jaw clenches.

"Somebody needs to take a pause and really listen to their Ancestors, because this ain't it."

Her expression is pinched, and I genuinely can't tell if she has any idea what I'm talking about, but I wanna say no.

"I showed you the Knights because everyone else seemed to want to rehabilitate my image by centering what I suffered. Or let's be real, *that* I suffered. They were merely an example you were meant to follow."

I deposit my napkin on the empty plate before me, and stand; Courtney immediately follows.

"It's definitely not the only way we can tell your story," Leona says, getting to her feet before I can step away. "But if you're scared, and no one's saying you shouldn't be—"

"Oh my gawd."

"We'll make sure the world knows that *you* are Eloko."

Wow.

"Is that what people think?" I ask. "That we'll trade it all—everybody else—if we can just get ourselves to the other side. Like I don't have a mother, or cousins, or like even if I didn't, any of this would be okay."

Leona doesn't answer me, she just exhales a long breath. I can't tell if she's fed up with me or herself, until she speaks again and her raspy voice is tight.

"You're the one who said you're Eloko first."

"I did. And the world set me straight, but that's okay. I don't need to be. Don't let me keep you from the pleasure of your own company," I say as I leave the table.

Leona Fowl gets nothing else from me. Not even a Good Night.

Chapter XXI

Knights of Naema Post

KEEP PORTLAND SAFE

Cursive_Signature [no shield] [metadata: posts (1)] [upvotes: 235]

I heard a new movie is in the works, to tell Naema's side of the story. And from what I hear, you guys are right. Tavia definitely went after her.

LePeintre [bronze/9]: Are you in the industry?

Anon: Is Naema involved in the movie?

WyteKnight [silver/32]: Why not just make it a documentary, so it'll really be her?

LePeintre: How did the siren go after her?

Lancelot [silver/41]: She made that snake turn Naema to stone?!

WyteKnight: Who didn't already know this? Sometimes assuming is just using common sense.

Hood&Helm [no shield]: Anybody else worried about who's gonna protect Naema when the siren finds out people know?

Greaves [silver/42]: There needs to be a presence in PDX, so the siren knows not to mess with her again!

NaemasNobleman [gold/47]: Don't worry, buddy, there is.

LePeinture: Is #Justice4Naema actually happening?

SilverSchalem [gold/46]: Yes.

NaemasNobleman: Some of us are real Knights. [upvotes: 249]

Hood&Helm: Where do we find out how?

SilverSchalem: This isn't a conversation for the forum. If you want to earn your shield, PM. [upvotes: 301]

Anonymous: And are you doing anything about the sirens swarming to Portland because of that first movie??

NaemasNobleman: PM.

Chapter XXII

NAEMA

Courtney is surprisingly quiet on the ride home, but I'm too shook by Leona Fowl to bug him about it. Or maybe more so by my inability to ignore the cyclone stirring inside me. I've pushed back before, but the Ancestor wind has been churning deep in my gut ever since leaving the restaurant, and no matter how many times I replay my epic Leona takedown, they don't agree. It feels like the Ancestors are warning me, like suddenly they're telling me something definitive about what someone will do, in a clairvoyant way they haven't before.

Maybe it's because she's Eloko, too.

Maybe the Eloko are more a collective than we've known, or behaved.

Maybe it's possible to be connected to one another by the Ancestors.

I'm not saying I believe it, but if that's true, I wonder if it means there's some Ancestor-attuned Eloko somewhere else who knows all the things *I've* done. I'm no villain, obviously, but. I can think of one or two things I've done that I wouldn't want passed around in the Ancestors' eternal memory.

Courtney raps his knuckles on Little Bit's bedroom door and interrupts the stock-taking I'm not sure I really wanna do in the first place. *I'm* in tune with the Ancestors now, after all. There's no keeping secrets from them, or with the potential Eloko collective, however few it may be these days.

Despite our talk about privacy, Courtney still opens the door a bit and peers in. His little sister has one leg hooked around the sheet, the cover aggressively kicked toward the foot of the bed whether I wanted some or not, and I hadn't even noticed that she's snoring into the side of my face.

"Can I talk to you about something?" Courtney asks, his bright hair the only part of him I can see with the rest of his body still hidden behind the door.

I nod and wave him in, putting my finger over my lips before pointing to his sister.

"Oh, you ain't gotta be quiet on her account. Nothing wakes her but the sound of the school bus leaving her behind so I'm forced to drive her. Knucklehead."

"What's up?" I ask him, sitting up. But it's like once he has my attention, he clams up like he did in the car. I almost snark at him about it, except he's looking at me like he's gonna try to hug me, so I think something's actually wrong. "Courtney."

"I just wanted to check on you."

"Again."

"What do you mean, again?"

"Wasn't it you who came and checked on me before? On the back porch?" I mean it affectionately, but he nods and looks like maybe I'm talking about privacy again, and starts to turn back toward the door. "Courtney, it's cool. I told you. I'm not especially used to being checked on. I appreciate it."

He takes a breath and nods again.

I mean it when I say I appreciate the way he looks out for me. I haven't told him half the things going on inside me, the way I don't tell *anybody* everything, but it's like he's this unique breed of person who doesn't treat me like uncharacteristic unloading is the toll I have to pay to gain access to consideration. He just offers it.

"I could see you were more than capable of shutting that chick down," he says. "But it must've been disappointing, the way she twisted your story. I know I'd be upset."

"I am that," I concede, through an exhale that's not at all cleansing. The nausea and turbulent wind is still wreaking havoc on my insides, so I tell him: "I'm even more upset because I'm almost certain I did *not* shut her down."

"What does that mean?" Courtney asks, and his forehead folds.

"I don't know," I say, and reach behind my neck to unclasp my necklace. I hand it to him, and he cocks a perfect brow. "But I need to ask the Ancestors."

"And you can't do that with this on?"

"I love how you have no questions about asking the Ancestors something, just about taking off my bell charm."

"It sounds pretty self-explanatory, Sheba. That and I was at the BBQ when you gave your little presentation."

"How's a presentation gonna be little, Courtney?" I say as I close my eyes.

"'Little' coulda been a synonym for, brief, in that context, sorry, I win that one."

"Quiet, please."

"Right."

I don't know what I'm doing. I have no idea why I closed my eyes, except that in the inevitable movie version of my life, it seems like what Movie Naema will do. Usually the Ancestors speak to me; I've never spoken to them before, if that's what I'm trying to do. It shouldn't be hard, since I gave them space inside me. The wind of their undecipherable voices can gust through my core at will, swirling sometimes in what feels like a cyclone, like something's literally climbing my esophagus, looking for a way out. The least they can do is answer when *I* want a word.

I need them to help me understand what Leona Fowl is trying to do.

Except when I think that, the unease gets stronger. So much stronger, so quickly, that I feel myself lurch toward Courtney. He catches me by my shoulders and, thankfully, I do *not* hurl on the bed between us.

The tornado in my abdomen keeps pulling. Like it wants me closer. Like it wants me to give in. Again, only this time it's unpleasant. Which, in my experience, from my Portland bubble perspective, is the least Eloko thing I could possibly do. Where I'm from, we don't pursue discomfort. We are light and carefree. Or we fake it, anyway. Fine, maybe it's true for some people. Maybe somebody got to be light and carefree for real. But it wasn't me.

So I give in. I lift my chin and breathe deep, and I make room for the gusting wind again, even though my guts feel like they're in knots. Even though I think I'm gonna vomit all over my cousin and his little sister's bed. And their voices get clear.

"The Knights," I say aloud, like I'm confirming that I heard them.

"What about them?" Courtney asks, but even in his concerned expression, I can see his irritation.

"She brought them up both times we spoke. At the restaurant and on the phone, when she tried to explain bringing up my Stoning." I shake my head, and it's like it's clearing away the nausea. "She knew about the subforum. Where they posted those pictures of me while I was gray. And I had to make an account to get there, so she must've, too."

Courtney's face doesn't change.

"You know, you seem to know a lot of stuff before I mention it."

"Whatchu mean?"

"Like sirens having protection, for one thing." But I know I can't push him on that, being expelled and all, so I add, "Or like there being Stoned pictures of me on the Knights site, or like the fact that I made an account. None of this seems surprising to you."

"Okay, so don't get mad," he blurts.

"Oh my gawd—"

"I'm NyNative. And I know you're Sheba503."

Son of a—

"Wait!" I punch him in the arm. "You're the dude who said my picture was Photoshopped?"

"I mean, more importantly, the dude who said he saw Priam with somebody else," his voice goes up exponentially with each word and he rises from the bed to stop my pummeling him. "I had to say something to keep anybody from believing you! The whole reason I joined was to keep an eye on it, and you. I didn't think you'd suspect Priam of stepping out!"

"Courtney! You said you saw him out with me, and I'm me,

so I know it wasn't me, so what else could that mean? Are you *kidding me*!"

"Stop hitting me!"

"What does NyNative even mean?"

"Oh, I just figured you'd think I was some New Yorker."

"That is the weirdest—"

"So you wouldn't suspect it was me!"

"You're the actual worst."

"Okay, but it's a good thing, right, because c'mon. Why'd you try to out yourself to them?"

"I don't know!" My playful exasperation doesn't really convey the truth, so I just confess it. "I guess to prove they couldn't be so bad. When I was already pretty worried that at least a few of them might be."

He's quiet for a moment, and then he tells me.

"She's on there, too. Pretty sure."

"Leona?"

He nods, but I've already grabbed my laptop and am pulling up the site.

"I checked when we got back from the restaurant," Courtney says as he watches over my shoulder. "There was new activity by someone with a pretty new account who hadn't made any previous posts or comments, *and* they have an auto-generated name."

"What does that mean?"

"Like, they just accepted the suggested name the site generates for you, before you type in your own. It's just a pair of random words."

"So that's where you got NyNative," I say as I peruse the site.

"No, Naema—"

"Oh! The *n y* means Ny, you're saying you're native to me, because we're related!"

"I told you it— Please shut up." He reaches around me and types a name into the search form.

Cursive_Signature.

"You can see everything she's posted, and the fact that she has zero comment or post history before tonight. And she doesn't make one post without using the Justice for Naema hashtag . . ."

And I see what he's talking about. On a number of posts, Cursive_Signature has recently been sharing Buzz They've Overheard. Finally, on a post about keeping Portland safe for me, the comment catches the forum's attention and spurs an excitable conversation.

"Oh my gawd," I mutter.

"Yeah, it's . . . not great," Courtney says.

"What swarming?" I almost shout, as I read. "There are no sirens swarming to Portland, what the hell is wrong with people?"

And then I pause. I mean. I don't *think* there are. To be fair, since being expelled from the network, I don't see how I'd know. Except I feel like it'd still be pretty hard to miss—an influx of Black folks anywhere in the Pacific Northwest? I'm extremely sure I would've noticed.

"The scary part is Leona's not even the one who posted that comment," Courtney says, like I can't see the user handle. "The Knights jumped to that all on their own. She voices one terrible thought, and inspires a dozen even worse. These people are wild, Sheba."

"I know," I say, because there are more comments to read . . . and if I'd eaten any of the rich hors d'oeuvres Leona ordered at the restaurant, I wouldn't be able to keep them down. "They're acting like all this sensational fearmongering is really out of concern for me."

And then I see it.

If it makes you feel any better, Naema's not in PDX right now. She's staying with family down south, someone says.

Southwest, NaemasNobleman corrects them.

W. TA. F.

There's an upvote on the correction, and I know it's her. I *know* that Cursive_Signature is Leona Fowl, and that she's confirming information about my whereabouts to a bunch of anonymous internet admirers.

The strong wind returns to settle in my chest, and the queasiness is gone. I'm enraged, and the Ancestors are raging inside me in agreement. If I open my mouth right now, I'll release a chorus of screams, theirs *and* mine.

Because *that's* the member she decided to connect with. Of course it is. The dude who convinced another member that I *want* to be found.

There are a half dozen trains of thought taking place in this one conversation, and before I explode, I try to catch up on the others.

People need to know she's not just some run-of-the-mill girl.

They hate her because she's Eloko.

She needs to be protected from the rest of them.

It's almost worse that nobody comes right out and says what they're very obviously saying. Nobody uses a slur, or references race. They don't have to. And most of them probably think themselves more intelligent or aware than the kind of trash who would. But at least I would've known what those people were on sight. At least I wouldn't have taken comfort in the adoration of people who came right out and said I was the exception that let them feel good about themselves.

I don't think I can feel any more angry, but that's only because I've once again underestimated Leona Fowl. It appears she isn't satisfied being mere inspiration after all. Despite how quickly the thread became unwieldy with almost frothing indignation and rampantly escalating paranoia, her final comment is an unveiled call to action:

It's time to take this out of the shadows, if we really want to protect our girl, Cursive_Signature writes. *Naema isn't safe until people know what happened to her. We *need* to make sure this film gets made! #Justice4Naema needs to go viral! Are we Knights or not?*

That's when I notice the shield by her name. One day of membership, and she's already climbing the ranks, being bestowed what I can only assume are reputation or clout points, probably for sharing information about me in private messages.

"Look at the time stamp." I don't know where to anchor my outrage. I'm gobsmacked. "If this is really Leona Fowl—and it is—she posted this before we'd even made it home from the restaurant."

"I'm pretty sure it's her," Courtney says, like he's less sure than he wants to be.

"No, Courtney. I'm *telling* you. This is her. I don't think I'd know for sure about anybody but another Eloko. I think that's how the Ancestor connect works. But trust me. Cursive_Signature is Leona Fowl."

"I trust you," he says. "But I don't think she's taking no for an answer, Sheba."

My hand is covering my mouth, and I read the comment again and again.

Our girl.

I think tf not. I do not belong to anyone, and I certainly don't get put to their purpose. Leona Fowl underestimated me, too.

"She thought. I really wanna see this chick make a Justice For Naema movie without a Naema."

I keep seeing Leona in the restaurant, perfectly put together, and far more ruthless than she appeared. I have so few regrets, but wishing I'd splashed that white wine in her pretty face is one I feel viscerally.

"I can't even dunk on Tavia Philips because of her." I have to ball my fists and seethe for a minute, Courtney jumping at the unexpected growl that escapes me. And then I'm back. "Fine. Whatever. Screw this movie. I'll have to settle for getting a book deal," I say as though these things fall out of the sky. But there is nothing on earth anyone can dangle in front of me and think I'm ensnared. This flashy producer type is about to find out that if Naema Bradshaw wants something, I will make it happen. Please. I have an in-home life coach and business mentor who also happens to be my dad.

Every Empire Begins With A Brainstorm—Darren Bradshaw.

Don't Nobody Need You, Leona—Me.

We've got this. I really just hope Leona Fowl has promised her production team she'd close the deal. I don't know *exactly* how these things work, but I really like the idea of her being lambasted in a boardroom, and then having to do a walk of shame from her desk to the elevators holding a cardboard box full of knickknacks and a desk plant. And it's raining when she gets outside the building. Because regardless of what they say about Southern

California, it'll do me this one solid and wash the waves out of her hair.

I sober. Because she's not just trying to plant grassroots movie support. She told someone where I am, where my family lives, even if just in general regional terms. Like she has no idea about the danger of doxing, and how many Black women and girls are targeted online for the absolute slightest provocation, and she sure as hell doesn't care.

And then it's like we really are connected.

There's a cross-posted link from a new subforum in Leona's #Justice4Naema post.

#SecretSirens.

"What fresh hell is this," I mutter. But it really isn't complicated. In fact it's exactly what it sounds like.

Someone's taken Cursive_Signature's call to action seriously, and it's NaemasNobleman.

I click through to the brand-new subforum, and Courtney and I are faced with pictures of Black women, with their full names, ages, and descriptions of the behavior they've exhibited.

This is a place to identify suspected sirens.

"Oh my gawd." The words slide out on a long, low breath, and I hear them before I realize I've spoken. Because, according to the Knight who began the collection, these are all Portland locals. And they're not even all women.

"There are kids on here, Courtney," I say, as though he's not staring from behind my shoulder. But he's gotten so quiet I can't even hear him breathing. "Courtney . . ."

"I see it."

There's a ten-year-old girl, with pictures that look like they've been taken during recess either by someone with a really powerful lens, or else by an unsuspecting person on the same premises.

"He's listed a possible address." I hear Courtney say it, but I don't understand.

The girl is playing on uneven bars in her school yard, and her half dozen braids and the brightly colored bobbles used to fasten them are hanging in the air as she dangles upside down.

She's another family's Little Bit. It's as bad as seeing my baby cousin being stalked. Who knows how bad this can get.

The little girl in the pictures is suspected of being a siren because—

"She won the school-wide spelling bee," Courtney reads. "That's all he wrote. She won the spelling bee."

I'm still looking at the little girl playing, completely oblivious to the photographer, or at least to the threat they pose. I don't remember who won my elementary school spelling bee, but I remember it happened during the school day. And I don't think it was publicized.

"There have to be hundreds of schools in Portland," I say, but I'm talking to myself. "Who would even know she won, unless they work at the school. A parent?"

I want to know who's watching this little girl. I need to. My heart is doing a weird flutter-pulse inside my chest, and it's such a rabid pace that it vibrates at the back of my throat and I almost have to cough.

That's when I wonder.

"What does it mean if *these* are the people on your side?" I ask the question even though I'm sort of hoping the Ancestors won't answer. "The only people who don't think I deserved to get Stoned . . . and they're monsters."

"Don't," Courtney demands. "Ain't even that simple. People can overlap in one thing, and still not be the same. Even a broken clock is right twice a day."

It's not like his words don't matter. But his voice is the only one I hear, and I want to know what the Ancestors would've said that night at prom. Because now they feel so supportive, so pleased with who I am—but I couldn't hear them in Portland. What if the person they like is the one who came out of the gray? What if Tavia's attack really did make me a better person?

I need to know.

"I wore a collar to prom," I confess, so they'll hear. "It's common knowledge. Or should be. Even the Knights have a picture of it, but no one's really criticized it specifically."

Courtney's brow cinches, and I'm telling the Ancestors, but I prepare myself for his response, too.

"I *did* antagonize her."

He doesn't say anything at first, which leaves a lot of space for the voices—but suddenly there are none. There's no swirl of warmth or comfort. Which shouldn't surprise me. I'm recounting the worst thing I think I've ever done, and I didn't even realize it at the time. Lying on Effie to provoke Tavia wasn't exactly a stellar move, but it could be considered your run-of-the-mill antagonization.

The collar . . .

That was something different. Courtney and the Ancestors are silent because that was borderline evil.

The only thing worse than their voices falling quiet is what they might say when they speak again.

"That's messed up, Sheba," Courtney says, deliberately. *"And* that doesn't make what she did okay. It's two awful things, and they don't justify or cancel each other out."

I can still see the photos in my peripheral vision, but I can't look at them or at him. It's another first for me, this ugly shame. It's like I've never felt regret before. There's no more need for regret in the vapid ease of Life In The Eloko Hotbed Of Portland than there is for discomfort. Despite intentionally giving in to it a moment ago, I still might not be built for it—but I'd rather chance it than be the kind of person the Ancestors won't speak to.

"I don't get along with Tavia," I say, careful to breathe. "Just her, as a person. But wearing that collar was a threat because she's a siren. I didn't get how messed up that was because there is no threat like that, for me, as an Eloko. Whether I'm a Black girl or not."

And nobody cared that I did it because they don't care about the people who know what it means.

The thought that is somehow both the Ancestors' and mine at the same time sounds like a defense, like a shifting of blame, but I immediately know better. It's blunt and honest, the way I say I am, pointing out the way my act of terror depended on the fact that no one cares about that kind of victim. And amazingly, it sounds like my voice, but it feels like theirs. A swell inside that's the same as Knowing. As being known.

I'm not a crier, and thank God. When I closed my eyes just now, a tear would totally have slipped free.

They're still there.

I breathe in and out, eyes closed, and feel a faint throb behind my sternum. I listen to the voices that become portraits, to the sounds that become energy. Because I've confessed my worst thing and I can still hear them.

I come back to myself and Courtney's studying me. He's still here, too.

"Between Tavia and me, it's too messy to pick a blameless victim," I say, looking back at the little girl being doxed on Knights of Naema. "But it isn't between Tavia and me anymore. These are pictures of people who have nothing to do with this; they're not siren or Eloko."

But they still belong to us.

That one's all Ancestors.

"What are they even gonna do with this information?"

As soon as the words are out of my mouth, I know I can't just wait and see. This subforum is supposedly brand new, but the research clearly isn't. This might have always been the endgame. Maybe if I could've seen any of the private messages, or someone had explained how the ranks were going to work, I'd have seen this coming. Because there's more than one member posting, and they're encouraging people to add to the collection.

The artist is here, too. The user who made the time-lapse video of a portrait of me. The one who didn't know whether or not he agreed with trying to figure out my location. He's in the new subforum dedicated to exposing the location and personal information of women and girls who have decidedly *not* posted their own photos, complete with supposed clues as invitation.

"You don't have to have proof," Courtney reads aloud. *"If she fits the profile and you get a feeling, post her here."*

They're saying they'll take the recon from there. Which means at least the user who started the page is definitely Portland local. NaemasNobleman is from my town.

"I'd be on here," I say. "If they didn't know I was Eloko. If it wasn't Justice For Naema, they'd be coming for me, too."

"No doubt."

"I have to go back to Portland. I have to tell somebody."

"Yep."

I snap the laptop shut, and the room goes dark and quiet. For a moment. "Uhh." Courtney smacks his lips. "How I'm 'posed to find the door, Sheba."

Chapter XXIII

Tavia Philips is the last person I ever expected to call, and when Courtney and I land at PDX the following afternoon, hers is the first number I dial. And then I close the app without completing the call.

I start at least three different text messages, too, but can't get the tone right.

Attempt number one is like, *I still think you're a POS, first of all, but can you give me a call.*

The second attempt feels more reasonable, if only slightly: *If I could afford to waste any time at all, I would not be reaching out to you, please believe.*

Draft number three begins with *You're lucky I don't put my hands on people,* and at this point I just have to admit that a phone call could have been started and finished in the time I'd already spent typing and deleting. So while Courtney—pardon me, Precious Heart—coos over Mommy's belly as he drives her car home from the airport, I just do the deed, knot in my stomach, and a hot stone ready to turn to a stream of cusses in my throat at the sound of her voice.

"Hello?" She seriously must have answered on the first ring. Absolute monster. "Naema?"

"Yep," I say through a sigh, because breathing deep feels very necessary.

"Wow, hi," she says, like we haven't chatted in such a long time, versus We Never Chatted On The Phone But You Did Text

Me That One Time Because You Used Your Siren Call On A Cop. Oh, and We Haven't Seen Each Other Since You Made Your Sister Turn Me To Stone And Then Awakened Me So The Ancestors Might Still Need To Hold Me Back.

Somehow her "Wow, hi" just doesn't capture it all.

"Are you back?" she asks.

"What?"

"Are you back in Portland? I heard you were—on vacation."

"Right, this is not a social call."

Her voice disappears and a soft static fills the vacuum.

"I met an old woman before I left, I think she's the head of the network in Portland," which is a ridiculous thing to say because I know she is, "and I need to know how to get in touch with her."

"Oh," Tavia says, but she sounds hesitant.

"I know I'm not in the network anymore," and then I lower my voice, just in case Courtney and Mommy are only pretending to be caught up in conversation in the front seat. "This isn't about wanting to get back in. I just need to talk to her. Like, today."

"Something's wrong." It's not a question, and the delicate, overly polite tone she's been using so far tightens.

"Yes, Tavia," and I enunciate, "I'm on the phone with you. Something's wrong. Can you get in touch with her or not?"

"Yeah, I've got it. I'll call you back."

"You can just text—" And she's gone. "Fine."

Tavia Philips is the literal worst.

She doesn't text. She does not, in fact, call.

Instead, she *shows up at my house*. Which is where I immediately went because until I do what I came back to Portland to do, I don't want anyone else knowing I'm here. So when the doorbell rings, I let Courtney answer it. Which was apparently a bad idea. He doesn't come back for several minutes, and when I get tired of waiting with our show paused, I go to investigate.

What I find disgusts me.

Courtney is super casually leaning in the entry, one leg crossed in front of the other, one elbow holding his weight against the wall, his blond coif hydrated and coily, and his fade clean because he doesn't go eight days without a touch-up.

I don't immediately see Tavia because she's hidden behind him, but when I call his name, he jumps like he got caught, and there she is.

Tavia Philips. Or should I say mini–Camilla Fox. She's wearing a striking African print headwrap around her topknot, big statement earrings, and a simple white tank with knee-length jean shorts. She certainly *looks* like an influencer now, and the outfit *is* fire, but I can't help rolling my eyes.

"Naema," she says, and her hands go behind her back, her posture straightening.

"I thought you were gonna call."

"Can we talk?" she asks without missing a beat, and annoyed is an understatement.

"It looks like you're already doing that," I say, shifting my disapproving gaze to Courtney, who doesn't even have the good sense to look guilty. So much for familial loyalty, I guess.

"I didn't wanna be rude," my cousin says, but he's speaking in a disturbingly unfamiliar voice, sticky sweet like someone poured Uncle Deric's homemade barbeque sauce all over it. It's disgusting.

"Rude is answering the door at someone else's house and not announcing the guest before you invite them in."

"Dang, Sheba," he says, and I shoot him a look. "Sheba" is for family. And Tavia Philips is not family.

"I know you hate me," Tavia blurts out, and draws our attention. "And it makes complete sense. Obviously." She's wringing her hands together behind her back, which I know because she's also apparently wearing what sounds like a small army of bamboo bangles. The girl is thorough, I'll give her that. "I've wanted to talk to you ever since . . . I just didn't think I had the right to reach out to you, but then you called—"

"I'm gonna stop you," I say, and stretch my neck from one side to the other, before letting my head fall back so I can stare at the ceiling while I mutter, "I do not want to be having this conversation."

Tavia opens her mouth again, and I throw up my hand. Despite the fact that I'm not as averse to difficult conversations as I once was. I don't think it's gonna overwhelm me the way it did at the Ninja Warrior place, and I know sometimes they're necessary if I want to hear the Ancestors clearly. But that doesn't mean I have to put up with it with Tavia Philips.

"No, seriously," I tell her. "You're not gonna sweep in here and make this your story, Tavia. I know you think it always is, but this isn't your big apology scene. I mean I got to see your remorse played out against a thoughtful montage of emotional indie music in the movie, with the whole staring out at the Willamette and standing on bridges"—I exhale and roll my eyes—"which just felt very extra, and I sincerely hope you didn't really do that."

"I'm sorry, Naema."

"What did I just say—"

"I mean, about the movie, too. I can see how it might've been salt in the wound."

My eyes drift around the room. I don't have an answer for that, which is annoying.

"I didn't really get how much license they take with those things, and once the ink is dry, 'meaningful consideration' and 'consultation' are apparently really subjective phrases." She says it all like she's still upset about it, her gaze slipping to the side.

"Buyer's remorse?" I ask, eyebrow raised.

"Yeah," she says through a sigh. "You could say that. I mean, it's been really useful, I guess. It's not all bad. I liked everything about Effie."

"Yeah, well, that doesn't surprise me." I cross my arms and feel my shoulders relax a little. Courtney seems to notice, too, which is when I remember that he's here. "Don't flirt with my cousin, by the way," I say, and lead them into the living room.

"Naema, no one's gonna replace you in my heart," Courtney says as he drapes his long legs across the ottoman. Luckily my mom's gone to a doctor's appointment, because Precious Heart or not, he's wearing sneakers and despite the fact that his foot is actually dangling clear of the upholstery, Simone Bradshaw's superpower is sensing dirt that might not even be there.

"I'm not gonna dignify that," I say before turning to Tavia. "So what do you want? I mean other than apologizing for the way your movie made me basic and jealous, which I have a hard time believing they did without *any* input from you."

"The only input I had was asking that your character not be Eloko. Just. So people wouldn't assume—"

"Wait, *you* did that?" I run my tongue over my teeth while I smile and nod. "Leona Fowl is *foul*. She made it sound like that was her decision," I tell Courtney.

"You know Leona?" Tavia asks.

"Yeah, I've had the pleasure. She wants to make a movie with me." And then I see the confusion on Tavia's face. "Lemme guess. That doesn't add up with whatever she said about me during *your* movie."

Tavia frowns like she doesn't wanna say.

"Girl, please, now is not the time to act like you're above the drama."

"Fine, Naema, yeah. That's a surprise. I didn't think she was a fan."

"Oh, I can promise you she's not anymore," Courtney interjects, wagging one of his feet, and looking like a lazy prince sprawled across the furniture.

"But then it seems her loyalties depend on the current paycheck," I say, snorting. "You're really not gonna ask me what I mean, Tavia? We're still doing that squeaky-clean, meek-mouth thing?"

"I showed up to your house unannounced, and you won't let me apologize to you, and you haven't told me why you called in the first place, except to say it's not good, so no, I'm not gonna interrogate you. If you want to tell me, I've no doubt you will."

Courtney's eyes volley between us, and he has a stupid smirk on his face.

"I don't need you to apologize to me, Tavia, because I don't forgive you."

The words may as well smack her in the face. Which is honestly fine by me.

"That's not really a thing you can apologize for, in my very humble opinion. You can't snatch someone out of the world and pin them in stone and leave them there, *no*where, and then go all neo-soul and want to walk it back. As you profit from Awakening me. And things turned out pretty spectacular for me in at least one particular way, but you don't get the credit for that. Me thriving can't make you right. It just makes me a queen."

She nods like maybe it's not the first time she's considered that, which. Good. What we're not gonna do is start thanking our attackers for our personal growth.

"Plus, sure, I'm the mean girl. But she's your sister. Did you ask Effie to forgive you? For using her power without her consent?"

Tavia's eyes are low, though they occasionally flick over to Courtney. I'm sure she wishes there wasn't an audience for this, but I mean, if she thinks Courtney's gonna politely excuse himself and go to another room, el oh el.

"Yeah," she says almost too quietly to hear. "But that's not really a thing you can apologize for, either."

She surprises me again, and the room falls quiet for a moment.

"But you guys are fine, right? I mean. Wherever she is, there's still that mutual obsession, that folie à deux you two do so well."

"Yeah, we're still everything," Tavia nods, but she doesn't make eye contact. It's not that the change in her isn't obvious, it's just that I refuse to do the whole Maybe the Real Feud Was The Friends We Made Along The Way, Made for TV reconciliation.

Still. Whatever her equivalent of being knocked out of my bubble and Eat, Pray, Listen to the Ancestors-ing my way through what I can't believe has only been the last week, Tavia's nothing like the girl I went to school with. Let alone the girl at prom.

Which reminds me.

The calm, constant rush of Ancestor voices, or just presence at this point, has been swelling and dissipating ever since Courtney and I boarded the plane to PDX this morning. Now I feel it more concentrated, as though despite how long they've been in residence inside me, now they're closer. Bolstering me.

"I regret what I wore to junior prom," I say, and then clear my throat. "The collar."

When her eyes settle on me, mine flick away, but I force them back. I force myself to look at Tavia Philips, even when I can feel Courtney's intensity beside me. He's as bad as my mother. But as comforting as the Ancestors.

"I won't ask your forgiveness, 'cause that's too big an ask, too," I say. My hand wants to reach for my necklace, but I keep it in my lap. I don't let my eyes roll, even to break up the tension. "But I have to apologize."

"Thank you." Tavia's face doesn't look like it's gonna crumple into tears, and she isn't wearing that Woe Is Pretty Me expression I thought was an irreversible feature these past couple of years.

"I guess it's only fair that you get to apologize, too, so." Now I roll them, Courtney snorting softly.

"Good. Because I really am sorry, Naema," she says. "That's not the kind of power I want. It's not the kind of *person* I want to be. I've done a lot of thinking, about myself, and. If I'm gonna use my voice, how big a responsibility it is. I know you've had followers a lot longer than I have. I didn't know how intimidating it can be. The way loyalties can change, the way one article declares you a heroine and the next calls you dangerous. But I'm worried about me, too. I worry every time I open my mouth. Is it a good use of my platform, is it true, did I do enough research?"

"I think you guys have really different channels," Courtney mutters, and I hit him. "Where's the lie?"

"I wanted to do a video about your support in Portland," Tavia says, like it's the perfect segue. She even reaches out and then withdraws her hand.

"What support?" I ask her, and I want to cut my eyes at Courtney, warn him not to mention the Knights before she has a chance to tell us what she knows.

"The stickers that started popping up? I saw it for the first time today, before you called, actually."

"What stickers?" I roll my finger, trying to hurry her along.

"The JusticeForNaema stickers? I mean, I only saw one, but I doubt somebody made just one." She pulls out her phone and searches the hashtag. When she turns it toward me, there's a whole account devoted to it.

Someone's going around Portland taking pictures of what

are clearly brand-new stickers affixed to lampposts, sidewalks, and even windows. Not one of them has faded, or had their color bleed from rain or, I don't know, urine. Someone did this recently.

Someone.

In the last twenty-four hours.

Even the account is new. Fewer than fifty follows, and only following one account. One called Knights of Naema.

"This . . ." I don't know what to call her. But the Ancestors don't even have to confirm that it's Leona. "She's really not gonna stop."

I look from Courtney to Tavia, but they're both waiting—Courtney, for me to say what he's not at liberty to share, and Tavia, to hear what's going on.

"Did you get me a meeting with"—I almost say the network donna, before I remember that that's not really what she's called—"the old woman."

"Ms. Donna?"

"What." Shut up.

"Little old lady who heads the network? Ms. Donna."

"I am a wizard."

"Uh . . . what?" Courtney asks.

Tavia's looking at me like there's a sprite on my shoulder.

"What? Sorry, that was just really funny."

"Whyyyy—"

"Shut up," I tell Courtney. "Can I see her or not?"

"She'll see you," Tavia says with a nod.

"All right. You better come, too." And before she can act surprised or stutter like some charmingly incredulous pageant winner, I head to the car.

"I just wanna be clear that this is the car you drive." Courtney looks ridiculous in the passenger seat of my beautiful Fiat. "And just for clarification, when we get out, we're expected to like, juggle and stuff, right?"

"I love my baby coffee bean," I coo, stroking the steering wheel. It's been too long.

"Tavia, back me up," Courtney turns in his seat, making a show of it like there's barely enough room.

"Your cousin and I have a tenuous cease-fire going."

"Smart girl," I say.

"Otherwise I'd tell you my sister said it looks like a dehydrated turd."

My eyes shoot to Tavia in the rearview mirror. "Jealousy is really ugly."

"Effie's words."

"Vivid and accurate," Courtney concludes. "I'll allow it."

"I'll allow you both to take the bus," I reply, but unfortunately we're almost to the senior center where we're meeting Ms. Donna.

I get nervous as soon as I step out of the car, as though the asphalt parking lot and extensive network of accessibility ramps leading to the front and side doors should be intimidating. Or as though the plethora of elderly who frequent the place—and if the signage beside the double doors is any indication, are preparing for a talent show—is something to fear.

Ridiculous or not, by the time we're inside, and an overly sweet smell mixes with what I can only imagine are overcooked green beans past their expiration, there are butterflies in my stomach. Or I'm queasy because these smells really do not complement. It's awful. I try not to scrunch my face, because there's a smattering of old folks sitting at tables throughout the room, or milling around near the kitchen entrance. I hope someone throws those green beans out.

Good gawd.

"This way," Tavia says as though she doesn't have a sense of smell, and leads us through the open space toward a hallway.

"You're holding your breath, right?" Courtney says to me quietly.

"I am near death right now," I say, which isn't good, because we have to choke back laughter.

"If you ever go to Aunt Toni's house for dinner, eat first. Everything she puts on the table smells like this."

I snort so loud Tavia glances back at us.

Her face still irks.

There's a light, airy kind of music coming down the hallway, and when Tavia turns into one of the small rooms with an open door, there sits Ms. Donna. She's got a music stand, and is playing a flute, her lips almost pursed, her breath escaping through the slightest part. Her hands look too delicate even for the slight instrument, but the sound is whimsical and lovely.

"Look at all these visitors," she says, with a smile, when she's finished whatever melody she was playing.

"That was beautiful, Ms. Donna," Tavia tells her.

"Thank you, baby." Ms. Donna says it like she already knows. "Practice every day, and you stay sharp. You can't get lazy."

The three of us nod like we'll take up the flute immediately after leaving today.

"You wanted to see me?" The woman's eyes fall on me, and there's nothing frail or fragile about her gaze. I remember it, and the way she said what she meant and meant what she said. And the way she still cared that I was okay.

"Can I close this door?" I ask, and the others sit. "Thank you for letting me come."

"I knew it had to be important, for you to ask. You don't seem the type to beg for second chances."

"It is. Important." I try not to look at Tavia, and gesture for Courtney to give me the folder he's got in his backpack. "I found out there's a group of people who think they're on my side. They started a site on the internet, after LOVE—our Eloko app—got revamped."

"Justice for Naema?"

"Just—" I motion for Tavia to hold on, because I don't want to get turned around in front of Ms. Donna. "Yes. I'll get to that."

Ms. Donna doesn't roll her finger in the air or hurry me along, she just keeps her gaze steady. It feels the way the Ancestors sound. Like confidence. Trust.

"I'm embarrassed that I didn't immediately get that something was wrong with them. But it turns out their defensiveness about me isn't so much *for* me, as it is against . . . us." I look at Tavia, which didn't used to be hard, but it was never a pastime. "It's just an excuse to hate Tavia. And sirens. Or anyone who could be a siren. And they've started accusing people. In Portland."

I open the folder with the pictures Courtney printed, and hand them to Ms. Donna.

"They're doxing women, and girls. Claiming they're sirens."

"What does that mean, doxing?" Ms. Donna asks, as she slowly goes through the pictures.

"It means they're sharing personal information," Courtney answers. "Like home and work addresses and phone numbers. Things people can use to contact or watch them. Or worse."

"They're claiming more sirens are coming to Portland, because of Tavia. And that I'm at risk. That sirens are out to get me, and that they have to protect me."

"And you don't know these people?" Ms. Donna asks, her voice as steady as before, without a waver or break. Whatever I expected her response to be, total calm wasn't it, I guess. It's almost depressing, how prepared she seems to hear something this grotesque. Like it isn't the first time, or like she's been expecting it. Like she always has to expect it.

"I don't. I wouldn't have known the site existed, but they posted a link to it on my LOVE account."

"So these girls are in their sights," the old woman says. She sighs then, and shakes her head.

"I know you can't tell me if they really are sirens. I don't think it matters. I just thought you needed to know."

"I'll let the network know," she begins, "and we'll watch out for them, whether they are or not. Doesn't matter."

"They're blaming Tavia for what happened to me," I tell her. "That's what Justice for Naema means. And I'm afraid there's a woman, another Eloko, making it worse."

"Why?"

"Because I told her what happened. She knows Tavia and I"—I look at Tavia—"don't get along. That's all I was trying to say. It was just supposed to be about us. But that's not the story she wants to tell. She didn't start the forum, but. She's using it, so people will think sirens have it out for Eloko, period." When Ms.

Donna's eyes meet mine, I hurriedly say, "I'm not gonna work with her. But. She's trying to break the story anyway, and I'm worried about who might get hurt because of it."

The old woman doesn't say anything for what feels like an eternity, and I remember choir competitions. Standing in front of a panel of judges when I've just performed a solo and I'm waiting to see how I ranked.

"I think they're building ranks," I blurt out, when I remember. "Like they're giving each other points or credit for the things they do. I know that sounds ridiculous, but. They have an incentive to one-up each other. That's what's got me worried."

"That tracks," Tavia answers, and now it's her giving a muted, knowing response to something terrible. Like she's learned a lot in this past year, too. "It's called 'gamification,' and believe me, I've had to get familiar. You can radicalize young white guys online pretty easily, as long as you make what you're asking them to do sound like a video game."

Courtney cusses under his breath, and then his eyes leap to Ms. Donna, apologetically. She doesn't seem offended, just serious.

"I see you girls, and I know how different you are," Ms. Donna says. "I know you're two individuals with your own personalities and ideas and thoughts, and I know that sometimes opposites don't attract." Her dark eyes are still so bright, and when she trains them on me, I can't help but listen. "But they don't see you. They don't see two high school girls with hormones and emotions and tiffs. They don't see a personal disagreement between you two because what's looking at you is an institution that's got designs on all of us."

I'm the only one standing, and it feels like the whole world can see me shifting my weight from one foot to the other. In her seat, Tavia's hands are clamped together in her lap, her bamboo bangles clicking against one another, so I know she feels as foolish as I do.

"You said this lady's an Eloko, too? The one stirring the pot?"

"Yes, ma'am. She's a movie producer named Leona Fowl."

"She doesn't care what the Ancestors have to say, I guess," Ms. Donna says, and folds her arms across her lap, her silver flute between them.

"I don't think everyone hears them," I tell her. "Portland makes it hard to hear them, and I'm guessing it's pretty similar where she's from. If we surround ourselves with too many outside voices, we don't have room for the ones inside."

I don't know why I look at Courtney. Maybe because I'm thinking of Great-Gram Lorraine and what she told me, that Eloko power isn't in speaking; we're supposed to listen. Anyway, my cousin smiles.

"I'm not an Eloko; I'm not a siren, either," Ms. Donna says. "But I've lived long enough to know something about both, about all of us, I guess. Your gifts aren't for you. A voice isn't power so you can keep it to yourself. And you aren't born with wisdom so you can be popular. We had oracles once, too, but they're gone now. Maybe because people stopped believing them, and maybe because they stopped telling." Her fingers move along the line of her flute, and she smiles a little, but she doesn't get lost. She looks back at me, and then at Tavia, and at Courtney, too. "Listen to the Ancestors and use your voice because you have the privilege of them—but also so the next generation does, too. Being an individual shouldn't mean you're not part of something. I know you know that."

I can only nod, but the Ancestors swirl up like a cyclone that lifts the uneasy knots in my stomach and untangles them inside my chest. I do know. Because they know. I didn't have words of my own, but I shielded Tavia because it didn't matter that I didn't adore her as a person. I still don't; I just wish I hadn't made genuinely disliking her the most important thing.

"You don't have to get along." Ms. Donna looks between Tavia and me. "But you have to be smart. And I know you can be. Because it sounds like the real trouble's coming from this lady. I'll get the network together on keeping these girls safe and letting their families know, but if somebody starts a national panic, we're all in trouble. You hear me?"

The wind swells inside me, and Tavia, Courtney, and I answer at once.

"Yes, ma'am."

Chapter XXIV

Katu News Segment

REPORTER (on scene, intersection of W Burnside & SW 3rd Street): Stickers on light posts and buildings and newspaper boxes are nothing new in Portland, but a new crop has appeared seemingly overnight—and a message that shouldn't be troubling is proving alarming to some.

Montage of sticker footage in the surrounding area.

ANONYMOUS LOCAL RESIDENT (voiceover): I think the issue is that it's a hashtag. That means there's more online, right?

REPORTER: The stickers read: Justice4Naema, and they seem to be in response to a recent movie depicting the Awakening, when local siren Tavia Philips released many Portlanders from a gorgon curse that had trapped them in stone. The stickers appear to reference local Eloko teen Naema Bradshaw. A recent Beckett High graduate, she livestreamed the terrifying Stoning episode that took place at last year's junior prom, before herself being Stoned.

Footage of internet search for #Justice4Naema and resulting hits.

REPORTER (voiceover): When the hashtag is typed into a search engine, social media accounts, blog posts, and even online forums appear in the results. Many of these accounts allege that Bradshaw's encounter was an intentional attack. Some even go so far as to blame Tavia Philips, a known participant in the event, and also the siren who later undid the curse.

REPORTER (on scene): Most people seem satisfied to ignore the smattering of stickers, including the newest which read ElokoFirst. There doesn't appear to be anything malicious in the message, particularly not in a town known for its Eloko adoration. At least a few residents, however, say it's unsavory, with University of Portland professor Heather Vesper-Holmes among them.

Brief footage of University of Portland campus, students milling. Footage of Professor Vesper-Holmes, at her office desk, working.

REPORTER (voiceover): Professor Vesper-Holmes has spent the past year investigating and compiling known recorded history of Eloko, particularly in Portland. Professor Vesper-Holmes maintains that her work has drawn criticism for asking what she calls "difficult questions about Portland's elite."

VESPER-HOLMES: Eloko are beloved, there's no shortage of evidence to support that. But I had to go back decades and eventually broaden my scope beyond the city before I came into contact with Eloko who showcased what we would consider traditionally magical attributes.

The mythos surrounding Ancestral Wisdom is true. Eloko were known to access and commune with the Ancestors, an entity that seems to be both personal to the specific Eloko's family, as well as universal, in that it operates similarly across cultures and continents. It even seems possible for the Ancestors to link Eloko to each other in a sort of network, although I haven't been able to find a present-day Eloko who experiences this.

REPORTER (voiceover): Professor Vesper-Holmes's study recently lost university backing and, with it, necessary financial support. While a representative of the university suggests that the move comes after an underwhelming review of her findings thus far, the professor blames the lack of community and academy support.

VESPER-HOLMES: Despite what happened last year and questions arising about one Eloko in particular, I think it's obvious that nothing substantial is going to change about the social experience and situation of Eloko in Portland. And I keep having to remind people, that wasn't my goal.

REPORTER (voiceover): When asked what was, the professor seems unacademically convinced of her moral position.

VESPER-HOLMES: The truth. I wanted to know why Eloko enjoy such observable privilege in society, and whether there's a cost, to themselves or to anyone else. Because that's what privilege tends to require.

If I could summarize everything I've learned, not just from what I was studying, but from people's reaction to what I was studying, I would say: everyone can calm down. I believe Eloko are magic. They don't have a magic that can be wielded in the same way that others do, but they certainly have a magic that can be weaponized. That's what those stickers look like to me. But I think it would take an Eloko saying that same thing to convince anyone in this town.

Footage outside Professor Vesper-Holmes's closed office door.

Chapter XXV

NAEMA

I always knew I would have to be the bigger person. As if I'm not already a pantheon of grace and mercy, when the three of us leave the senior center and Tavia suggests we share this information with one other person, I not only acknowledge that she's right, I let her come along.

"You're the last person I'd expect to wanna enlist Officer Blake's help," I tell her, glancing in the rearview mirror. Tavia's looking to one side, and then, as though there's a sprite flitting around that only she can see, she quickly checks the other way.

'Kay. Somebody's nervous.

"Are you sure this is a good idea?" I ask, trading glances with Courtney.

"It wasn't in the movie because I didn't tell anyone . . . but he knew I was a siren," Tavia answers, nodding. "That time I asked for your help," she says, like it was just the once. Like because that's the only time she explicitly asked me, that it was the only time I helped her. And then she corrects herself. "The last time, I mean."

"Yeah, I know."

Her gaze leaps to meet mine in the mirror.

"Priam told me. Recently. Literally last week."

She composes herself, but the anxiety is dripping off her. If her Magical Black Girl getup is meant to have some sort of empowering quality, it needs recharging. Tavia looks like a regular teenager, worried she's gonna miss curfew or something. But I've got an idea in mind for how we're gonna shut Leona Fowl up, and it involves the new and empowered Tavia Philips. I need her confident and convincing. Which is the only reason I play nice.

"Whatever happened to your gargoyle friend?"

"The one from your livestream?" Courtney asks, super helpfully, and I keep my eyes forward, enlarging them where only he can see. Thankfully, Tavia just carries on.

"Gargy's good. We still fly some nights."

I accidentally hit the brake for a moment and we all jolt forward.

"Sorry," I mumble.

"I think I speak for everyone when I say we'd definitely like to hear more about how you get to fly around with a gargoyle named Gargy," Courtney says, turning in his seat, and having remarkably less trouble doing so than when he was implying I drive a clown car.

"It's not that great," Tavia says with a humble shrug.

"You're a very bad liar," he tells her. For my part, I'm just watching the road. Try to cheer someone up, feel bad for them because they don't have their own car, and then you find out they've got their own personal Stone Monster Sky Tour.

"Is he your boyfriend or Effie's?" I ask, through a sigh.

"Effie's. Definitely." She almost sneers at the back of my head, but pulls it down just as quickly as it starts. "He comes to get me so I can see her."

"So is she still . . ." Courtney starts to ask and then loses his nerve.

"A gorgon?" Tavia asks, her eyebrow cocked. But she seems amused, and anyway, she's not looking around nervously anymore. "Yeah, that's sorta for keeps, I think."

"And she isn't coming back?" I don't realize I'm gonna ask it until the words are already out. I read the license plate on the car in front of mine to keep from looking at my cousin or the girl I really never intended to talk to, let alone chauffeur around Portland. "I mean, to be with you. And like, for university."

She's watching me in the mirror, but I don't look at her and I don't look down. Whatever she thinks she's picking up on, I'm not interested. I asked what I asked; I'm trying to be civil, not best friends. This isn't the part where I confess some vulnerability so she'll see that underneath my tough exterior, I'm really soft and scared, and just like everyone else.

When she hasn't spoken, and Courtney can only make so many awkward expressions with his mouth, I finally look up at her reflection. I lift my eyebrows like a continuation of the conversation, like I'm waiting expectantly and, above all, innocently for her to answer my totally uncomplicated question.

"I don't think so," Tavia finally answers. "No, probably not. I'm happy she has somewhere else that's home."

I nod because I don't want somewhere else, but I get it.

We arrive at the Blake house, and I pull into the circular driveway.

"I'll be right there," I say, expecting the two of them to get out of the car ahead of me. Which is just ridiculous on my part because while I'm sure I'm not some great comfort to Tavia, there is no way she's going up to Priam's door without me. So after Courtney opens the passenger door and realizes he's the only one who did, he slowly pulls it closed, but not hard enough for it to latch. Whatever smooth he had, Tavia and I are seriously dampening it.

I put the phone on Speaker since everybody's staying, and when Leona answers, she sounds as surprised as Tavia did. Folks are just not ready for the gift of my attention. I get it.

"Naema, I'm so glad you ca—"

"I know you're in Portland." All the eyes in the car exchange looks, and wait for her to deny it. But despite all of Leona's foolishment, she's no fool. She'll assume I've seen her, if I'm accusing her of being in town, or that someone I know has. So I know what she's going to ask next.

"Are you?" Even with her rasp, which is still dope by the way, she manages to make the question sound light and innocent, like we weren't just together at a posh restaurant in a different state yesterday. If she's smart, she'll think about why she's here, and then wonder what equally compelling reason I could possibly have to come to the same place in the same time frame. And I know she's smart.

"Let's get lunch. The BV on MLK in two hours."

"The—"

"Burgerville." And I hang up, like it's a TV show and people don't use salutations, or like it's a movie and I've just arranged The Drop. Anyway, I expect my companions to comment on how badass I sounded, and am immediately disappointed.

"Yeah, 'cause we've been here for hours and ain't nobody fed me yet," Courtney says. "Y'all ain't got no hospitality up north, I know that."

"You haven't eaten?" Tavia asks, like he's gonna keel over and die.

"He's fine, can we get out of the car?" I ask and just do it, walking up to Priam's Craftsman bungalow, and then bypassing the front door for another door on the long porch. It's almost hidden, since there's an unexpected corner that you don't notice on approach. I guess Tavia didn't come here often, or she'd know the Blakes never lock this and no one ever uses the front door.

I knock and open the door at the same time.

"Hello?" When I don't feel anyone behind me, I turn and find that Tavia and Courtney are still on the porch. When I motion them into the house, neither moves.

"You said an Officer Blake lives here?" Courtney asks, both hands in his pockets like he refuses to touch anything. If he could hover above the porch, he would. "Yeah, I'm good. Imma hold down the porch. Out here."

Tavia doesn't say anything, but she's got her lips pulled into her mouth and her hands are behind her back again.

"I'm not the kinda Black that goes into police officers' houses unannounced," Courtney continues.

"Shut up," I say, and roll my eyes. "It's my boyfriend's house."

"Ex-boyfriend," he says, and I cock my eyebrow at him just as Tavia's eyes get momentarily wide and then look away.

"See, this is why I don't tell you anything." When I turn around, Priam's jogging down the stairs across the room from the nook through which I'm *try*ing to get everyone to enter.

He says my name under his breath, and pauses on the bottom step like I'm an apparition, which is fair. If I were back on LOVE,

I totally would've captured this Surprising My Boyfriend Who Doesn't Know I'm Coming To Town moment because those videos do serious numbers.

"Hiya," I say, and wave, grateful that the other two are still behind me and can't see the completely idiotic smile I'm wearing. He looks so disbelieving, like seeing me is too amazing a prospect to be real.

One minute he's across the room and the next, he's almost to me. Too greedy to make it all the way there, he grabs my arm and pulls me into a kiss, one hand immediately holding my cheek.

"You're home," he says when he releases my lips, our foreheads still resting against each other's.

"Is your dad?" I ask, which, admittedly, is a weird way to reply.

"What?"

Before I can explain, Courtney finally comes inside.

"Hey, Priam, what's up, man?"

"Hey, Courtney, that's so cool you came up—"

"Is this the kitchen?" Courtney slaps hands but never stops walking in the direction he's guessed houses the food. "This way?"

"Yeah, that's—"

"Oh, now you're fine to come inside."

"Yes, Naema, now that a legal resident of the home is present and aware of my entry, I'm fine to come inside, geez." He's in the other room before he finishes, and Priam looks back at me for an explanation.

"We just came for the day. Like you did." I poke his stomach through the striped T-shirt he's wearing.

"So you do miss me." He wraps his arms around me and pulls me tight before dropping his nose into my hair and breathing deep.

"Yes, *and* that's not why we're here, but I do absolutely miss you." My conjunction does not have the desired effect and he pulls back, quizzically.

Which is when there's another, timid knock on the already open side door. And I'm about to tell him who else is here, but when I open my mouth, he's already looking around me, and I can tell precisely when he sees her. I don't know if there's a hitch in his breath or whether I'm imagining it because I'm holding mine.

"I'm lost," he says, and looks back at me for a moment.

"Tavia, come in already, gawd." I really did not think it would be this awkward for anybody but me, and then I remember that I finally know what happened between them. "Since we're doing apologies now, Priam do you wanna apologize to Tavia for biting her and then dumping her like it was her fault?"

"And maybe for saying you wish you'd never met me," she offers.

I look back at Priam with a half grimace, half cringe.

"Yipes. Okay, I didn't know you told *her* that. I thought you were supposed to be the nice one."

"This is a really interesting visit, getting ganged up on in my own house." But when no one caves to his defensive pity party, Priam nods. "And yes. I do want to apologize. That had nothing to do with you, Tavia. I just didn't want being Eloko to suddenly change, which I get was irrational since no one cared about our lore until now. I also didn't know you were a siren at the time. So I get it if you can't forgive me."

"I pretty much forgave you immediately," she says, gently. "I'm living what you were scared of."

Okay, that was a boss line, I'll give it to her.

"Cool, that was my good deed for the day," I say, turning back to Priam with steepled fingers. "For real this time: Is your father home?"

Officer Blake takes a full twenty minutes to arrive, and that time passes much more enjoyably when the four of us just incidentally pair off, and Priam and I escape to his room, while Courtney and Tavia do whatever I interrupted at my house. I just assume.

"You're really not gonna text Jamie?" Priam asks once we're cuddling on his cushioned window seat.

"I am, Prism—"

"Oh, I like that one."

"I'm just not gonna text her until I can afford to be pounced on. Don't insinuate that I don't miss my friends."

"I'm insinuating nothing," he says, and draws his fingers through my hair as I lay against his chest. "You've just been extremely missed, and as much as I'd like to keep you to myself, it doesn't feel fair."

"You mean, you got in a lot of trouble when you got back from visiting me, and you're trying to avoid that happening again."

"That's basically what I said."

"Right," I say, but I'm smiling. The sunlight is falling across our legs, and there are little particles in the rays, falling or floating in slow motion. I can feel Priam's chest rising and falling behind me, and it's making my breaths fall into sync with his. He keeps smelling my hair, and it's just very good to be home. Even if it is already a little louder, but I don't have a second world oasis like Effie does, so I'm going to have to learn to balance the cacophony of my city and the voices of my Ancestors.

"And you're not gonna tell me why you need to see my dad?"

"Ugh." I let my head fall to the side, and pull his arms around me. "It'll be bad enough repeating it a second time, don't make me do it three times."

"Who'd you tell?" he asks, and I hesitate. I know he knows about the network already, but I'm almost hoping he's forgotten. "Ny?"

"Remember how I said normal was gonna be different now?" I ask, lacing my fingers through his.

"Yeah. If that still stands, this is really confusing, Naema," he says.

"Okay, so obviously, the different isn't gonna be us, because clearly that's not what I want."

"Okay." He breathes. "So what then? Are you and Tavia gonna be friends now or something? Because that's really confusing, too. Showing up with her when the last thing you asked me was whether I have a problem with you exposing her to the world."

"I could just tell you if you'd shut up for a minute." I close my eyes, and bite my lip. "Sorry."

"Please tell me *that*'s not the new normal."

"What."

"You and this apology tour," he snarks.

"Wow," I say through a laugh. "And you didn't even hear the big one."

"I'm assuming yours was to Tavia, too?"

For some reason I freeze up. Like my knowing about my regret, confessing it to the Ancestors and Courtney, is bad enough, but thinking that maybe Priam knows that what I did requires apology will be the embarrassment that breaks the camel's back.

"Yeah," I finally say.

"Does she at least know the collar wasn't real?" he asks, and I hesitate.

"I don't think that matters."

"I mean. It kinda does, if she still thinks you got it from me or my dad," he says. "Seems like you should tell her my dad didn't actually give you one. If you're going for New and Improved Naema."

There's a swell in my abdomen, and I already know what it is. They're present but calm most of the time, but the Ancestor chorus swirls around until I can hear them.

I shift in Priam's arms.

"I'm a work in progress," I tell them all. "And anyway, that wasn't my point. My point was that the new normal isn't about Tavia. It's that I'm not Portland's idea of Eloko anymore. I don't wanna be."

This time it's Priam who freezes up. "What does that mean?"

Part of me is glad we're not facing each other. It wouldn't change what I'm saying, but I'm pretty sure I would've just seen my Eloko boyfriend wince.

"Don't sound so hurt. We both know I'm not what Portland wants in an Eloko anyway. Shallow, Prom Queen, Influencer types—"

"Naema, you're literally all of those things."

"What I'm saying," I sing, because it sounds sweeter that way. "Is that those things aren't even what Eloko *are,* Priam, they're things we *get* because we're Eloko."

"You sound like that professor," he says. Which means he's been paying attention. Not like we have a choice when all we've ever known is Portland; the city and its celebrity are deafening—or at least they used to be.

"Anyway," I say. "It's ridiculous, and it's fake af. If we're gonna be envied, shouldn't it be for what we actually are?"

"We're Eloko," he says, exasperated.

"Right, and what does that mean? We have a melody, and we're charming, and we get good grades without trying." I know that what I'm saying sounds like enough because it was, all my life. "And we chalk it up to Ancestral Wisdom, but we don't actually *hear* the Ancestors?"

"Maybe that's not a real thing," he says, and I feel him shrug behind me.

"It's a real thing," I say. "And it's . . ."

I don't have the words.

It's stabilizing. It's invigorating. It's humbling. It's comforting.

It's healing.

"It's everything," I say, quietly. "It's transforming."

"So, what, are you gonna be a different person now?"

"If anything, Priam, I'm more myself—"

"And if I can't hear the Ancestors, am I not Eloko then?"

Now I turn on the window seat and he has to move one leg, put one foot on the ground to make room.

"Am I not Eloko enough?"

"Hey." I stop him. "That's not what this is about. I wouldn't do that. I know what it's like for people to treat you like you're doing your identity wrong, okay?" I smooth his brow with my finger, and kiss him. "I'm just saying, we've been missing something we didn't even know exists. And when I heard it, it wasn't just about one piece of me. It was about all of me." I think of the forum, and have to fight not to grimace. "I'm never gonna be okay with people trying to erase the rest of who I am," I tell him. "Never again."

"That's not too much to ask," he answers, and I smile.

"I know," and I kiss his nose. Below Priam's bedroom window, his dad's patrol car pulls behind my Fiat in the drive, and I part the blinds to watch him. "Fuggin' finally."

And then I remember that if Officer Blake gets inside before we get downstairs, Courtney's gonna have a heart attack, and I hurry Priam down to the living room. Which means when we meet his dad in the nook, it absolutely looks like we were fooling around. Not that his dad would ever say anything to us about it.

"Hey, Priam, what's up, buddy." Officer Blake is reading his phone and hasn't looked up. "I've got about an hour and then—Naema!"

I shove Priam out of the way and smile.

"When did you get back?" He gives me one of his Dad Side Hugs. "Thank God, too, because this kid was killing me with the moping and the broken heart."

I laugh, and we both look back at Priam, who would never survive my family given how red his face has gotten already. And we both know his dad's not saying anything that isn't true.

"I'm just visiting. And I brought some people with me," I tell him, and with a look of intrigue, he follows me into his own kitchen, where Courtney and Tavia immediately jolt upright from their previously relaxed position eating grapes at the farm-style table with chairs on one side and a bench on the other.

"This feels like a really weird surprise party," Officer Blake mutters, and when I turn to face him, he's looking just at Tavia. "Ms. Philips. Is it safe to assume you kids had Priam call me home because something's wrong?" He nods along with me. "Is this something we should do at the station? If you need help—"

"We need *your* help," Tavia blurts. "Because we already know we can trust you."

"I'm not the only police officer you can trust, Tavia." And I have to assume everybody but Priam rolls their eyes with me.

"Okay, we don't need to have a whole discussion about the obvious," I say, making the universal and universally annoying gesture for Let's All Calm Down with my hands, fingers splayed. "But this involves unsavory white guys, and we all know the Portland PD has a habit of helping them avoid arrest, so. Yeah, we just need to talk to you."

"Hi, I'm Courtney, by the way." Everyone looks at my knucklehead cousin. "It just feels like everybody knows everybody. And I ate some of your grapes, I hope that's cool."

"Do you have an office?" I ask Priam's dad without waiting for anyone to respond to Courtney. "And a laptop I can use?"

There's nothing new on the Knights of Naema forum, or it's subforums, and what's terrifying, I've already seen. When I pull up the site, and ignore both Priam and Tavia's not exactly subtle expressions of WTFery, it's just the same brand of obsession. Sharing photos I've shared somewhere before. Polling on topics they can't possibly verify. Fan fiction.

Shields, and points.

The only difference is that now it makes my stomach hurt. It's not the Ancestors or their wind, either. It's just a combination of anger and disgust.

I don't check in on anyone's reactions until after I've scrolled through the Secret Sirens page. My stomach is in anxious knots hoping there aren't any new women or girls listed, and there aren't. But it doesn't make me feel any better.

When I turn to look at Officer Blake, his face is blank. Priam looks like he wishes he hadn't heard it all, but his dad looks like he already has.

"This isn't news to you," I say.

"I was debating whether or not I should let you know this website exists, but then you left town, and I thought I'd wait at least until you came back. I know how hard this past year has been for you."

I don't look at Tavia, but I'm sure that doesn't make it any easier for her to be in the room right now. She is, after all, the reason this past year has been the worst. Even with how quickly I tried to move between posts and pages, it's really unlikely she hasn't noticed the siren bashing, and mentions of taking action.

"We were hoping you could find out who these people are, because at least some of them are local." I stop. "You know that, too."

"Listen," he says through a deep breath, and now it's his turn to do the whole Let's All Of Us Hold Our Horses gesture. "It's probably time I talk to your parents, both of you," he looks between

Tavia and me, "and let them know about this, and the folks I've identified. Just as a courtesy, not because I think there's anything actionable going on."

"Should we wait? Would you?" I ask. "If it was your kid being discussed on the internet by a group of grown men? Are there not enough examples of these exact circumstances turning very bad?"

"This is where white domestic terrorists are being radicalized," Tavia says, and I think of the Knight artist, and how quickly his mind was changed. And how he now has a bronze shield in the corner of his avatar. "If it was anybody else gathering, and curating lists, and talking about vigilante justice, SWAT teams would've busted down their doors, and we all know it. The fact that you already knew isn't heartening, not to me."

Everybody stops, and it feels like we're all waiting for something, but I don't know exactly what.

"Dad," Priam says, and it's a complete sentence. "If Tavia or Naema see these guys on the street, they don't have a right to know they're there?"

Officer Blake studies his son for a few moments, but it's clear he's doing more than that. If I'm being totally honest, I don't understand what the dilemma is. Maybe Priam's dad doesn't know the network exists, but I think everyone who *wants* to know knows that police don't protect and serve everybody. That they're as likely to be hiding behind this forum and the Knight shields as their own. Officer Blake must know some of us survive by looking out for ourselves, and one another. And if the police force isn't gonna do anything with the information anyway, why wouldn't he give it to us?

"You're gonna tell our parents, right?" I ask. "Because clearly it's serious enough for that."

"Yes, Naema. I'm gonna tell your parents."

"And you know they're gonna tell us, for our own safety, 'cause it doesn't matter that I'm still a minor, people like this have proven they'll go after us anyway, yes? So can we skip the part where the kids are kept unnecessarily in the dark by the people who are supposed to help them? It doesn't make us feel innocent, it just wastes time."

Officer Blake motions for me to roll his chair back so he can open the top drawer of his desk. "I am the adult here, I just wanna make that clear."

"We know, Dad." Priam pats him on the back for good measure. "You're totally in charge."

"You can always say I made you do it," Tavia says, arms crossed over her chest, and Officer Blake immediately stops and looks over his shoulder at her. "Too soon?"

"My partner still thinks that was his idea, you know. Not giving you a ticket."

"I didn't deserve one, as I recall."

"Hi, was there something in the drawer you wanted to show us?" I ask, impatiently, just as Courtney mutters:

"I feel real unspectacular right now."

"Don't worry about it," Priam says, nudging him with his elbow. "Apparently I haven't been Eloko-ing right."

I cannot, and I refuse.

Thankfully, Officer Blake has retrieved the three thin files and set them on the desk in front of me. When I glance up at him, he looks over my head and nods like he's still not sure about this. I'm not waiting for him to reconsider, so when he moves out of the way and the others gather around me, I flip one open.

The first two don't yield much but a photograph in each and a lot of boring paperwork. I make mental notes of the men, just in case I ever see them around town, and I commit their names to memory. From Officer Blake's notes, one of them is the Knights of Naema user who posted the pictures of me while I was Stoned, and the other is the one who assured someone that there's a presence in Portland, ready and willing to defend me against a horde of imaginary siren warriors. To absolutely no one's surprise, he's a complete poseur, with zero ties even to the several ugly collectives in and around Oregon. It doesn't mean he's harmless, just that for now it's probably bluster.

I don't want to look at either any longer than I need to, but I also don't want to see the picture of Stone Naema Officer Blake's included. I slide it out of the paper clip and turn it over before sliding it back into place and handing off the file to whoever else wants a look.

I'm expecting the same nauseating but manageable experience with the last file.

There's a picture again, and a name, and neither of them is familiar. Guy #3 looks like another run-of-the-mill white guy. Beard. Moustache. Plaid button-down and a tie. If anything, he's younger than the first two, and looks like an elementary-school teacher.

Because he is.

His occupation is listed, and the school. And I've seen it before.

Before I look at the associated username, I already know who he is.

It's the radicalizer, the Southwest corrector. The Secret Sirens forum starter.

NaemasNobleman.

The Ancestors don't need to speak. I already know. I see the little girl, hanging upside down, braids and bobbles dangling below her smiling face.

I look at Courtney, and even though I don't say a word, he understands.

That's how he knew. That's how he knew she won the spelling bee, and that's how he got the photos he posted of one of the students at his school.

I'm not sick to my stomach now. I'm pissed. I want to rage-scream at the top of my lungs, tear his picture to shreds, show up in *his* Safe Spaces and prey on *him*—

"Thanks, Officer Blake," I say, slapping the file shut and standing. He's walked out of the office and back into the kitchen like he's trying to maintain some sort of plausible deniability. Now he comes back toward me wearing a still-conflicted expression, so I decide to really test my acting chops and try to put him at ease. "It makes me feel better putting faces to the usernames. So I know to go the other way if they ever get too close."

It's funny because it's a lie. I'm not going to wait for Plaid Shirt to get close to me, because he's already too close to someone else, and she probably thinks she can trust him.

He's the most average-looking dude—but aren't they always? He's average height, master's-level education, no scars, no tattoos, no record, no bad credit. Isn't it funny how the narrative is always that no one would ever have guessed, when really, statistically, we all should've? He Doesn't Look Like A Bad Guy only makes sense if you're a complete Fox News zombie, parroting back whatever you're told. He doesn't look like the guys we're *told* are bad. He doesn't look like the people we're *supposed* to mistrust.

He looks exactly like a bad guy. And I'm gonna let him know he's not anonymous anymore.

XXVI

LOVE Press Release—Immediate Publication

Eloko Verified has always been about magic and love. Our genesis was in identifying and sharing an adoration for Eloko that feels uniquely Portlandian. We are therefore troubled by the recent spamming of profiles and posts with the #ElokoFirst hashtag, and are disallowing the use of this hashtag going forward.

While it seems very straightforward to us, we are aware this will seem confusing and potentially off-brand. We want to assure our wonderful community that this could not be further from the truth. We feel a responsibility to communities who have not experienced the unfettered admiration that Eloko have, and have been intentional about listening to groups outside our own in deciding how best to move forward. The work of Professor Heather Vesper-Holmes at the University of Portland has been illuminating, and history is very clear on the damage and danger that can arise when any privileged demographic is intentionally framed as lacking it, or requiring protections already inherent to their experience.

We are asking our fellow members to stand with us against any radicalization that would mar the love we have for Eloko, and to broaden the scope of our community as we seek to learn more about others with magic of their own.

Effective immediately, *Eloko Verified* will be *Magic Verified*. We hope our Eloko influencers will not only remain, but also welcome others as we grow together, in love.

Chapter XXVII

NAEMA

School's out for summer. Obviously. But apparently teachers still go there during the break? The things you learn when you're hunting down a decorated Knight—excuse me, *Noble*man—who takes pictures of little girls who threaten him by out-spelling all her white schoolmates.

The network told us where to find him.

As in the siren-shielding network I used to be part of. It was Tavia who snapped a picture of his picture from Officer Blake's file and texted it with his name and occupation to everyone who still gets those texts—but when the reply came in, it came to my phone, too.

When it vibrated, I looked at my phone and then—involuntarily!—shot a glance at Tavia, even though I sincerely hope I recovered before she noticed.

Anyway.

It hadn't taken long to find someone who lives near the school, and knows teachers had already started showing back up. Someone even did a preliminary drive-by and verified his car and room.

When we arrive, Plaid Shirt is apparently still putting his classroom together, and knowing he teaches fourth grade makes me want to burn things. I consider it. His car is parked on a side street closer to his classroom door than the faculty parking lot would've been, and there's no reason I couldn't at least bust out a few windows, but I won't. Not because I have a ton of respect for his personal possessions. Just because I think talking to him will make him a lot more anxious, and I don't feel like giving him cause for a police report that would really highlight the way I might be Eloko, but there's still a Right Phenotype and he's rocking it. Better not to test the past year's damage.

Which is also why I've assembled the Eloko, with whom I'm posted up across the street from Plaid Shirt's car, parked under an Oregon white oak, basking in the shade.

"Your channel is so dope, Tavia," Jamie's saying, inching closer every time Tavia casually steps slightly away. "I loved that episode about the history of siren calls."

"Thanks," Tavia says, almost standing on Courtney's feet in her attempt to maintain some degree of personal space. For his part, my cousin doesn't scooch at all, like if he's patient she'll just end up in his arms. Turd.

"Have you learned any more since—"

"Nope." If that was supposed to end the conversation, it doesn't.

"But you still see your grandma in the water? You should ask her to teach you a new one, that's so cool."

"That's weird, sirens and Eloko both have an Ancestor thing," Priam says, and then, as though he didn't mean to say it out loud, "I mean, kind of."

"Yeah, but we just get their smarts, we can't actually talk to them," Gavin says from his seat on the roof of my car. He's here, but he's totally moping because when I called and told him and Jamie that I'm in town and that they needed to meet me at a random elementary school, I declined his offer to bring New Girlfriend.

"Well, actually," Priam starts, and I give him a Not Now glance. I'll have plenty of time to espouse the We Must Return To Our Roots And Forgo The Trappings Of Celebrity Culture If We Want To Hear The Ancestors doctrine after today's festivities. "How many of Tavia's videos have you watched, Jamie?"

Flawless segue.

Jamie's shoulders leap up to her ears, and she looks at each of us. We're definitely a clique from a high school movie, Gavin on the top of my car, Priam and I leaning against the hood, and Jamie, Tavia, and Courtney taking up the side. Which isn't difficult,

Fiats being diminutive and all. My point is that when Plaid Shirt finally comes out, he'll think he's walked onto a film set.

"I've seen all of them, I think, right?" she asks Tavia, like she should know. "But that's okay now, I thought!"

"You didn't just watch them today, Jamie," Gavin says, dropping his chin like he's chastising her. Which he's only doing in case *I'm* going to, which would supposedly be worse. Ever the nice guy. The nice, love-crazy guy with terrible but thankfully short-lived taste.

"Are you sure you wanna do this?" Priam asks me quietly while the bickering continues.

"You don't have to," I say.

"That's not what I said. I'm saying do you and Tavia really wanna meet this guy face to face? What if instead of ending this, it makes it worse for you two?"

"There's no end to this." I watch his brow buckle, and then shrug. "I mean, probably. We're both visible, and neither of us is gonna stop being visible, and new dudebros are being radicalized online every day . . ."

"So what's the difference? Why take the risk of antagonizing him?"

"The difference is these people are doing it in my name," I say. "That doesn't work for me. What, am I gonna be *less* brave than Tavia Philips? How dare you."

"This isn't funny, Ny." He pulls me closer.

"I'm not laughing. I'm just not gonna hide on the off chance that they disappear."

"I totally get that you're *the* Naema Bradshaw," Gavin chimes in because he's never not eavesdropping. "But I still say we should be entrapping this guy. Am I the only one who thinks it might be helpful for other people to see this?"

"So Officer Blake knows I came straight here?"

Jamie cringes.

"Exactly. I'm good. It's like you said, Gavin. I'm *the* Naema Bradshaw. We don't need everybody to see this, we just need this guy to see *us*."

"I'm just saying—"

"It's time to use your Eloko swagger for something other than hooking up with randos. After all: when they go low, we step on their necks."

"That's not how that saying goes."

And across the street, Plaid Shirt returns to his car for another box of whatever.

"It is now," I say, and wave until I get the man's attention.

At first he just squints at us, half waves in case he should know who we are, and why a group of really attractive teenagers is hanging out on a super-clean Fiat.

"Hey," I call, all jovial and misleadingly. And he figures out who I am.

"N-Naema?" he asks, and then his whole face lights up, and he starts across the street. "You're Naema, right?"

"That's me," I say, finger hooked around the necklace I put on for this occasion while I reach with my other hand so he has to come closer still.

"This is wild, do you live around here?" the moron asks, barely taking notice of the four other people with me while he first shakes my hand, and then holds it between his.

"I mean, yeah, I live in Portland." It's amazing how easily I still slide into my trademark charm and infectious smile, even while delicately retracting my hand.

"But near here? I teach here," he says, pointing back at the school. "I'm a teacher at this school."

Should I be impressed?

"That's so cool," I say, and then thrust my phone at him. "Can you take a picture for us?"

"Oh," he says, but it's less a word and more an exclamation of obedience. "Yeah, of course, whatever you say."

"Make sure you get all of us," I chirp, and the five of us snap into model mode, changing poses slightly a few times while Plaid Shirt captures them with my phone. "That's perfect."

I reach for the device and he makes another monosyllabic burp like the bumbling sack of pathetic that he is.

"You're good at that," I say, scrolling through the pics. "At taking photos of people, I mean."

"I'm like an amateur photographer—"

"I'd believe that. You have that amateur vibe." And then, while he's smiling strangely, like he's trying to make sense of what I've said, I add: "Nobleman. But you're not very smart, aren't teachers supposed to be smart?" I ask Tavia.

Which is when he sees her. I have to say, I love the way she waves like the motion is moving through one finger at a time.

"Yeah, how exactly would you have explained being that excited to see me, by the way?"

"You did seem real eager," Courtney quips from his very relaxed lean. I notice one of his arms dangles over Tavia's shoulder now.

"Right?" I ask. "So we've established you're a Knight," I list it off on my fingers, "and you're an amateur photographer, and you post pictures of little girls online because they're too smart and that's not fair."

"I don't know what you're talking about," he says, and Plaid Shirt finally finds his bearings and starts to cross the street toward his car.

"The police do," I call, and he glances over his shoulder. "And that producer lady who I'm guessing got in touch with you. Plus some other people." When he looks at me with concern, I shrug. "I mean, I wouldn't be surprised if it gets out. 'Schoolteacher Doxing Little Girls In His Own School' sounds like something that might capture a news cycle or two."

"Especially if it gets amplified on some really popular social media accounts," Tavia offers, strolling up behind me in the middle of the street.

"That's *going* to happen, by the way," I say. "These aren't hypotheticals."

"Why?" he asks, pushing his head forward in my direction like maybe the others won't hear him.

"Why am I going to make sure the media, the school, and various other interested parties know that you're trying to earn clout by terrorizing people?" I ask. "Is there some reason you thought I wouldn't?"

"You're—" he starts because he's really incredulous. Which

I refuse to take as a personal indictment. None of these losers asked if I wanted to be their Token, and the fantasy they've concocted has very little to do with me.

"Eloko?" I finish for him. "I am. So are they," and I gesture toward the others without specifying whom. "That's part of why this is gonna go so badly for you. The Knights aren't the only ones who can weaponize Eloko celebrity. We're why people are actually going to listen."

"You're an ungrateful bitch," he spits, his face instantaneously bloated and bloodred. As teens are wont to do, we ruin his moment of impotent anger with howling laughter, and then Tavia and I step into him.

"You know, Tavia, I'm shocked—*shocked!*—that a man who anonymously went after a little girl online and separates Black girls into Exceptions and Sirens thinks I owe him a debt of gratitude because he wants to terrorize everybody who looks like me. Aren't you?"

"No," she says through a low breath. "I'm just bored."

We turn back toward the others, but I twirl around for a moment and flash Plaid Shirt a killer smile. As soon as I see him again, I'm on the verge of nausea, and there's a ridiculously loud rush that sweeps up from my chest and all the way to my head.

I take an involuntary breath, but then I lift my chin. I don't want Plaid Shirt thinking his seething is having any impact.

I just want him to know I will.

"I wouldn't bother decorating that classroom, but"—and I shrug, ignoring the way my ears feel packed again—"who am I to tell you how to waste your time."

Plaid Shirt is still standing in the street not quite to his car when I snap a picture of him.

"We're not all amateurs," I tell him before we all pile into my Fiat and bid him a fond farewell, horn, music, soul-slicing teen laughter, and all.

That went exactly the way I planned it—but something's wrong.

The Ancestors bellow, they swirl inside my guts.

This isn't enough.

But I know that. I was never going to assume it was enough

to face Plaid Shirt down. That was for me, and the spin I'm planning, and sure, embarrassing dude is the cherry on top.

"Jamie, my love," I say, thrusting my phone over my shoulder to her in the back seat. "Pick the best one and post it?"

"I can't believe you made him take our picture first," Courtney says, and he and Gavin burst into laughter, which only makes Tavia more squished. My car is not made for six people and our arrangement is all kinds of illegal. I'm also sure it's the only reason Tavia's on my cousin's lap with her legs across the other two.

"Post it where?" Jamie asks, like she needs to hear me say it.

"LOVE, Jamie," I say, rolling my eyes and smiling like there's not a chilling cyclone inside of me. "Or Magic Verified, or whatever."

"Wait, Jamie knows your passwords?" Priam asks when she squees.

"Do you know how best friends work?" she snaps at him.

"Be nice," Gavin and I say together. Jamie waves us off and then her fingers return to my phone. She comes up with my best captions, I have to say. She's also my preferred photographer, lighting adjuster, videographer.

"Make up a good hashtag about my relaunch. And don't forget to tag Tavia," I say, because maybe now the Ancestors will understand what I'm doing and calm the hell down.

Only they don't.

Their voices spark now. They snap against me like a reflex hammer and I jump—which is like nothing I've ever felt. I don't know why, so I don't want my friends to know yet—but it's kind of scaring me.

There's still phase two of my plan, though, and my pulse is quickening. I hope it satisfies them. Because the alternative is permanent fear. The alternative is that people get to gather, and plot, and seethe, and the rest of us are supposed to just ignore it and pray they're all talk.

Plaid Shirt's reddened face, bloated with embarrassment and anger, materializes in my mind.

LOVE—or Magic Verified—was right. There's power in platforms. There's legitimacy and encouragement, if the shields and reputation and ranking scheme the Knights enacted wasn't proof enough.

I vaporize Plaid Shirt's menacing face, and think of all the innocent and unaware faces of the women and girls on the Secret Sirens page. I focus on them, on the fact that I want that forum down, and there's a warm swell as the wind moves. But there's still the nausea, and the cold.

"Okay, we're really eating now, right?" Courtney asks, one arm across Tavia's legs, and the other around her back.

"Are you just perpetually starving?" she asks him.

"Y'all just do not eat often enough, I feel like I'm being pranked, I swear."

"We're gonna eat right now, Courtney, calm down," I say, and if anyone notices the distraction in my voice, they don't let on.

"Yeah, well. We're going to meet Leona Fowl and, in my experience, we don't actually end up eating."

"I promise you we will eat this time. It's Burgerville—"

Except we pass something and Courtney makes Tavia hit her head on the roof, trying to twist in his seat to confirm.

"Was that a Popeye's?"

"Courtney—"

"Girl, if you don't turn this car around!"

"Seconded," Gavin chimes in.

"I mean." And Priam shrugs.

"Will you guys please stop taking his side, I already told Leona—"

"A real boss would text her a new location at the last minute and you know it, now Naema, I know too many things you don't want these people finding out for you to pretend you ain't gone turn the car around."

"I'm gonna turn—"

"Turn the car around!" he yells, and even if I wanted to make a retort no one would hear over the raucous laughter, so I settle for shaking my head and breathing deep while I look for an opportunity to make a U-turn. I can't argue with my cousin *and* the Ancestors right now.

"Watch what happens when we get out, though," I say, nodding now.

"I eat at Popeye's."

Tavia snorts and then tries to pretend she was sneezing.

"That's what happens when we get out. Y'all play too much."

I'm trying to quell an anxiousness that threatens to become visible at any second, so I just leave it and text Leona Fowl a brief *We're down the street at Popeye's* once everyone's begun piling out of the car. Just inside, Courtney goes straight to the counter, Priam tagging along, and Jamie and Gavin go grab seats at both a table and a counter so we make sure to get enough space.

Tavia idles until I catch up.

"I'll get out of your hair after this thing with Leona," she says.

"What's Courtney gonna think?"

"I'm sure you'll explain that this whole reconciliation thing is a ruse."

"Oh, he knows that already," I say, brows bunched. "I meant he's gonna think you're not into him."

"I'm not."

"He was right, you *are* a bad liar. What's the matter, you don't like blonds? Is it because his hair and skin are basically the same color?" She looks like she can't figure out exactly how to respond, or to what, and I wave her off. "Whatever, I'm not gonna beg you to date my cousin. I'm just saying, I don't care."

"I will . . . keep that in mind," she says, and when her eyes accidentally glide over to the counter where he's placing an order, she jerks her whole head and makes her earrings dance.

I'm about to join Courtney and put in my order, when she stops me.

Like, she grabs me. Tavia Philips's hand is snap-bracelet-cuffing my wrist so fast I don't even have time to resist.

"Are you gonna tell me what's wrong?" she asks quietly, and then gives me a look before I can deny it. So I don't.

"I'm not sure."

Her look subtly transitions into something more serious, like she knows that's not good.

"Something didn't go to plan back there, with the Knight. I thought scaring him off would feel better, but. The Ancestors don't seem to agree."

"Ah." There's a look of recognition on her face. "That's what he meant. When Priam said we both have an Ancestor thing."

"Yeah. I'm supposed to hear them, but I can't make sense of it. Sure, being back in Portland has packed my proverbial ears a bit, but. Right now they're just freaking me the eff out."

"Well . . . are you listening?" Tavia asks, and she clearly thinks she's being delicate, the way her brows lift.

This—

I've officially let Tavia Philips get too comfortable with me. She *just* got a handle on her thing, now she thinks I need her help figuring out mine.

"Do I answer to you?" I ask, and yank my wrist back before joining Courtney at the counter.

A few minutes later, there's half-eaten fish and chicken and a half dozen sides scattered across the table and counter we're using, and to onlookers, we're being completely insufferable, though with the multiple trills dancing through the restaurant because of the Eloko presence, no one seems to mind. Personally, I just want Leona Fowl to show up so I can quiet the Ancestors and calm my guts, but I've gotta stay on plan.

The number of notifications I've received just since Jamie relaunched my account is unbelievable. I forgot what a dopamine rush it is to post something and know that thousands of people are gonna gush, and comment, and consume whatever I want to say. They want to know where I've been, to tell me that I look better than ever, to ask if that's really Tavia Philips hanging out with my crew.

It's so addicting, the electric feeling every time a notification banner bubbles up at the top of my screen, even while we're trying to take short, nonsensical videos, and post more pictures.

Siren + Elokos! #ALLTheMagicalBlackGirls

Serious FOMO! someone comments.

Can this be an impromptu meet-up?

I tell them that Tavia and I will consider organizing a meet-up before the summer's over, and that today's just about Old Friends Reconnecting. They do not, of course, see the way I dry heave while I type it.

If you guys are friends, what does #Justice4Naema mean?

Is someone trying to stir up drama??

They are indeed, faithful subscriber. They are indeed. And now it looks as flimsy and contrived as it is, because I'm still Naema Bradshaw. I'm still an influencer regardless of a little LOVE app revamp, and I am more than capable of shutting down a false narrative.

What the Ancestors don't seem to get is that I know how to Social Media. What I'm doing today has a purpose, even if they can't understand it—which honestly might be a symptom of the whole Ancestral Spirits From Who Knows When. It wouldn't shock me to discover they aren't exactly tech-savvy enough to appreciate my strategy.

"Here she comes," Courtney croons, and whether we're eating, laughing, or dancing in the space between the table and the counter but under the red light shades, we all watch Leona Fowl enter the restaurant and approach.

I'm impressed. She's definitely good at what she does, fitting in no matter where she goes. At the posh restaurant, she was dressed exactly as I would've expected, blazer and stilettos included. For today's field trip to the PNW, she's wearing a V-neck that looks sheer and expensive, paired with high-waist, wide-legged dark jeans that look like she's thrifted them since being in town, and a pair of canvas shoes. Her hair's in an intricate mess of braid and bun, with Not Quite Wayward tendrils framing her face, and she's wearing small earrings and a long, simple necklace. And discreet bronzer. And eyeliner. She's absolutely awful and I can't help but respect that she nails it.

The stutter in her step is almost imperceptible, but a smile tugs at the corner of my lips. Nobody stands to greet her, but I drape my arm across Tavia's shoulders.

"Leona, what's good?" I say in salutation.

Anyone else would see me and Tavia together, and walk out the way they came. Anyone trying to sell a movie about a rivalry that extends beyond us and into sirens and Eloko as a whole, anyway. But Leona's not anyone else, and her recovery's smooth and immediate as she proceeds to the area we've claimed.

"Naema," she says. "Friends."

"You remember Tavia," I say, refusing to let her escape the awkward. "You guys worked together on that movie. Cordially, I'm told."

"I remember," she says, hands in her pockets, legs looking long and denim and modelesque. "In fact I'm having some déjà vu here. This is the scene where Tavia and Effie did their big reveal for the news cameras and simultaneously saved both their reputations." I don't say anything, just smile calmly. "Right? Isn't that what this is supposed to be? Personally, I try to avoid sequels following the same formula, but that's me."

"Then you're gonna hate this," I say, without mentioning the fact that Jamie's livestreaming with my phone. Super redundant, I know. "To be fair, using a Black girl as a shield while you attack her community feels overdone, too. So I mean you're not against *all* formulas."

"There you go again, making it about something it's not. I just see another Eloko when I look at you, Naema. You're the one stuck on race."

That one's just too boring to dignify.

"If you don't want to share your story out of some misguided sense of duty, that's your prerogative, Naema. But don't try to rewrite my concern into something ugly—"

"What's Justice4Naema?" I ask.

"You know what it is."

"Right, but how'd you get involved?"

"Who said I am?"

"The traffic cams that caught you putting up stickers."

"Oop," Courtney says, setting off a ripple of only slightly restrained laughter.

It's a total bluff, but I mean. Entirely plausible.

"You're just a one-woman publicity campaign for a movie that doesn't exist and never will."

"Imagine jet-setting around the whole West Coast tryna secure a bag that ain't even yours." Courtney's fingers are laced around Tavia, who hasn't said a word. Not that she needs to. Her colorful headwrap, and earrings, and pursed lips are saying plenty.

"But you're not a one-woman campaign anymore, are you?" I correct myself. "You've got the Knights all riled up."

"You sent *me* that website," she snaps.

"Yeah, but then you made an account. And you got them all frothy and aggressive about protecting me from Tavia, and a bunch of other people who have nothing to do with this."

"I don't know—"

"What I'm talking about, I know." I roll my eyes. "But you used the hotel's internet when you told NaemasNobleman where my family lives, and made all those Scary Siren posts, so I mean who else could Cursive_Signature be, amirite?"

"It's pretty serious, inciting hate crimes," Priam tells her. "So is intimidation. Which is a felony."

"There haven't been any hate crimes," she says, but her raspy voice is a little less confident.

"You better hope there aren't. Like, that's a ton of trust to put into every individual member of the forum who might have seen your posts. That *nobody* is capable of doing something heinous and, above all, criminal?"

Leona is actually chewing the inside of her lip now, so appearances be damned, I guess.

"And I mean, even if your posts were taken down, hard to convince people that one had nothing to do with the other, I bet. Forget a movie and a personal career being tanked when people find out you're affiliated with a site where grown men sexualize a minor, I'd want the whole thing deactivated before I got indicted if I were you. Which honestly shouldn't be too difficult to get done since it's borderline pedophilia, but I don't wanna step on your toes. I'm sure you've got a plan."

She shifts her weight, and her eyes roam for a moment.

"I do. And. If you guys would rather tell the story of your reconciliation—"

And every one of us erupts into groans and exclamations.

"Ma'am." I shake my head.

"Can't stop, won't stop," Tavia says, incredulous.

"It's the saddest thing," Courtney agrees.

"We're already telling our story, Leona," I say, pointing to Jamie, who giggles behind my phone. "Just go put out your fire."

The look on her face when she figures out what Jamie's doing. She jerks her head to the side, forgetting her hair's up and can't guard her face.

"Why is she still here?" Gavin cries, and we laugh as she turns on her heel and heads back toward the door.

"And done," Jamie says, ending the livestream. But I barely hear her.

Because the Ancestors.

Once again, the wind is a chorus is a bellow, and it's moving with a strength so overwhelming that it actually makes me stand up. And when I do, yet again, there's something new.

It must be happening behind my eyes, because there's no way the entire restaurant dims. There's no way a shadow like dark clouds sweeps from one side to the other without anyone else noticing. It's the wind, the chorus, the Ancestors trying to get my attention. They're trying to compete with the loud and the cacophony that I'm so accustomed to. I've given in to them twice now, and it's still not enough. Apparently, Great-Gram Lorraine was right. (She said it way before Tavia.) I'm not listening.

So I do.

I let the shadow fall. I expand my chest and let the wind manifest outside me, where only I can see it. When it overlays the whole world, it's not like being Stoned again. It's deeper. It's darker than gray. And I'm not alone.

The wind is still a chorus of voices, and the shadow that mutes everything else is like being attuned to the Ancestors. This dark isn't terrifying; it's being close to their spirits. I wonder if this is what I would've seen if I'd known how to answer them the very first time they passed through me. Maybe I could've been here a long time ago. Maybe this past year didn't have to be so bad.

I can still hear my friends, but now they're the background. And they're totally unperturbed that I not only stood but have stepped away.

"Did anybody watch?" Priam asks, and several of them snort.

"Did anybody watch," Courtney repeats. *"My cousin has fifty thousand subscribers, my dude."*

"Had," I correct him from inside the shadow, but it's his voice, it's the mention of a cousin that makes what the Ancestors are saying make sense.

You're not alone.

And when I'm listening, when I'm one of them, and near enough to see the shadow place, I've put the world in the background and I know the words they say mean a half dozen things.

They're closer now.

I'm not going to lose them just because I'm back in Portland.

The network helped us find Plaid Shirt today. Ms. Donna said they'd look out for the doxed, whether they were sirens or not. Maybe that means that just like LOVE, they know we need to expand our definition of what the network means, and who we protect.

And it's "we" again, because without ceremony, they let me back in.

We're all in this together.

Look. I'm still Naema, and yes, I'm a strategist, but the Ancestors tell me I'm not alone. Which means I don't have to execute every plan on my own. I'm not supposed to. There are limits when I do.

Like facing down a Knight, and hoping he'll scurry off the grid, never to be heard from again without double-checking that he did.

The shadow's gone. I'm standing in a very brightly lit Popeye's surrounded by friends who are excited about my comeback and the internet's reception. And Leona Fowl is almost in her car.

I run.

"Leona!" And when I yell, I throw the trill in my voice but not to charm passersby. As a reminder. So that Leona Fowl knows why she's supposed to hear me out.

She pulls her shoulder back like being trapped between me and her open car door makes her nervous. Because she can convince herself she's in harm's way after I have a strict word with her, but she doesn't get what's so wrong with venting about wanting to Take Action against Black women and girls.

"I need to see the direct messages," I tell her.

She gives me a skeptical side-eye.

"Leona. I know you're in them. We're talking about a little girl, and a grown man who wants to prove he's a Knight. You need to tell me how they make rank."

"All the ridiculous ways? . . . Or the big one?"

Chapter XXVIII

Magic Verified Collaboration—Tavia and Naema

NAEMA: Welcome back to my magical space, friends!

TAVIA: Hi!

NAEMA: This is the long-awaited, much-requested—

TAVIA: So much requested.

NAEMA:—magical collab! I'm joined by siren superstar Tavia Philips, who of course you all know very, very well. Tavia, thank you.

TAVIA: It's finally happening. Very glad to be here, and glad to tell our own story ourselves, right?

NAEMA: Girl. So listen. We know it's been in the news, but if this last year has taught me *anything*—

TAVIA: Right?

NAEMA: It's the importance of having our own space to tell you guys the real, without intermediaries and third parties putting their spin on it.

TAVIA: Or interjecting with product placement.

NAEMA: That, too.

TAVIA: Okay, should I start?

NAEMA: Girl, this is not your channel.

TAVIA: My bad.

NAEMA: Please look around. This is not Siren Speaks. This is Naema B.

TAVIA: All right. I got it.

NAEMA: Let *me* begin. So once upon a time there was an Eloko princess named Naema B—

TAVIA: Oh lord.

NAEMA: And some super corny internet bros decided I needed a pack of self-proclaimed Knights—

TAVIA: Oop. Air quotes and everything.

NAEMA: To defend my honor or something. Because of a whole Awakening thing that's old news. Anyway, it quickly became evident that they were really just very pressed about our girl Tavia's popularity, and everything she stands for as a siren.

Tavia: True facts.

NAEMA: And stanning a Black girl Eloko was supposed to keep anyone from figuring out that they were anti-Black af.

TAVIA: All the tea.

NAEMA: So then came the hashtags—

TAVIA: Justice for Naema, ElokoFirst.

NAEMA: Thank you. And one more that no one but fellow Knights were supposed to know about.

TAVIA: Secret Sirens.

NAEMA: And friends, it's exactly what it sounds like because the mediocrity knows no bounds.

TAVIA: They started making a list of Black girls and women they supposedly suspected of being sirens. And in order to earn reputation points and improve his ranking, one of them decided to be a hero and collar one.

NAEMA: You probably heard all of that on the news. What you probably didn't hear is that it was me and Tavia—

TAVIA: And a crew of Eloko—

NAEMA: And a lot of people who look out for us. *We* took him down.

TAVIA: Shout-out to Officer Blake of the Portland PD for showing up, and believing us when we said we knew where dude was headed, and why.

NAEMA: Which reminds me—the other part you probably didn't hear about on the news is that another Knight earned his rank by hacking the schematics for a siren-silencing collar like law enforcement uses. So the collar the guy took to a little girl's house? It was real. Just like the rope that was found in the back of his car.

TAVIA: Don't worry, gang, the little girl is safe. Her family had been alerted ahead of time, and she was taken elsewhere while we waited for the cavalry. We're eternally grateful to the dedicated community members who worked with us not just to warn the family, but to track the so-called Knight's movements and unmask his secret life as a domestic terrorist.

NAEMA: One down, so many to go.

TAVIA: But we're not letting that discourage us. In the next few video collabs, we're gonna be explaining how Naema and I are planning to continue this fight, from supporting local legislature aimed at suspending the use of siren-silencing collars, to working to free activists like Camilla Fox—

NAEMA: To creating a watchdog network to make sure the forum where these guys assembled doesn't go unnoticed when and where it inevitably pops up again.

TAVIA: Definitely that, too.

NAEMA: We're going to be making our digital home here on Magic Verified, and we're so excited for you all to get involved in keeping Portland magical for everyone.

Chapter XXIX

NAEMA

We're back at the airport several days later, but it's not just Courtney and me this time. Dad's tipping the skycap, and chatting away, while they take care of my parents' totally unnecessarily huge luggage, and beside me, Mommy is rubbing her tummy apprehensively.

"Don't worry," I tell her, snaking my arm through hers.

"I'm not worrying," she lies, and then glances up at me and Courtney with a timid smile.

"I know you want the baby to be Eloko, and I know Portland's supposed to be the magic place," I begin.

"But you didn't know what being Eloko was really like until you left," she finishes, recapping what I told my parents after the hoopla of Ms. Donna, and Officer Blake, and Leona Fowl.

"No," I say, gently. "I was gonna say that being with your family matters a lot more. Mommy, I know you miss them, or you wouldn't chip in to reunions you never attend, or fill out visitation paperwork when you had no intention of being in town. You're giving up too much."

"I'm just trying to make another you," she tells me, and puts her head on my shoulder. Which is good because she can't see the way the setting sun glints off my eye and almost makes it water.

"I mean. That's totally fair."

I don't tell her what I already know. That part of hearing the Ancestors is a kind of Eloko network, joining us together. So I know already that my little sibling is Eloko just like me. I don't tell her because I want her to be willing to leave Portland regardless. I want her to be ready to let go of all the fawning and pedestaling that it took the stone to dislodge me from.

"You are the actual worst," Courtney says, wearing my travel pillow on the back of his neck.

"You're lucky I'm even talking to you," I reply, digging a finger between his ribs.

"What are you even talking about?" he asks while he grimaces. Like he doesn't know.

I know they exchanged phone numbers at Popeye's, and I saw them this morning, when she came by and he snuck outside to meet her. The way they talked for a few moments, twirling hair around fingertips, and rubbing a clean-shaven chin with the right hand so she'd see the thick silver watch glint. Then he'd extended his arms in a clear invitation. The worst part was the way Tavia giggled, covering the bottom of her face with one hand, while she looked over her shoulder like she didn't want anyone to see—and clearly didn't look in the right direction to see me. When she finally slid into Courtney's arms, they were all sunlit melanin, and hair and headwrap silhouette, and my cousin's handsome grin over her shoulder.

Idiots.

"Everybody ready?" My dad asks as he comes back, shoving his wallet into his back pocket. "First vacation in—man, I don't even wanna count."

"We already missed the family reunion," Mommy pouts up at him.

"It's a family reunion because we're going," he says, and kisses her forehead before popping down and kissing her tummy.

"*They* are the actual worst," I tell Courtney, and head into the airport.